ANNA

LAURA GUTHRIE

D1099858

gob stopper

First published in 2020 by Gob Stopper

Gob Stopper is an imprint of Cranachan Publishing Limited

ISBN: 978-1-911279-66-2

eISBN: 978-1-911279-67-9

Cover Illustrations © Julia Dreams

Cover Design © Anne Glennie

www.cranachanpublishing.co.uk

@cranachanbooks

cranachan

For my Grandpa - Teddy Garden

There was a huge summer storm as I was coming up on the bus—splattering rain, and flickers of lightning every thirty seconds or thereabouts. It was dark enough outside that I could see my reflection in the window, and the cars coming in the other direction all had their headlights on. I was happy that I was warm and dry, and not being soaked with rain or splashed with spray from lorries and cars.

I didn't really know where I was going—only that I was going north across the border to the Scottish Central Belt. I was happy that, unlike me, the bus driver knew exactly where we were going. At least, I hoped he did.

I'd travelled without Dad before, but never so far, to somewhere totally unknown to me, and never with people to whom Dad had not entrusted me. I tried to be happy that I was doing so well on my own, and that there hadn't been any hitches.

The man next to me had his head tipped back and was snoring gently. His hair was curly and brown. Dad had curly brown hair too—like a Jersey cow. Every time I saw this man out the corner of my eye I thought I was sitting next to Dad. Then I'd turn to look and see that it wasn't him. Then I'd remember that I could never sit next to Dad again. One of his elbows was sticking into my side, but it seemed selfish to wake him. Besides, waking him would mean I had to talk to him.

The first time I went somewhere without Dad was two years ago when I first tried secondary school, aged eleven. I went on the school bus. He bought me a phone specially, so that we could talk to each other throughout the day if I got scared. It wasn't a very fancy one—it looked a bit like one of those walkie-talkies policemen used to use—but it was good for texting. I never added any other contacts or texted anyone else. The pamphlet the school had sent when my place was confirmed said phones were banned, but Dad said that if I put it on silent, turned it off during class and handed it over if asked, he would 'face the music'. During that bus trip into school the driver had shouted at me because my bag was in the aisle. I'd wanted to curl up or run away, but instead I'd texted Dad.

I still had that phone. Now I took it out and accessed the old message in the inbox:

Dad: "Why did he shout at you?"

I came out of the inbox and accessed the outbox:

Me: "My bag was in the aisle."

Back to the inbox:

Dad: "It could trip someone up. Why not be happy they don't want you to trip! Xoxoxoxoxoxoxox".

A minute later he'd sent a second reply:

"If you're sitting beside someone, introduce yourself. They're probably just as nervous as you are. Xoxoxoxoxox".

We hadn't texted very often, so there weren't many messages. There would never be any more. I had barely looked at them since leaving the flat—I wanted them to feel fresh when I really needed them. Except now I felt like a pumpkin being turned into a lantern. I put the phone away, and swallowed down a sick feeling.

The bus lurched to one side. The driver really should have been going a bit slower. The curly-haired man sitting beside me jumped awake.

"It's ok," I said, "We just aquaplaned a bit because it's raining."

"Ah, yes." He rested his head against the seat and closed his eyes again.

I held out my hand. "Hello," I said. "My name's Anna Whitear. It's very nice to meet you."

His eyes snapped open. He looked at my hand, then gave it a very short shake. "Ben Strachan. Nice to meet you, too." He turned away.

"I'm on the bus up to my mum's house."

His eyes flicked back towards my face, but they didn't meet mine. "I see." He hunched forward and picked at the right side of the thumb on his left hand with the thumb and index finger on his right. This conversation was not running along as smoothly as Dad's message had made me think it would.

The other passengers murmured in the background, along with the hum of the engine and the rain which now pattered, rather than pelted, against the windows. I pulled out my pen and writing pad.

"Want to play noughts and crosses?"

He turned to me and put his head on one side, eyes narrowed like Dad used to narrow them when he was trying to deduce whether I'd washed my face that morning. Then he gave a smile and his shoulders seemed to relax. "OK then."

We played fifteen games. I won eight, we drew in five, and Ben won in two. About an hour later we got held up in a mile-long traffic jam. The bus driver made a phone call, then announced to us that a lorry had jack-knifed, and that we were waiting for the rescue services. I decided to be happy it wasn't anything more serious.

"Nobody's going outside to smoke," I said.

Ben craned forward to look. "Too rainy."

"At least that means they're less likely to get cancer."

"Well that's one way to look at it..."

"Dad smoked," I told him. My chest hurt—it was the

first time I had referred to Dad in the past tense following his death. "Never inside though, because of me. He had those self-roll type cigarettes. The kits all came with huge health warnings on them. Why do you think people still do it when everyone knows how bad it is?"

"It's an addiction, isn't it?"

"Yes. They're hard to overcome. I know—I sucked my thumb for ten years."

When the bus pulled into the station I collected my two suitcases and looked around for someone that could be Mum. I'd never seen any photos of her. Dad once told me we didn't have any. I asked him why not, and he started looking for some in his desk, but instead found tickets he'd managed to get for us to see the Royal Philharmonic Orchestra playing Tchaikovsky.

We wouldn't have been able to afford that sort of thing usually, but Mrs Taylor's mother's friend had come down with pneumonia, and had passed her ticket on to Mrs Taylor's mother (who couldn't go because she was going to be away in Italy at the time), who passed it on to Mrs Taylor, who would have gone but thought I would appreciate the music for what it was better than she could have done, because I was so much more knowledgeable—and she knew that Dad would want to go with me.

Dad had been so excited about the concert that I'd

decided not to ask anything else about Mum, because it might have seemed ungrateful and obsessive—and I knew from my outreach worker that being obsessive could alienate people. That night when he had tucked me in, he told me that Mum was fine, and that we were fine, and that I had nothing to worry about. He also said something about not rocking any boats. I wasn't quite sure what he meant, but I didn't ask again, because he used the same tone of voice he used to end a conversation when I'd talked too long about the same thing to someone, without letting them have a turn.

I had another surreptitious look for photos when Dad was out at work and Miss Corrigan was babysitting—but I didn't find any.

Dad taught me a fail-safe trick for being happy, no matter what. We simply called it the Happy Game. It was to find a happy aspect in everything, no matter how dire. Like a riddle to crack. It was easier just after he had died—the whole thing had been so horrific that I was just happy he wasn't suffering any more. It was also easier because I knew all of his worries about money and me and getting recognition for his paintings were now over, but, me being still alive, I had a lot of new things to worry about. So much had happened in the last two weeks that I still hadn't had time to assimilate all the ways my life would change from hereon in.

Dad's jaw was square-ish, and he had freckles like me,

but not as many. It was impossible to tell whether Mum would have any freckles, because freckles are as much environmentally-determined as they are hereditary. However, she probably had a round face, because I did. I also have more red in my hair than Dad did—although my hair is still more brown than red—so Mum probably had red hair. That's not because she's a Scot though—not all Scots have red hair. Dad's family came from Glasgow before his great grandparents moved down to London. That's why he wanted to study at the Glasgow School of Art, which is where he met Mum.

There were no round-faced, red-haired women waiting in the stance. I sat down and watched as people passed, and tried to think of a happy thing about that. Someone tapped me on my shoulder.

"Is somebody here to meet you?" Ben asked.

"Well, Mum should be here...I was just going to wait until the crowds died down."

"Have you got her number?"

"No. I've got her address, though." I rummaged in my pocket and pulled out the post-it note Alison had given me. "Sixteen McCallish Court."

He blinked, then stared at me intently. My face grew hot.

He sat down. "How old are you, Anna?"

"I turned thirteen on the 6th of August."

"I see." He rubbed his temples, then tapped his forehead rhythmically with two fingers. "Well, let's give it a few more minutes." We played rock, paper, scissors for about fifteen minutes, until the people had nearly all gone. Ben kept looking up and around, until finally he glanced at his watch and got to his feet.

"Right. You can't wait here alone. There's no telling what types might come skulking around."

"What do you mean?"

"Some people... well... they're less than savoury." He bit his lip. His shoulders looked very tense. "We need a plan," he said, speaking very slowly. He continued, with lots of hesitation. "Tell you what—there's a taxi rank at the front of the station. Er... how much money do you have?"

"Five pounds emergency money."

"That's not enough." He seemed to be speaking to himself—Dad often spoke to himself when he was cooking or cleaning. "Look, I'm not sure if this is the right thing to do, but... well... not much choice, really." He reached into his pocket, took out his wallet and extracted a ten-pound note. "Here." He handed it over.

"Oh, that's far too much!" That's what Dad said when Miss Corrigan gave me sixty pounds one Christmas. I think it's what you're supposed to say when someone who isn't family gives you money.

"Don't worry about it. Needs must. Your five, plus

my ten. Fifteen should be more than enough to cover all possibilities. Have you ever taken a cab before?"

"Yes. Dad used to send me home in one with the flat key when he was working late."

Ben frowned. "Well… I'll help you get started, even so."

We left through the double sliding doors at the front and came out onto a curved street lit by the glow of the bus station's lights. We were first in line, but there were no cabs.

"Shouldn't be long, hopefully…" He hugged himself and shivered. Every now and then he darted little glances at me, bit his lip and rocked back and forth on his heels. A strand of hair blew across my face, and a lone spatter of rain hit my cheek.

"I've found something else to be happy about," I said.

"Fire away."

I flinched, but tried to push the associations out of my mind. "Well, Mum may not have been here to meet me, but you were!"

"Er… yes. I suppose so."

A cab rounded the corner and pulled up. On impulse I gave him a hug. He gasped and stiffened, but patted my shoulder when I let go.

"Fare thee well, Anna," he said. "Perhaps our paths will cross again sometime."

Sitting in the back of the cab I got my first good look

at the town. The junctions, traffic islands and lights faded in and out of view, like drawings on an infinite, unravelling scroll. The houses were a mix of very old and very modern, and the streets, though urban, were quiet, less packed and more interspersed with wild greenery than those of London. The street lamps glowed orange against the blue of oncoming night. Mostly we were travelling too fast to pick out much detail, but twice I was able to take a peek when we stopped at a red light. There was a yew tree in the garden of 22 Stuart Lane which cast a shadow across the lawn. I could see into some of the ground floor rooms. Through one window I saw a woman holding a baby. Another older child stood close by. There were lots of shops too. Most looked like general newsagents, but one read 'The Auld Toy Shop'. There was one with a tourist information sign, and another with a selection of fruits and vegetables piled in the window.

We turned right, off the main road into a narrow alley which was not well lit, then left again into a sort of courtyard with groups of houses either side, each facing the car park. Most windows had their blinds down or their curtains closed, but yellow light shone out from behind these. Each house's lawn was small, and had a wooden fence with a gate in it along the front. Two had high hedges either side.

"There you go, doll," the driver said, pulling in.

"That'll be nine pounds sixty."

I handed him Ben's ten-pound note, and took the change. Then I waited while he extracted my luggage.

The sky was almost black now. The silhouetted outline of a low hillside was just visible. The rain had stopped, and a soft breeze blew across my face. It smelled of grass, and something unidentifiable to do with the countryside. Apart from the distant sound of traffic and the shifting of leaves on the hedges, there was silence. This threw me—the part of London where we lived was never quiet. It felt as if a chunk of the world had gone missing. However, like eyes becoming accustomed to the dark, I found myself settling into it as I stood on the tarmac and got my bearings. Without traffic to fill my mind, I imagined I could cock my head, see the constellations circling the pole star, and feel the Earth shifting beneath me, like standing on the back of a blue whale.

The gate of number sixteen was painted white, but had several chipped and rusted areas. I dragged my wheelie-suitcase behind me, and lifted the other in short bursts. It was difficult to know what to do once I was at the door. It seemed rude to simply walk in, but I wasn't sure whether I should knock, given that this was now my home and the person inside was my mum. It was beginning to get cold. Summoning up my courage I knocked three times. The silence seemed to extend as my anticipation mounted. Then there were gentle footsteps, and the sound of a lock turning. My mouth went dry, my hands went wet, and the door opened.

She was only about half an inch taller than me, and wore a pink fleece dressing-gown with purple, squashy slippers. And she did have a round face and straight, red hair! She also had big, brown eyes which were highlighted with mascara.

"Mum…?" I swallowed back a lump. Her eyes stretched very wide and she took half a step back. Her expression reminded me of the face Mrs Taylor had made when she walked into the Intensive Care Unit and saw Dad lying on the hospital bed, the day after the fire in the flat. Her face had turned white too. Mum didn't look much older than me—certainly not old enough to be my mother. She didn't look nearly as old as the mums of my school friends.

"Ah." She cleared her throat, her face settled back, she dropped her gaze, and nodded. Her cheeks were colouring. It was an 'ah' that seemed to struggle to get out of her mouth, and ended with a hitch in her breath. She raised her eyes slowly, and looked me up and down.

"Anna. You are Anna, right?"

I nodded.

"Good. Well…" It was a whisper that trailed off, followed by a nod. Her whole frame suddenly looked very spindly and frail.

I wanted to hug her and tell her how I had been

looking forward to meeting her, as well as how happy I was to be coming to live with her. On reflection, I also wanted to know what she had been doing all this time, why she hadn't come to the bus station, why she had never written or come to visit, why I'd never seen a picture of her, and why she and Dad decided to separate. However, I didn't seem to be able to move or speak. She lifted her chin, turned away and checked something which seemed to be stuck onto the other side of the door. The way she had gone from spindly to smooth-moving reminded me of how actors get into character before auditioning.

"You're supposed to come tomorrow. They said tomorrow! Oh God, this is…" She trailed off and passed a hand over her face. I copied her accent under my breath. Then she stood looking at me for a long time, her eyes darting over my face. "How did you get here?"

"In a taxi."

"Right. Come in then. Take your shoes off, please."

I heaved my suitcases into a bright, cosy little kitchen. There was a gas cooker in the corner, a wooden pulley for hanging clothes on, and a tall, humming fridge-freezer. A big freezer looked fun—you could make lollies in it. We had only a tiny freezer compartment in the London flat. The TV was on in the living room of Mum's house— which had a thick, cream carpet, and a sofa against the wall with the door in it. Venetian blinds were drawn over two large windows set in the wall facing the door.

"I was right about your hair," I said. My outreach worker told me that if I'm stuck for conversation with someone, or I don't know how to proceed within a situation, paying compliments is a fairly safe bet. "It's really pretty. Some people say red's unlucky, but Dad said that was just a superstition. Will you let me style it? Please? I love styling hair." I reached out, but she cringed away and picked up my non-wheelie suitcase.

"Let's just get you sorted."

I followed her through a door on the other side of the kitchen, which opened into a hall dominated by a flight of green-carpeted stairs. This seemed a strange way to design a house—if it was raining hard people would have to trample across the kitchen, getting water and mud everywhere, before they could take off their boots and hang up their coats. I dragged the wheelie suitcase up behind her a step at a time—THUNK—THUNK—THUNK—pulling myself forwards with the help of the banister. The walls of the hallway were papered in plain white, with raised floral patterns on them. It would be a good pattern for a blind person's house—they could feel the pictures with their fingertips.

There was only one bedroom. A huge double bed covered with a white, lacy quilt had its headboard against the wall opposite the door. The window was set to the left, and the curtains were white. Although they were closed I could see pink ribbons on either side, which held them open during the day. Two wooden chests of drawers sat next to a full-length mirror, and there was a dresser for make-up near the door. Next to the double bed there was a bedside cabinet, and a desk with a laptop on it, with an office chair pulled up. Then there was a wardrobe, and a bookshelf which was stuffed and piled all round with books. It reminded me of the year Dad challenged me to read my height in fiction over the twelve days of Christmas. I'm fairly tall for my age but I managed it, just. I'm quite a fast reader because I read a great deal. On the floor, at the foot of the bed there was an air mattress, with a sleeping bag laid out on top of it. Mum gestured at this.

"You can have that. It's not much, but then... this was all kind of sudden." She perched on the edge of the bed, shoulders hunched, hair hanging lankly down past her shoulders, and watched as I kicked off my trainers, plonked myself down and drew up my legs.

"When Dad and Mr Langton were doing up my room I slept on one of these."

"Oh." Her mouth went very small, and her eyes flicked round the room.

I felt a sudden urge to cry, but Mum seemed so fragile already that I thought doing so might break her, so I held it in, forgetting in that moment that I, too, was very fragile. But unlike me, she didn't have the fail-safe game of being happy in any situation. I scrunched my hands up and pressed my tongue against the roof of my mouth, concentrating my mind on the fact that I was safe and warm and dry and home. It certainly was a great blessing to still have a home of some sort.

Her gaze wandered over me again. "Well… welcome home." She made a strange, strangled noise, jumped up and ran from the room, slamming the door behind her and leaving my mind feeling like it had just been pushed over the edge of a cliff.

My room at Alison's had been more like a hotel room. For all that she was so good to me, she was a short-term foster carer, and children like me passed through her care like products on a factory line. Now I had somewhere to really make my own. I knew this should have been a happy thing. Maybe happiness just didn't feel like how I thought it ought to feel. It certainly seemed a small reward for such a lot of chasing by so many people in so many different times and places. But if Dad seemed to think it was worth chasing as hard as he did, for as long as he did, and in the many different ways that he did, then there must be something to it.

I recalled every aspect of the day—especially Mum—and listed on my fingers the many things to be happy about. Meeting Ben, the light on the lawn, the farmland… Dad had used the expression 'turning over a new leaf' in one of his texts, to help me feel better about starting secondary school. I pulled out my phone and stared at the message for a long time. Well this was definitely a new leaf. But in all honesty, I wasn't sure I liked it.

When I woke I had a moment of blankness, before the heaviness that had lodged in me every morning since Dad's death came rushing back in, like water to a sand-hole. I let it settle, then tried to work out what was going on. The bedroom window in Alison's flat was at the head of the bed, whereas here it was at the foot, so at first I thought I was upside-down. Then I remembered. I struggled into a sitting position. Mum was still asleep, even though the clock on her bedside table said it was quarter past eight. Her red hair was spread across the pillow, like Ariel from The Little Mermaid. I wanted to touch it, but I didn't—Dad and my outreach worker once explained to me about personal space.

The kitchen wasn't nearly as bright as the bedroom, but it was light, and the air was fresher and cooler. I got to work learning my way around. There were eggs in the fridge, and coffee and sugar in one of the cupboards. I found cutlery in a drawer near the bin, and a gas lighter which was also a bottle-opener. Pots and pans lived in a cupboard to the right of the sink. I twisted the knob for one of the cooker's rings to turn the gas on. There was a gentle hiss, and as I clicked the lighter next to the ring, it ignited with a quiet wumph. I cracked two eggs into the frying pan, and whilst they were cooking I found a pink tray patterned with green frogs. Just as I was filling a glass with orange juice there was a loud beeping from the hall. Remembering Dad's way of stopping the smoke alarm in London before he got fed up with it and threw it away, I quickly lifted the pan off the hob, picked up a dish towel, went through and waved it back and forth in front of it. The noise stopped. I listened hard, but I couldn't hear any sounds from upstairs.

The eggs weren't burned—it must have just been the hot oil. I turned the gas down, put a slice of bread in the toaster, stuck my fingers in my ears until it popped, and checked the eggs again. The whites had gone opaque and jelly-like, and the yolks were round and globby. I scooped them out onto a plate, along with the toast, then put the orange juice on the tray. Very carefully I carried everything upstairs and put it down on Mum's dresser. The alarm clock now said it was twenty to nine. Since most people start work at nine o'clock I violated the personal space rule and shook her shoulder.

"Mmmmurgh…" She opened one eye a slit and saw the clock. "Oh sugar!" She shot out a hand and banged the clock three times against the bedside table. I cringed at the sound. "Stupid… darn… thing…" Then she jumped up and pulled off her nightie.

I had changed in front of Dad many times for

swimming and getting into clothes and jammies, and he had changed in front of me, and had supervised my bath times until I turned eight, when I started showering instead. I must admit, though, I was a little curious to see what an adult woman looked like without her clothes on, simply because I had never seen one before and yet I would soon be one. I'd seen the blurry outline of Mrs Taylor in the shower before, and then seen her later in just a towel, but that was all.

Mum had a curvy, hourglass figure. Her skin was pale, as though it had rarely been exposed to sunshine, and around her neck she wore a thin, metal chain with a tiny, square-shaped pendant on it. Across the lower half of her abdomen, just under her navel, there stretched a thin, horizontal line—almost like a smile. I wondered if I would grow to look like her. My body seemed very stick-like and flat-chested in comparison to hers, but then, I think I'm something of a late developer, and anyway, I had no other female family members to consult or compare with.

She opened the first drawer in one of the chest of drawers and took out a pale-blue, lacy bra. Sliding its straps over her shoulders she tried unsuccessfully to do up the catch. I went round and hooked it into place, but she didn't say thank you, or even pause. Instead she pulled on a long top, black tights and high-heeled boots, tied her hair back, picked up her handbag and went clattering down the stairs. I ran after her and watched as she struggled into a black felt coat. Then she slapped a twenty-pound note on the work surface. "That's not for you," she said, and rushed out.

I drew in a deep breath, and let it out again. Mum's behaviour reminded me of my friend Jenny when she and I fell out. Except with Jenny I knew what I had done wrong. I extracted my phone from under my pillow and scrolled through the inbox. One message from Dad, dated 20th of July, simply read: "I love you!" From outside there came the noise of a car engine starting up, then of wheels grinding, before the engine revved once more and faded.

The tray was still sitting on the dresser. I carried it into the garden and, after checking the grass was dry, sat cross-legged on the lawn. A chaffinch called, and a blackbird, and a thrush. There were no gardens in our part of London, so hearing birdsong was a rare treat. Now I would be able to hear it every day. A black and white cat with no collar sniffed around outside our gate.

"Puss-puss-puss!" I stretched out my hand. It turned towards me, rested on its back feet, then slid under the gate. It crept towards me on its belly, eyes wide, pupils fully dilated. Once it was almost within touching distance, it stretched its neck out and sniffed my hand, but when I tried to tickle its cheek it ducked out of reach and ran away.

The streets were empty. The curtains in the bottom window of the house next door were drawn, but the car was in the drive. Even if the people who lived there were out on a walk or at work, you would expect them to pull the curtains back to let the sun in. Dad always said that made a difference to how a place 'felt'. I watched as a van pulled up, and a man in a blue boiler suit heaved a huge, rectangular cardboard box from the back. When he rang the bell a woman answered. I was too far away to hear what either of them said. The woman took the parcel in her arms and kicked the door shut, leaving the man standing on the step. He shrugged, then got back into the van and drove away.

Once I had made my bed and brushed my teeth and hair, I decided to explore. Opposite McCallish Court there was a sloping patch of green, with a play park at the bottom surrounded by a bank of trees. I did what Dad and I had done at Richmond Park when we went for trips there early in the morning; I spread my arms out, tipped my head back and ran across the grass, shouting "WAHOOOOOO!" We would run in wide circles, sending birds scattering, and then chase each other until he caught me and pretended to be a monster, slinging me over his shoulder and growling, and we would laugh and laugh and laugh. Then we would explore and play football or just walk around, or I would go to look at things, and he would take out his sketch pad and draw me. We called this ritual 'breaking in the morning'.

Now I reached deep for that feeling again as I ran and shouted, but I just felt like a noisy siren, and couldn't help imagining people looking at me like I was strange—they didn't know. There were cans and bottles scattered across the grass, along with bits of newspaper and polystyrene take-away boxes—the kind that hamburgers and chips come in—as well as plastic cups and wooden stirrers. The two square meters surrounding me contained a cola can and a polystyrene box. I picked these up and moved on to another patch of the same size directly in front of me, which had a broken glass bottle in it. To avoid getting cut I stood as far away from it as I could and picked it up with the tips of my fingers. There was no bin so I walked up the road, hoping to find one in somebody's garden.

At the top the road split into a T-junction. On the opposite side from me, and slightly to the left, there stood a gigantic house—also with all its curtains closed. In its driveway there were two green council bins. I hesitated, wondering if what I was about to do constituted trespassing. But then, I wasn't going to move or even touch anything other than the bins—which weren't his anyway—and the gate. Even so, I tiptoed in and lifted the lid as quietly as possible with my elbow. Unfortunately the glass bottle made a crash as it hit the bottom, and suddenly a dog was barking—a deep, low bark that sounded like an Alsatian. A man with wild black hair and grey whiskers, wearing a dark red dressing gown, opened the door.

"What do you think you're doing? I'll skin you alive!"

I ran for it. Of course, he would go to jail for murder if he skinned me alive, but that wouldn't make the experience any less painful.

When I stopped running I was on a street I didn't recognise. There was a second play park, but smaller than the one opposite McCallish Court. It was empty too. I sat on a swing and wondered where the other children were. Pushing myself back and forth with one foot I sang *She'll Be Coming Round the Mountain When She Comes*. As I was in the middle of the second verse I heard mingled voices shouting. The front door of a house on the street opposite opened, and a man in a pinstriped suit strode out. He was followed by a woman dragging a small boy by the hand, with a girl toddler at her side, and a baby in a sling.

"You flipping blanket!" she shouted (I have substituted the last two words). "I just can't deal with this anymore!"

"Good! That makes two of us! Do what you want, Joanne, I'm off to make money." The baby began to cry, the toddler began to march forwards towards the road, and the older boy tried to wrench his hand free. I stood up and jogged across the street as the man got into a black car. He slammed the door, and was revving the engine when the toddler reached the kerb.

"Emily!"

Joanne sprang forward, but I reached Emily first and swung her out of danger, just as the car sped off. She went rigid in my arms and let out a screech. A baby's cry is the same volume as an electric drill. The woman ripped her out of my arms and pushed me back before running inside.

I stood on the pavement, stunned. If anything I was entitled to a humble 'thank you'. I had actually risked getting run over to save her, after all. It would probably only have been a small knock for me, but she could have been killed. I clenched and un-clenched my fists a few times. Why was everyone here so cross? I started to walk slowly away.

"Excuse me...?"

I hesitated, but it could have been any woman's voice, talking to anyone.

"Hey! Excuse me?"

This time it was louder, and had an edge to it. I turned round, saw Joanne waving, and ran back to meet her. Her cheeks and the rims of her eyes were red. The boy leaned against the doorway.

"I'm... I'm sorry." Joanne sniffed. "Sam's supposed to stay until Molly gets here. Not that he ever does stay..."

"Who's Molly?" I asked.

She passed a hand over her face. "What a mother I

must seem! Can't even keep my own house in order! And a right besom." She paused. "Thank you… for what you did, just there."

"What's a besom?"

"A grumpy old birch."

I haven't substituted any words this time. I knew 'birch' was the wrong word. I think she did, too.

"That's ok! I like babies. Especially not-squished ones."

The boy walked up and tugged her arm. "Mum…"

"Actually, I was just wondering where all the other children were," I said.

"Lots of families are still off on holiday," she replied.

"Mum…"

"Didn't you want to go on holiday too?"

"Uh-oh…" She patted the baby. "I smell trouble. Again."

"Do you know how to get to McCallish Court?"

"MUM!"

"What, Skylar?"

"I'm thirsty!"

"Then get a carton of juice! I'll be there in a minute!" She turned back to me. "McCallish Court… That's up near the big house, isn't it?"

"You mean the place where the man lives who skins people alive?"

"Eh?"

"At the top of the junction. He set his dog on me. I ran away and ended up here."

"Oh, that man! He won't hurt you. All bark and no bite. Anyway, McCallish Court, you say?"

"Yes. I live at number sixteen."

"Patty Harrington's?" Her eyebrows jumped up.

"Um…" I dropped my gaze, realising I didn't even know Mum's name. Presumably Harrington was her maiden name and she had changed back to it after she and Dad had split up.

"What's your name by the way?"

"Anna."

"I see…" She gave her head a little shake. I couldn't deduce what the expression on her face meant. "Right. McCallish Court. Hang on—I'll show you." She crossed the lawn to the gate and pointed up the road. "You see that pedestrian crossing? Well, you turn left when you get to it, then you basically keep following the hill up, and turn right at the top."

"Thanks!" I said, "I'm very happy to have met you."

I followed Joanne's instructions and found my way back to Mum's. The black and white cat was lying curled against the gate. Its hips and shoulders poked bonily out from under its skin. I put my hand down to stroke it, but it flattened its ears, gave a hiss, and swiped at me. I yanked my hand back, and saw three little lines of blood arcing across the back of my hand. It jumped up and ran. I was about to go inside when I heard something, and stood very still. Although Mum's car wasn't in the drive, there were footsteps coming from inside the house. I wanted to run, but as Mum's daughter I felt I had a duty to protect her and all that was hers. I looked around for something heavy, wishing I had kept the broken bottle from the green. All I could see was a medium-sized branch in the gutter of number eighteen. There must have been a storm earlier in the week. I picked it up, went through the garden gate, flung the front door open, and strode in, brandishing it.

The person inside didn't look very burglar-ish. She looked as if she was in her twenties, with short, bouncy hair. It was red too, but unlike mine and Mum's it was dyed a dark, artificial red. Her round, pale face looked strained, but she had smile lines around her eyes, and a dimple in the left corner of her mouth. She wore a sky-blue blouse, an ankle-length black skirt patterned with white polka dots, and shiny red Doc Martens. She was wiping down counter surfaces with disinfectant spray, but dropped the cloth when I barged in.

I lowered the branch and cleared my throat. "Hello," I said.

She hesitated. "Hi." She gave a tentative smile. Her eyes were milky-blue.

"Who are you?"

"I'm Molly." Was this the Molly Joanne had mentioned?

"When will Mum be home?"

She put down the cloth and held out her hand. "So you're Anna!" I took it, feeling hugely confused. She gave it a vigorous shake with both hers. "Patty's told me all about you. It's an honour!"

"She has?" This seemed unlikely. Mum had hardly said anything when she saw me, much less spent time getting to know me. I couldn't imagine her chattering away to someone about me. Still, at least I now knew Joanne had been right about Mum's name.

"Yes. She phoned last night. She was all worked up."

"Why?"

"Nerves, I think."

This made no sense. "Why would she be nervous of me?"

"Well you did just rush in waving a branch..."

My face grew hot.

She gave a light laugh. "She couldn't stop talking about you. What happened to your hand?" She was looking at the lines of blood the cat had left.

"Oh, there was a cat outside. I went to stroke it and it hissed and scratched me. Then it ran away."

Molly flicked her eyes up. "Ah, that cat!"

"Do you know him?"

"He's a stray. At least, none of my clients know who he belongs to. Been trying to get a good meal into him for weeks. He keeps hanging around my place, but he swipes if I try and touch him."

"Why?"

She shrugged. "I think he's in pain. A lot of animals are aggressive when they're in pain. Self-defence. If he'd only let me touch him I might be able to help."

I thought about this. Then I realised my thinking was causing a silence that might feel awkward to her, so I decided to break it by making polite conversation. "Are you married?"

Her face coloured. "Aren't you Little Miss Forward!"

"Ah." I clenched and unclenched my fists. "Mental Personal Space—that's harder, isn't it?"

"Don't worry—I'm not offended. And in answer to your question, no." She wiped the table top vigorously.

"You could marry my friend Ben," I suggested. "I met him on the bus yesterday."

She burst out laughing. "Well, let's see!"

Mum didn't come home before I went to bed. It was incredibly stuffy upstairs. I opened the window, lay down and dozed off, but was woken by something fluttering back and forth across the light at high speed. At first I thought it was a large moth, but as it flew past my face I realised it was in fact a pipistrelle bat.

"Silly bat," I said. "You can't live here! There aren't any insects and there's no water. Besides, you'd miss your friends." I tried to wave it towards the window, but it was darting all over the place. Mum was on the phone in the kitchen. Perhaps Molly was telling her about our encounter. I tiptoed to the cleaning cupboard in the hall, where I found a plastic bucket near the back. Once in the bedroom I stood on the bed and tried to trap the bat. It kept getting away, and I found myself jumping around, clapping the bucket against the ceiling.

"What are you doing?" Mum's voice sounded from the doorway. Then she saw the bat, and flung her arms up around her face. "Get it out! GET IT OUT!"

"It's only a little bat!"

She had gone all pale, trembly, and glassy-eyed. I made a quick decision to temporarily disregard rules about personal space, took her by the arm and marched her into the landing, before returning to the bedroom and shutting the door.

"Come on little bat," I said in a soothing voice, though I was shaking all over. After about a minute it stopped its fluttering and clung to the curtain with its tiny thumbs. I was able to get the bucket over it, cover it with the curtain, and guide it out the window.

I found Mum leaning against the landing wall. She had a little more colour in her face, but was still shivering.

"Wash your hands."

"Why?"

"Just wash them!"

I ran to the bathroom and did as she said. When I got back she was sitting on the bed, taking deep breaths.

"Bats aren't scary," I said. "They're just little mice with wings. They can eat up to three thousand midges a night—except for fruit bats and vampire bats, but you don't find either of those here. They navigate using echolocation because they've got very poor eyesight. And they're wonderful mothers."

Every muscle in her body seemed to go tense at this last sentence, and she seemed to struggle for breath. For a second something in her eyes looked like how the cat had looked just before it had scratched me. Then she stood up and, hiding her face, ran from me for a second time.

The next day Mum wasn't in her bed when I woke up at 5am. I went downstairs and found her coat and bag gone, as well as the twenty-pound note laid out on the work surface. I wasn't sure why she had gone so early, since, as far as I knew—which wasn't very far—her work began at nine and she hadn't usually been leaving that early. Perhaps there had been a work emergency.

Mum returned home at half past five in the evening. I'd spent the day clearing more rubbish from the green—there really was a lot of it—and had found some lovely yellow flowers in the long grass and bushes that ran alongside the river. I put them up my sleeve and got back to the house just as Molly was about to leave.

"Are you friends with my mum?" I asked.

She smiled. "Our parents were friends. We went to the same school too at one point, but she left when I was nine so we didn't overlap there. Also my gran was on the same chemo ward as…" She stopped, and her eyes darted in the way mine do when I've said something wrong. Then she went back to normal again. "But yeah, we're still friends."

"If she's friends with you, why do you charge her money to clean her house?"

She scratched the back of her neck and wrinkled her forehead. "I wish she'd let me do it for free, to be honest. I'm happy just to help—she could do with the company. But she insists. So I charge her a very discounted rate. And she gives me more and won't accept the change back."

"Why not?"

"She says she wants to help!"

After Molly had gone I put the flowers in a purple vase I found in the same cupboard as the glasses, and put the vase in the middle of the table. The purple of the vase was a soft, pastel shade, and the bright yellow of the flowers, as well as the blue of the table cloth, looked pleasantly artistic. Then I went upstairs and wrote in my notebook. When I heard the key in the lock an hour later I jumped

up quietly and padded downstairs to watch—unseen—
Mum discover them. Then she would know that I was
sorry about the whole bat thing.

She hung up her coat and started to go through to
the living room, but then she turned and saw them. She
stopped and drew near, her head cocked to one side. She
wasn't smiling—she was actually frowning, but not like
she had done when she was cross with me. She took one
out and rubbed the stem between her finger and thumb,
so that the flower twirled round one way, and then the
other. Then she smoothed her hair back behind her right
ear, and poked the stem of the flower through it, like a
Kirby grip. The yellow of the flower stood out against the
red of her hair. Then she pulled it back out, put it in the
vase, gave the vase a quick pat, and started towards the
door behind which I was hiding. I ran away before she
could see me watching.

I spent the evening in my room. Mum didn't speak to
me when she came in to get ready for bed. She bent her
head as she squeezed past my bed. I wrote in my notebook
and she read, and when she turned the light out I kept
waking up to check if she was still there. At four in the
morning, just to be sure, I got up early, showered, dried,
dressed, made myself some hot chocolate, and waited in
the kitchen. At six she clattered down the stairs looking
flustered.

"Hi," I said as she hurried into the room. She let out a

breath and put a hand on her chest.

We looked at each other for a few seconds, but I couldn't think of anything else to say. I've never run dry on stage before, and I've never frozen up playing the piano. But now I felt like a cornered animal. And then the moment passed, and as she made breakfast it was as if she was one of Alexander Fleming's bacteria and I was the penicillin mould—wherever she went her body seemed to lean away from me, and her face seemed to always be turned sideways to me, or else her eyes would look just past me over my shoulder.

We watched television together that evening. I say 'together'—we were in the same room, on the same sofa, except there was about four feet of space separating us. Mum had her knees drawn up so that she was curled into a little ball. She was wearing her pyjamas, dressing gown and slippers, just as she had been when I'd first arrived. I had the oddest sensation, for a moment, that perhaps if I got up now, packed my things, thumped my suitcases back down the stairs and backed out the front door, the taxi would be waiting for me, and then I could get back on the bus and go all the way back down to London, and Dad would be waiting for me and we'd go back to the flat and this whole thing would be a strange kind of waking-dream. But my clothes were in the wash. The rubbish was gone from the green. The flat was a hundred miles away. And Dad was… I didn't know where he was now—the real him.

Mum's eyes never left the screen. Her face was impassive as she watched. When I was four, Dad used to read me stories. I don't remember a lot of them because at that age I was much more interested in watching his face as he read. His eyebrows would jump and raise and lower. His mouth would grow and shrink. His forehead would wrinkle and smooth. Sometimes his nostrils would flare. I learned those facial expressions later, with the help of my outreach worker and some photographs of situations and people. I also taught myself how different facial expressions are connected to different feelings, and different feelings are reactions to different information being received. It's an ongoing process.

That night as I dozed I sensed her crouching beside me, and considered whether or not to open my eyes. In the end I decided I would, but my courage failed me. When I was pretending to be asleep she stood closer to me than she ever had before; I felt a hand rest for a second on my shoulder, and then it lifted again. I lay extra still, hoping that she might keep it there for just a little longer. But she didn't.

When Dad was alive it had never felt like hugs were an essential thing—not like food and water. Now, however, I felt like how I imagined it to feel to be withering away from famine. In the quiet moments I would look at the texts, and I would try and get back a sense of him, but it didn't work.

The phone was an old model—older than Mum's—and I didn't have a charger for it, nor did I know where to get one. The only reason it had survived at all was because I was holding it when I jumped out the window to safety, having used it to call 999. I tried to be happy about it having survived, and about still having the texts. It was like trying to be happy about getting a new doll when you thought you were getting a little brother or sister.

Did Mum even want to hug me? Perhaps. I hoped so, but I couldn't be sure. Maybe she just wasn't a hugging person. To try and help her feel more relaxed I resolved to make up another game, which I played during the following day to the best of my ability—the Avoid Provocation Game. One point for every morning I managed not to get in her way or make her shout. Each time I did annoy her or get in her way I subtracted a point from my total score. I didn't speak to her. I didn't cross her path. I didn't try and catch her eye. I didn't do any surprises. And I have no idea why, but it didn't make me feel more relaxed, at any rate. It should have made things happier and easier and more relaxed for both of us—I'd taken away all the things that made her shout after all—but it didn't.

The weather quickly turned colder and cloudier.

Alison said you don't get a lot of dry days in Scotland, so on good days I took my breakfast outside. My favourite breakfast is ham with fried tomatoes, cheese, a slice of buttered toast, and some hot chocolate. It's lucky that most people have most of those things, and it's something I know how to put together myself. It was never long before there was a high-pitched 'meow', and the black and white cat came trotting over the grass towards me. I'd offer it a shred of ham, and it would stretch out its neck and sniff, before taking it from my hand. Soon it let me pet it properly. One morning it jumped onto my knee.

That morning it must have rained during the night, because when I ran across the green my feet squelched, and cold, slimy water leaked through my trainers between my toes. The green sloped down towards a wooded river bank, and as I inched closer, picking up cans and an old nappy along the way, I saw something in one of the trees. I pushed through the tangle of shrubs that surrounded it and saw a human leg, clad in khaki trousers, with a foot on the end wearing a muddy black trainer, hanging. I approached with tiny steps, my heart palpitating.

"H-hello?" I said

"Who's there? Identify yourself!" demanded the other person. I let my breath out, and approached with more confidence. The reply was muffled by leaves and branches. It was a child's voice, unbroken but in the alto range—and it sounded cross, but this time in a way that made me smile.

I called up once again: "What are you doing?"

"Being away."

"Who are you?"

"Nobody."

"That's your name?"

"No, stupid."

"I was making a joke. So what is your name?"

"Jamie."

"It's nice to, er… meet you…" I took hold of his foot to shake it. He gave a yell and kicked out, making contact with my lip. There was a searing pain and a salty stickiness in my mouth. A drop of blood landed on my sleeve. The owner of the shoe on the foot on the leg dropped down and stood facing me. He was about ten years old, with large front teeth, thick, dark, scowling eyebrows, quite brown skin, and big, brown eyes. He had a little knobbly nose and round cheeks. He was wearing baggy tracksuit bottoms with a really stained, grass-green, too-big fleece. Its sleeves dropped past his hands, and it had a zip that went from the top of the collar down to about his breastbone. His hair was blackish-brown, too long, tousled, and was covered in little knotty balls.

He glared at me. "You made me lose the game!"

"Game…?" Did he have his own Game, too?

He held up an old-fashioned Game-Boy-type thing, knocked my shoulder with his and started to walk away. Then he stopped and looked back, before turning round and retracing his steps, eyeing my lip.

"How'd you get that?"

"You kicked me."

"Oh." He cocked his head, and his eyes flicked between my mouth and the Game Boy. "You're not crying."

"It's not that sore." More blood dripped onto my trainer, briefly forming a red blob before the mud and water diluted it.

"You should go to the doctor. I had a cut that big once. I had to get stitches."

"Does it hurt?" I asked, slightly timidly.

He grinned massively. "Oh, yeah! When I had it done they used a big needle. They stuck it into me and pulled the thread through like an operation, except I was completely awake. And if they break one stitch the whole lot comes undone like knitting, and then they have to do it all again, except if they do it too many times over the same spot the skin all mashes up into a humungous big mulch!" He spread his arms.

"Ouch! I don't think I'll go then."

"If you don't you'll bleed and bleed until you shrivel up!"

I had never heard that before, but decided not to risk it. "Where's the nearest surgery?"

"Follow me."

I leaned my bin bag up against the tree. Jamie led the way back up my street, past the wooden fences, the brown concrete houses and the little gardens with flowers and patios and white plastic chairs, up to the junction where the man who skinned people alive lived. We turned right, down a foot path at the side of the road, where there was a flower bed and a green, fluffy looking hedge, and then right again. All the while Jamie was playing on his Game Boy. Drops of blood splashed my shoes, the road, and my tracksuit. I dabbed my lip again with my sleeve, and winced as some of the fibres stuck.

"Shrivelling up yet?"

I held a finger up to check. It was pink and full. "Not yet. What's the game you're playing?"

"Snake."

"What d'you have to do?"

"Make it eat the dots so it grows. Now shush."

I tried to be quiet, but it's so much harder when somebody tells you to. We passed down a street called North Street. The houses here were bigger, and were all joined together in a row. Then we came to a couple of shops, and a pub called 'The Corrie'.

I leaned over to look at the Game Boy screen.

"You're putting me off!" He stepped into the road. There was a "MEEEEEP!", a scraping of tyres, and a high-pitched squeal of brakes. I grabbed his arm and yanked him back onto the pavement. He wrenched himself free.

"OW, get off me… what?!" He stared at the screen, then glared at me. "I was heading for top score!"

"You almost got hit by a car!"

"Stupid car."

"You didn't look both ways."

"So? It should've slowed down when it saw me."

He sat on a flat, low wall which ran alongside the pavement. I dabbed my lip again.

He pointed up the street. "Keep walking that way. It's a big white building."

"Can't you come with me?"

"No. Now pee off."

The streets were mostly empty here too. I was happy for them that they were all probably having a lovely time on holiday, like Joanne said. Still, I thought, it would be so nice to meet just one person—especially someone my own age—who didn't keep going all scowly and cross at random times.

I carried on until I came to a white building with a sign above the sliding doors saying: 'North Hill Group Practice Surgery'. Inside were six chairs and a coffee table with magazines, and a central desk at which sat a woman who had slightly greying, wavy brown hair and a pointy nose, talking on the phone.

"No, no we don't have any appointments for tomorrow, I'm afraid. Friday? Yes, we can fit you in for nine. Date of birth? Fantastic. We'll see you then, Mr Fraser. Take care. Goodbye. Bye." She put the receiver down. "What?"

"I've cut my lip."

She raised her eyebrows. "So I see."

"I just moved here, so I'm not registered, but I think it needs stitches."

She took a sheet of paper from a stand, and handed it to me. "You fill that in, and I'll see what I can do with slots."

I filled in my gender and previous address. I had known the latter ever since I was five. Dad taught it to me after I got lost in Richmond Park. More blood splashed onto the form as I bent over. I wiped it with my sleeve and checked my fingers again to see if I was shrivelling up.

"I don't know who my old doctor was," I said. "Someone in London..."

"Well that narrows it down. Er, right, well... You're going to need the name and address of a parent or guardian."

"Oh, that's easy—I found out Mum's name yesterday from a neighbour. She's called Patty Harrington. She lives at number sixteen McCallish Court."

"Right, I'll photocopy it and you can take the original back with you. Just make sure you bring it back filled in. Excuse me." The phone was ringing again. "Hello? Uh-huh. No problem, would you like to reschedule?

OK, well why don't you get back to us when you know? Thanks for telling us. OK. Bye now."

She turned to me: "Cancellation."

"Ah, sorry to hear that."

"Sorry? That means the doctor can see you now— here he is now."

Someone had come out from a side room. It took me a second to recognise him, but when I did I had to check again to make sure I wasn't seeing things.

"Doctor Strachan, we have a damsel in distress."

Ben pointed at me. "I recognise you!"

I pointed back. "I recognise you!"

"Come on through. That cut looks nasty."

I followed him, feeling happy because now I could introduce him to Molly. His office was quite small, with a computer, a bed with a curtain round it like a shower curtain, a desk and three chairs—one on his side and two on mine.

"Take a seat, Anna." He sat down. "What can I do for you?"

"I've cut my lip," I said, although because of the swelling it sounded more like: "I cuh why liw".

"How did that happen?"

"I got kicked."

The smile disappeared. "Is there something you'd like to tell me?"

I frowned. "What do you mean?"

43

"Has anyone done anything to you which… which they shouldn't have?" I looked down and sorted through everything that had happened since I'd arrived, whilst trying to work out what he meant. "You can tell me. It's OK."

"N-ooo… At least… I don't think so. Well, the man who lives in the big house threatened to skin me alive when I put some rubbish in his wheelie bin, but he didn't go through with it. Does that count?"

He laughed, breathing a long breath. "No—no it doesn't count. I just had to make sure—professional obligation, you understand. And neighbourly concern, of course. Would you mind telling me who kicked you, and what happened?"

"It was an accident. There was a boy in a tree. I tried to shake his foot to say hello, because his hand was too high up to reach. He got a fright and kicked out, and his foot hit my lip."

"Well, at least it was an accident. But it's a significant cut. I'll need to clean it before I do anything else. Let me just get my things together." He fetched a cardboard tray and some antiseptic swabs, washed his hands and put on his gloves.

"So… you found your mother's house?"

"Yes. It's so clean. The living room has a thick carpet and a big squashy sofa. And I get to sleep on an air mattress in her room!"

"Hmm."

"My mother's… interesting."

"Is she?"

The hairs on the back of my neck prickled. I wasn't sure why. "Yes. She works a lot. She's usually really tired when she gets back, so she shouts at me and doesn't have much energy left to talk. And she's terrified of bats."

"Yes, I remember that." He tore open a sterile swab.

"Do you know her?"

He nodded. "Hold still." He dabbed my lip, and I winced. "Right! That's the sore bit over. Now comes the main act."

Jamie had been completely wrong in everything he'd said. Not only did I not shrivel up, but the stitches didn't even hurt—apart from the disinfectant. The needle didn't turn anything to mulch either. Ben made me lie down, then sprayed my lip with cold spray, which seemed to numb it. The needle going in and the pulling tight of the thread just felt like two tugs. Once he had finished, I sat up.

"Now, you book another appointment in a week or so to come back and get those taken out. OK?"

"OK. And thanks. I'm happy we'll get to chat again!" I reached the door, and remembered something: "Do you know Molly?"

"Molly who?"

"She's a cleaner."

"Oh, that Molly! Yes, I do." He smiled, the corners of his eyes crinkling like paper. "She's lovely."

Back at the house I found Molly vacuuming the living room. I stuck my fingers in my ears.

"HELLO!" She waved, then gestured at me and pointed to her lip.

I made a gesture which I hoped conveyed that all was OK. "IS MUM HERE?"

She pointed upstairs.

"WOULD YOU LIKE SOME HOT CHOCOLATE?" We had run out of milk the previous day, but instant drinking chocolate has milk already added.

She shook her head and gestured at an ironing board, which was set up along the wall with the window in. Sitting on the end was a cat-patterned cup, filled with plain hot water. She turned off the vacuum.

"Sorry… trying to get this done before the hour. I'm meeting up with a friend. What happened to your lip?"

"Someone kicked it. He was in a tree near the river."

"Ah, Jamie Bean?"

"Yes. But it was an accident."

"I see."

I paused. I had never had any coaching on how to ask the question that I now wanted to ask her, and so I didn't know if it was OK to ask it, and I didn't know anything about the right time or place to ask, or the right way to go about it.

"Molly?"

"Yes?"

"How… how can a person be happy?"

Her eyebrows went up and her mouth opened a bit. "Uh," she said, as though she hadn't meant to make a noise, and then she closed it, frowned, and put her head on one side. Then her shoulders drooped, and she ran a hand slowly down the handle of the vacuum cleaner, as if it were a cat. "If you find the answer to that, Anna," she said at last, looking almost like Mum because her eyes were looking off somewhere and her smile had vanished, "Tell me. Tell all of us, in fact."

I made a cup of hot chocolate for myself, then swithered for a long time. Since I couldn't control what Mum did, but I could control what I did, I made a second mug, took off my shoes and went upstairs, taking care to avoid the creaky step at the top. The door to Mum's room was ajar, and computer keys clacked inside. I poked my head round and saw her sitting at her desk, typing. I pushed the door open with my elbow.

"Hi."

She jumped. "Don't blooming do that!" There was a very long, very awkward silence before, slowly, she turned round. Then she stood up quickly and swept towards me, eyes glinting. "What happened to your…?"

I couldn't work out what she meant until she stretched out her fingers towards my lip.

"Someone kicked me."

Every part of her seemed to go tense. In fact, she seemed to grow in size too, though that must have been an optical illusion. "Who?" she snarled.

"A friend."

"Which friend?"

"Jamie. I met him in a tree. It was an accident—he's just little. He didn't realise my mouth was in the way of his foot. Don't worry—it's not bad. It doesn't hurt much now."

She drew back and sat down, not taking her eyes off me. It felt good to be having a proper conversation with her again.

"Where did you go for the stitches?"

"North Hill Group Practice Surgery."

She nodded. "Well, we'll get you registered with my GP in Livingston. Not at North Hill."

"Why not?"

She shivered. "I just don't feel comfortable there, ok?"

"But I've already filled in half the registration form…"

"Don't worry about that. We'll get you a new form."

Her voice sounded strained. Her shoulders looked stiff. I put the hot chocolate down on the table. She tutted, and moved it onto a coaster which had printed on it a picture of an owl and its baby.

"This desk belonged to my mother. It's worth about five hundred pounds."

"Is it? I didn't realise you were putting it up for sale."

She closed her eyes. "I just mean I don't want stains on it. OK?"

"OK." I sank down onto my mattress and sipped my hot chocolate for a few minutes. She turned back towards her computer screen and keyboard as though she were about to type, but instead she just sat there. "Mum?"

"What?"

"What is it that you actually do?"

"Administrate. For a charity in Livingston."

"What does 'administrate' mean?"

"It means I do the dirty work nobody else can be bothered to do."

"Like what?"

"Book meetings and transport... organise events... type minutes... get flyers and other things printed... take personal calls... get food in... God knows what else. Truth be told, I'm getting blooming fed up of it. Was going to quit. Then I get a call saying you're coming to stay, so..."

"Why are you getting fed up? Don't you like the job?"

"Oh, it's not the job—it's all the stuff around the edges. The nit-picking and bickering. It's not even about doing a good job, it's just about getting one over on each other. I try and stay out of it—keep my head down, but..." She shrugged. "You can't, really. They hunt you down and drag you into it."

"School was a bit like that. Well, now I can understand why the fridge is so empty and everything is off." I put a hand on her shoulder.

"Hmm?" She took my hand gently, and moved it away.

"The milk was all curdled yesterday, there was only one slice of ham and we're running out of eggs. But if all you do all day is get food in for other people then I can understand why you wouldn't want to do that in your Golden Time as well. That's what Dad calls it. I mean—called it."

"Anna." Mum's voice sounded like the effort to speak was comparable to the effort of hauling a sack of potatoes up a ladder. "Look, I know you must be hurting. I know you loved your dad. But I don't want to hear about him, OK? Or his flat. In fact, I don't want to hear about anything touching upon your life together."

"Why not?" It was as if she had punched me in the chest.

"He hurt me very much."

"How?"

She turned away, then started to type, then stopped again. "When you were a baby and he decided he wanted to leave, he sued me for custody of you." She sipped her hot chocolate. "He won."

"Why?"

Her face went very blank and her voice sounded a bit like one of those automated phone network voices that do your top-ups for you. "The case your dad's lawyer built," she said—and I remember noticing how crisp and clean each word sounded, like it was a hedge that had been carefully pruned to exactly the right shape—"Was that because I had chosen to work full time, and because I'd been showing symptoms of severe depression, and because I wasn't breastfeeding— all those things combined meant that you and I hadn't developed a proper sense of attachment to each other, so if I got custody of you, you would be emotionally starved. He argued that you should be cared for by the parent who had the most chance of ensuring you thrived both physically and emotionally."

"But I do feel attached to you!"

She was quiet for several seconds. Then she continued as if I hadn't said anything: "Have you any idea what that feels like?"

I shook my head.

"I watched him gather up all your things and pack them into two big suitcases. After he had done that he stowed them away in the boot of his car. Then he took your car seat out of my car and secured it on the back seat. Some of the neighbours were watching—it was like the air was saturated with their judgements. He took you from the social worker's arms and he strapped you into the car seat. Then he got into the driver's seat, started the engine, and drove off." She was shaking. "I stood in that driveway for an hour after he left. When I went back inside it was like I'd never had a baby. Until I found one jar of baby food still in the freezer. Imagine how that feels."

It interested me how she spoke about the air being saturated with judgements—as if feelings were like radio signals one could tune into without words if only they had a working satellite dish. I'd never thought of feelings in that way. Perhaps my dish was faulty. My hot chocolate was far too sweet, and it coated my mouth gaggingly. Out of habit my hand started to inch towards the pillow for my phone, but I caught myself and thought better of it. After about ten minutes Mum got up, went over to her bag, took out a twenty-pound note and put it into my hand. "Here," she said. "Stock us up."

It hadn't been a pleasant conversation at all. My mind tossed and turned as I walked down the road to the shop. Dad had been my every other thought for the last month, but in light of what Mum had said I now felt guilty for dwelling on his memory. It felt… tainted. Would I gain the same comfort from his text messages now? If I had been in his position I wouldn't have found it as easy to abandon Mum as he had seemed to find it.

I didn't feel like smiling. I didn't feel like breaking in the morning. I didn't feel like dancing or skipping. I didn't feel like all my worries had disappeared. And yet... In Biology I watched a documentary about the desert. At one point the presenter walked up to a clump of totally dead-looking plants and, by flicking his fingertips, sprinkled a few drops of water over them. You can't usually see plants moving and changing but these ones did. The leaves all uncurled with a gentle crackling, and brightly coloured flowers sort of oozed up out of them like blisters from a burn. That's how I felt after the conversation between Mum and me. But I didn't know why.

The wind had picked up and had blown the clouds away. The sun shone low and glinted from the west, but it was still bright and warm. I sort of hoped, as I turned into the junction and onto the main road, that I would see Jamie playing on his Game Boy. But he wasn't there, so I went into the shop, picked up a wire basket and walked up and down. There were essentials like fruit, which sat in wooden boxes, bread which was up on the shelves, and juice and milk in the yellow-lit fridge area. I put a carton of fresh orange juice into the basket, and picked up a jar of red and a jar of white pasta sauce. I also got some tinned pineapples and peaches, as well as some new potatoes and sardines, some cheese, some lettuce, a smoked sausage and a pack of sliced ham. For snacks I picked up a bag of chocolate chip cookies and a multipack of crisps. All together it cost sixteen pounds and thirty-eight pence.

When I got back Mum was sitting on her desk chair, her head resting on her arms. I thought she was crying at first, but when I got closer I saw that her eyes were closed and her breath was gentle. I tiptoed round her, perched on the edge of the bed and put a hand on her shoulder, thinking of those times she had sat with me while I pretended to be asleep. It occurred to me that at this moment, the roles might just be reversed.

It was raining the next day. I woke up to it splattering on the window. The wind gusted the ventilation system, rattling something I couldn't see. When I looked outside, the shrubs and bushes were swaying back and forth, and a plastic bag whirled in the road. The window itself had streaky droplets running diagonally down to the left, and the sky was a deep shade of purpley-grey. The house next door still had its curtains shut in one window, just as it had done all day the previous day, and the day before, and the day before that. I went downstairs in my nightie and found Mum in the kitchen, putting on her coat.

When she saw me she gave a quick nod. "TV guide's on the coffee table. Help yourself to snacks. Oh, and have you got that GP form? Might as well register you today. I'll just copy the info you put down."

I fetched the form and handed it to her. "I didn't know all the answers, but I filled it in as best I could."

She took it and skim-read it. "What's that?" She asked, pointing to something I had filled in. She started to giggle.

"What are you laughing at?"

Something hot rose up inside me. Dad had told me off very severely for laughing at the medical word *'squamous'* when Mr Langton once used it in front of me. Mr Langton had been talking to Dad about Mrs Langton, back when Mrs Langton was still alive. Dad had said that it was extremely wrong and hurtful to laugh at somebody's diagnosis, especially that one, and double-especially if you don't know what it is—no matter how funny it might sound—and that I should make every effort to control myself. But when I used to go to school the other children still asked me all the time if I pooed burgers, and if they could have some brown sauce for their chips when it came to my diagnosis. Then they'd roar with laughter, and my ears would go so red that they would burn me. But I quickly learned that I couldn't just ask them to make an effort to control themselves. That only made them laugh more, and then my ears would go even more red and that would make them laugh too and call me things like 'traffic lights', which became my nickname. It got used more than my real name in the end. Eventually, I forced myself just to laugh along whenever it happened, which Dad said would make us friends instead of enemies, so that is what I did.

"I know," I said, keeping my voice as relaxed as I could, "I think it sounds like a fast food restaurant for donkeys!"

She waved a hand in front of her face, blew out slowly through pursed lips, and when she had stopped laughing she said, "Sorry."

I blinked. I'd never heard her say sorry before. In fact, nobody had ever said sorry before for laughing at my Asperger's.

She folded the form up and zipped it into the main compartment of her handbag. "So, when were you diagnosed with this... Asperger's?"

"When I was four," I said, noting how intently she was staring at me. I didn't know why this was gripping her so much more than any of our previous interactions, but it felt good to have her attention so completely.

"How... Why? I mean, what is it? Fill me in!"

I hesitated before answering. How could I describe in a few minutes something that had taken nine years to live? Most people who'd found out about my diagnosis had already heard of it, and most of them already knew all they wanted to know, or else it wasn't a good time. It was quarter to nine now. Mum was going to be late for work. Nevertheless, she'd sat down at the table and was looking at me. It felt odd to be looking back at her—

actually looking into her eyes instead of watching her look somewhere else. I sat down too.

"Well," I said, "It's a thing that makes you a bit different in how you look at the world, and also how you learn and talk to other people. It's named after Hans Asperger. I don't know if it's a hard or a soft G."

She nodded. Of all the conversations that could have made us start talking to each other again, I'd never imagined that it would be one like this.

"Sometimes it makes you think very intensely about things," I continued. "And sometimes you don't always understand people, so you accidentally say things that upset them."

"Like what?"

This question surprised me. I'd thought I'd said plenty to upset her since arriving. Maybe I'd read her wrong. "Um, well... Once my friend Jenny drew a picture of me and she drew my head really big. And I thought it was a caricature so I laughed and said the head was far too big. But it wasn't meant to be a caricature. And she didn't speak to me for a week. My outreach worker told me what I did wrong—I didn't figure it out for myself."

"Maybe Jenny came down too hard on you anyway. It was just a misunderstanding." It came out of Mum's mouth as a whisper. She dropped her gaze. Her cheeks went a bit red. She looked like a boy in my class once looked after he'd accidentally made the teacher cry.

"Who is this outreach worker, then?"

"Oh... I had two I used to go and visit. They helped me learn some things about how most other people work, and how to know what they need and expect, and how to reach out to them. They said it was because I'll have to be around them my whole life, and most of them don't think like me, so I might as well learn some general things to help me get by. That's the other thing about Asperger's—people don't always understand you either, so sometimes you have to teach them, and to do that you have to know what they need in order to learn, because they don't always know themselves. But sometimes they're not interested anyway and won't listen. But that doesn't matter. It's good to give them the chance. And Da… I mean… I think it's fine to be a bit different anyway—no matter what people say—as long as you're honest and careful and kind."

"Ah. OK." She fiddled with a thread on her sleeve. "There's a lot I've missed, isn't there?"

I didn't know what to say. I wondered how this was going to end.

There was a noise outside. We both jumped up. Mum opened the door, and we peered out. I shivered and hugged myself. The bottom of my nightie flapped around. I held it down. The delivery van was back in next door's driveway. Two men were staggering in with another box.

"Were those the ones who stared at you?"

"Hmm?" She turned to me briefly.

"You know… when Dad left."

Her lips went very white and taut. "No."

"What do you suppose is in the box?"

She paused, shook her head, and then shrugged. "They don't even have jobs!"

"Perhaps they work from home. Or… or maybe they have a rich relative!"

She gave me a sideways look. "Well then, how come Molly sees the daughter at the benefits office every week?"

I didn't know what to say in reply to that.

It was far too wet to eat outside, so I stood by the window and watched for the black and white cat. Nobody deserves to be left outside in a freezing deluge—even if they did scratch you out of pain. Of course, I'd have to make sure it didn't walk on the living room carpet. It didn't turn up though—it must have found somewhere else to shelter.

I went through to the hall to see if Mum had any waterproof coats. There was a wooden panel bolted to the wall, with a lot of shiny gold metal pegs screwed into it. An oilcloth waterproof hat hung on one of these. I picked it off and put it on my head. On the floor immediately below sat a pair of green wellington boots.

They looked brand new. Perhaps Mum had been given them by someone, but wasn't in the habit of wearing wellingtons. Otherwise she would certainly have worn them on a day like this.

There were no spare coats on the pegs, and I wondered what to do. Then I remembered the cupboard under the stairs. When I'd got the bucket to get rid of the bat there'd been a bit of oilcloth poking out from the bottom. It could have been a sleeve. I found a camping torch hanging from a hook on the inside of the cupboard door. It kept flickering on and off, and the light it cast was dim, but it was good enough to shine around until I found the poking-out bit. I gave it a sharp tug. A heap of things fell forward, but since everything was so disorganised anyway I didn't suppose Mum would notice. When the whole thing came free it was indeed an old, green oilskin coat! The lining was maroon and dark green checked on a white base, and it had a gold zip and poppers down the front for extra waterproof-ness. There was no hood, but that didn't matter because I had the hat which went perfectly with it. When I put it on, the sleeves came all the way to halfway down my fingertips, and the bottom reached my knees. Since Mum wasn't much taller than me, and it was not the style of coat designed to reach to the knees, it must have been too big for her too.

Before I could wonder about this any more, I heard another sound outside—a bumping noise, and then a rumble, like wheels rolling across tarmac. I rushed down the path, banging the front door of the house shut behind me, hid behind the wooden fence and peeked into next door's garden. The gap was so narrow I couldn't clearly make out details, but the woman—who wore a long, black coat—was wheeling a bin down the driveway whilst trying to shield her head from the rain. She left the bin outside the gate and retreated back inside, banging the door.

As soon as she had gone I crept round the fence, through the gate and up the concrete path, which had a knocker on it in the shape of a horse shoe. I knocked three times, and watched the rain run down the window pane. Quick, light footsteps approached, and the lock turned. The woman had a long, thin, pinched face with coarse skin, and downward sloping creases at both corners of her mouth. Her hair was dirty blonde, her cheekbones were high, and her eyebrows were low.

She looked me up and down. "What?"

"I'm Anna," I said. "I live next door. It's nice to meet you." I held out my hand. "Can I come in?"

"No," she snapped. "We're busy." She started to shut the door.

"It's soaking wet…"

It opened a tiny crack. "Not my problem."

"What are all the parcels?"

There was a pause. "None of your business."

"OK," I said. Perhaps this was just a very private, unpersonable neighbourhood. Maybe that explained some of the things about Mum, too. "It's just that if the curtains are shut all the time but you're dressed, I wondered if you were looking after someone who couldn't get up. And that must be really annoying for them."

She gave a laugh, but it wasn't the kind you do when you're having fun. It was the nasty kind, like the kind my friends did at me when I used to go to school. "Ha! And what about the poor folks they drag down with 'em?"

"Maybe I could come in and cheer her up? I'm good at being cheery."

"Don't waste your time, Honey Pops—nothing's gonna cheer that one up." She jerked her thumb in the direction of the door. "Save those smiles for someone who appreciates them, because trust me—they won't make a blind bit of difference here." And the door shut.

The rain was really coming down heavily now. It reminded me of the car wash Dad used to drive through every Wednesday, but the drops of water were fatter and wetter. The oilskin hat magnified the noise until it sounded like there was a waterfall in my head. The street was empty—or so I thought. I decided the best thing to do would be to simply go back to Mum's house and borrow one of her books. I squeezed back through the gate and splashed down the road, through the puddles that were collecting because the street was sloped and the kerb at the lower side of the road was high.

It was only when I got back to the front door that I realised how stupid I had been, banging it shut behind me in haste, without setting the latch so that it wouldn't lock behind me. Now it wouldn't open. In stories people are able to magically open doors using hair clips. I wasn't sure it would work with this kind of lock, but it was my only hope. I took the oilskin hat off and removed my butterfly hairclip. Then I tried fitting it through the keyhole, both in the open position and the closed, but it was too wide, even when I tried forcing it through. It sprang sideways and I cut the side of my thumb a bit.

Even after such a short time with the hood down my hair and back were completely soaked. There was no point in putting the oilskin hat back on, and my clip would most likely tangle in my hair, so I hung the hat on the doorknob, put the clip in my pocket, and went down the road to see if I could shelter under a tree.

I crossed the grassy area, which was now even squelchier than before. The rain was pelting directly in my face, and I was shuddering. The wind roared around my ears so that they ached and I felt dizzy. Someone tapped my shoulder. I gasped and jumped round.

"Are you deaf?" Jamie yelled.

"What? I can't hear you in this wind!"

"You're a freak!"

"What?"

"YOU'RE A FREAK!"

"Why?"

"Nobody goes out in rain like this!"

"You're out…"

"Yeah, only 'cause I saw you and had come out to call you a freak. Come on—this way…" He grabbed my arm and hauled me back across the green.

Jamie's house was a good deal smaller than Mum's. His parents were obviously not nearly as particular about muddy shoes or making sure the furniture stayed neat. The linoleum in the kitchen had brown stains on it, and there were cracks where the tiles met. The living room had a thin, faded carpet and a brown leather sofa with yellow foam poking through a hole. There were blinds on the windows instead of curtains.

"It must be lovely that your parents don't care if you don't take your shoes off," I said.

"Yeah, yeah. Here—this is my room." He pushed open a wooden side door, upon which "Jamie's Room" was carved in spiky capitals, using what looked like a kitchen knife.

His room was even smaller than the living room— just big enough for a bed, a chest of drawers, a laundry bag on a hook on the door, and a stack of shelves up the wall. The lowest shelf had a radio on it, and a very thick, heavy-looking mobile phone catalogue, as well as a tin money box. The second shelf held a pile of upturned drawing pins, his Game Boy and a head torch.

"You can wear some of my clothes." He wrenched open a drawer and pulled out a fleece and some trousers.

"Thanks." I pulled off my jumper and T-shirt.

"Wait a moment!" He threw his arms up over his eyes.

"What?"

"I'm a boy!"

"So? You're just little. I changed in front of Dad all the time when I was little."

"Family's different. And I am not little. I'm nearly eleven."

"Are you? OK then. But why is family different?"

"Because… because…" he faltered. "Look, I'll turn my back." And he stood in the corner, facing the wall.

Once I had changed I said, "You can turn round now."

"Are you dressed?"

When I said yes he turned cautiously, scowling. "Siddown." He gave me a push on the chest so that my knees buckled and I sat heavily on the bed. Then he sat cross-legged opposite me, and looked as if he wasn't quite sure what to do now.

"Did you ever make a den?" I asked.

"What?"

"Well, if you pin the duvet to a shelf with some of your drawing pins and hang it over the edge of the bed, you'll have a sort of tent, won't you?"

He picked up his Game Boy. "Let's see you do it, then."

I got him to stand up, then pulled the duvet cover off the bed. It was blue, with an orange stain near the poppered opening. I pinned two of its corners to the top shelf using six drawing pins—a red one, a yellow one, two blue ones and two green ones. Then I pulled the other end straight, so that it fell over the side of the bed. Now there was a wedge-shaped space where the pillows were.

"See? A den!" I sat back, admiring my work.

"Great—now I can't see the flaming game." As soon as I'd pulled the duvet off, Jamie had sat back down on the mattress and I'd worked around him.

"Here," I took the torch and forced it over his head.

"Ow—flip off!" But he let me pull it over properly.

"Budge up…" I squashed in beside him. The den was very warm with the two of us inside. "How's the game?"

"Not bad."

"Can I try?"

"Wait your turn."

I looked through the mobile phone catalogue. There were a lot of incredibly high-tech, fancy new ones. I turned to a random page and started reading information for the Polestar H7—a silver phone with a screen that looked like a very small computer. "Download games, apps and more!" the description read.

"Look at this," I said. "If you had this you'd have loads more games—not just snake."

He jabbed a finger at the price: £399.99. "As if Carol'd be able to afford that."

"Carol's your mum?"

"No fear. She's my foster mum."

"Really? I had one of those! She was called Alison, but she only did short-term emergency fostering."

"There's four of us—Alasdair, Jeremy, Joe and me, but Joe's almost sixteen now, so I expect she'll kick him out soon. Imagine getting paid to keep children! Like when there's a used car nobody wants, so they pay to get it taken away and stayed-away." He threw the Game Boy down and clenched his jaw. "I put it on level one for you. Arrow keys move it. You've got to get the bits of food and the snake gets longer and longer. If you touch the side you die. If you touch any part of the snake you die." I hoped he wasn't being literal. Life here was proving to be decidedly violent.

The snake was a thick, grey line made of squares. It was quite short, and didn't move smoothly. It travelled forward in jerks, about one every second, accompanied by a 'Bip… bip… ' sound. The 'food' was a tiny grey square in the top right-hand corner of the screen. At first it was easy, almost boring. However, as it grew longer it curled around the screen, and I had to think more carefully and plan ahead so that I didn't trap the head end. I lasted as long as I possibly could, spiralling inwards, until a piece of food appeared in the top right-hand corner. I aimed for an emerging gap, but missed and hit the body. The screen went blank. There was a "Dee-deedee-DEE!" noise, and the words 'TOP SCORE!' appeared, with an animation of a snake waving.

"I got top score!" I said.

"Impossible," he scoffed. "You were on the lowest level! Anyway—it was your first time." He snatched it off me and inspected the screen. His eyebrows and the corners of his mouth went right down. "Right," he said, "I'm setting that straight." And he settled back on the pillows and started a new game.

I don't know exactly how many games we played, but it must have been a lot because we got three more top scores between us, and when the knock sounded on the front door it was dusky and had stopped raining.

"Should we answer it?" I asked.

He shook his head. "It'll just be one of the others."

"They wouldn't knock, would they? They live here. You didn't knock." He didn't answer. "I'll get it if you like."

He shrugged. "Suit yourself."

I opened the door, and found myself facing a gigantic policeman.

"Are you Anna Whitear?"

"How do you know?"

"Carol only fosters boys. I've been sent out to look for

you. Been round all the houses in between this one and your mother's. What are you doing here?"

I began to sweat. I didn't see what I'd done wrong, since Jamie had invited me in and nobody had forbidden me from going out, but I still didn't want to be dragged off to prison. "I was just visiting."

"Aye, well, your mum's in a fair state, worrying over you."

My stomach felt like it was collapsing in. I never thought she might actually get worried about me. Dad knew I was sensible, and we had agreed rules so even if I did get lost—which hardly happened at all after the Richmond Park incident—he knew I could get back safely. Maybe now she would pay to have me taken away and stayed-away, like Jamie.

"Can I get my clothes? They got wet in the rain."

"All right."

When I went through to Jamie's room I found it empty. The window was open, and the white net veil that hung in front of it flapped in the breeze. It was as if he was a criminal, running from his own house. I recalled Molly's words—you never know from the outside why someone reacts the way they do. I gathered my clothes up. Then the policeman walked me home.

Mum was pacing up and down on the lawn. When she saw me she came towards us with her chin raised.

"Thank you," she said to the policeman. He nodded

and left. Then she took my arm and led me inside surprisingly gently. When we got inside, however, she pressed me down into a dining chair and stood over me. Now I almost wished she would shout at me. I would have deserved it. Instead her voice was level.

"Do you know how much trouble you've caused?"

I couldn't reply, even though I knew I owed her a proper explanation.

"The police had to come out, Anna. The police."

"I'm sorry." My mouth wobbled and I tightened it.

She squeezed her eyes shut. "You know, they say that if a missing child doesn't turn up within the first few hours, then something's probably happened to them."

I looked past her towards a painting of a farm which hung on the wall opposite the table. The cockerel looked as if it only had one leg, and it had its eye fixed on a nearby hen.

"I'm sorry," she added.

"What for?" I was incredulous.

"For leaving you alone. It was wrong of me." She sat down. Her nails were ragged and short.

I wanted to reach out and comfort her, but I didn't dare.

She lifted her head again. "Go to your room." Her voice sounded like a dog baring its teeth.

I sat in my room and thumbed through Dad's texts. The phone had twenty-eight percent of its battery left.

LAURA GUTHRIE

"Chips tonight? Xoxoxox" read one from last November. Another read, "Conkers match. Five o'clock, Regent's Park tomorrow. Prepare to get THRASHED! Xoxoxoxoxox". A third read "Don't worry about them. You're head and shoulders ahead—I believe in you. Xoxoxoxoxox".

I heard Mum on the stairs, and then the sound of the bathroom door, and a bath being run. It felt like someone was holding a glowing hot poker against my heart, except that pulling back and twisting couldn't shake it free. I wanted to keep reading, and yet doing so was unbearable. Instead, I took out my notepad and wrote.

Three paragraphs in, Mum knocked softly on the door.

"I ran you a bath," she said, and held out a large, fluffy purple towel. "Leave your clothes on the floor. I'll wash them for you."

Mum and I both settled down to sleep early. The excitement, the soaking and Mum's scolding had worn us out.

I spent the evening in my sleeping bag, writing. Mum sat up in bed, reading a book.

"Wuthering Heights," I read out, catching the title as she opened it.

"Mm-hmm," she confirmed.

71

"Mum? How did you get that scar? The one on your belly?"

Asking the question felt like throwing a newborn baby across a gorge. It was an all-or-nothing moment—like that moment when a cartoon character runs over a cliff and hovers for a second, running in mid-air, before either plummeting or grabbing on to something to pull themselves back up again.

She went very still, then slowly shut the book and laid it to one side. "When you were born."

"What do you mean?"

She was silent for several seconds. "Ever heard of a caesarean section?"

"That's where they cut the baby out, isn't it?"

"Yep. Well, they had to do that with you."

"Why?"

Her hands seemed to develop a slight tremor. "I was very ill. So were you."

"OK." I hoped she would elaborate, but instead she sat for about a minute, and then picked her book up again.

As I cuddled down into my pillows Mum turned off the light, slipped out of bed and went to the bathroom once again. There was the sound of the tap, followed by the toilet flushing. Then she tiptoed back into the room, opening the door only the tiniest crack to slip through. My eyelids were much too heavy to raise by now. Not entirely sure if I was awake or dreaming, I felt her crouch down once again at the head of my bed. Once again, a cold hand pushed a strand of hair behind my ear, and a finger traced the shape of my eyebrow. This time, however, she also spoke. Her voice was soft and low and lulling—and the words were in a language I couldn't understand.

"Get up, Anna."

Mum shook my shoulder, and started downstairs. I sat up, rubbed my eyes and looked across at the alarm clock. It was half past nine—far too late for her to still be in the house. Then I remembered it was a Saturday. I dressed and put my earrings in. My butterfly hairclip seemed to have gone missing since my having tried it out as a makeshift key. I searched through my laundry and in both suitcases, as well as in and around my bed. It wasn't there. I went to the kitchen and found Mum sipping coffee whilst bustling round the kitchen, a blue folded sheet of A4 paper in her hand. Her hair was wet, and she had a towel round her shoulders. She was wearing a knitted white top with wool bobbles spaced regularly in vertical lines down the front, and black corduroy jeans.

"I like your jumper," I said.

"Thanks." She pointed at a second bowl. "Eat up. We're leaving in ten minutes."

"Where are we going?"

"Edinburgh. I need to visit my solicitor."

"Oh. Why?"

"Just stuff. There's always stuff." She stuffed the blue folded sheet into her bag. "Also need to get you a coat and hat."

"I've got a coat and hat," I protested.

"You mean the oilskin ones? I put them in the skip."

The honey loops felt squishy against the roof of my mouth. I thought of my coat and hat lying amongst piles of rubbish, with the rain rotting the lining and gradually breaking them down into nothing. That's when I remembered I'd put the clip in the pocket of the coat. Dad gave me that clip last Christmas. Everything to do with him was slowly crumbling away. Probably one day my memories of him would fade, too. I should have been happy that Mum wanted to get me nice new clothes and spend the day with me, but instead I wanted to scream and hit things—the hot poker feeling was back, despite not looking at the texts. Soon it would be too big for me to hold it inside of myself any longer.

Once I had finished, Mum dumped my bowl in the sink. "Teeth and hair. Quickly now."

I took time alone in the bathroom to calm myself down by twisting the hand towel violently—as if I was wringing water from it. That was a technique my outreach worker taught me for when I needed an 'outlet' for anger. It seemed to help for this feeling too. Once I had wrung out all my upset I sat on the closed lid of the toilet seat, letting my breathing get back to normal and collecting my thoughts. The sky shone blue, framed by the skylight in the bathroom. Towards the end of summer the quality of light changes—it gets yellowish instead of white, and shines on things from a lower angle so that they have a sort of halo. Today there was a thin but dazzling glow around the edge of the metal window frame. I felt something inside me like chimney smoke, or leaves chasing each other on the pavement, or a flame in a dark room when the candle has almost burned out.

I opened the window, and thought I could smell the frost which would appear in later months, carried ahead on the wind. The radiator gurgled. There was a muffled flapping from within the sloping wooden ceiling, and I wondered if it was the bat settling down to sleep in some hidden cranny. I put my toothbrush back in its glass and ran down, out the front door, to where Mum was waiting in the car.

We drove past the house of the man who skins people alive, and straight ahead at two roundabouts. The houses thinned out, and so did the shops. I saw more farmland ahead.

"Do you like Queen?" I asked.

"No."

"What about Thin Lizzy?"

"Ugh. No."

"Starship?"

She snorted. That exhausted all the bands Dad and I used to listen to together. My interest and knowledge with regards to classical music, along with my piano playing, were things he approved of and had been proud of, but hadn't shared. Neither had my outreach worker. Neither had Mrs Taylor or Miss Corrigan. Neither had my teachers. Neither had any of my school friends. And thus far I had found no indication in Mum's house that she might share such an interest, either.

"So what music do you like?"

She shrugged. "Bjork. Florence and the Machine. Kate Bush."

"I've heard of Kate Bush, but I don't know any of her music. Can I hear some?"

"We're almost there. Perhaps another time."

The car jerked as she changed down a gear. To our right I saw a footbridge spanning two parallel railway tracks, with a platform and an outdoor shelter on either side. A portable cabin formed the station building, with a large car park in front which gleamed in the sunlight.

Once we had pulled into a free parking bay Mum pointed at a fat, blue metal contraption which stood at head height about fifty metres away.

"Machine's up there. Get us a ticket."

Five minutes later Mum was sitting in the outside station shelter reading her book, while I wandered up and down the platform. At each end where it sloped down to the track there was a white-rimmed, triangular red sign which read: "DO NOT CROSS THE LINE". The track curved to the left, and clumps of tall dock leaves and stinging nettles grew on either side. The train to Edinburgh was due in three minutes.

"What are you reading?" I asked, returning to Mum's side. It wasn't Wuthering Heights any more. She must be a fast reader too.

She held the book up. It was called Her Eyes, and was by Marion Carson.

I watched her reading for about a minute before she said, "You're giving me the heebie-jeebies".

"What are they?"

"Can you not sit still for two seconds?"

I tried really hard, but even in the shelter the wind was picking up, and although it was dry it wasn't as warm as it had been the day before. I swung my legs back and forth, and my teeth clacked together with every gust. Finally I stood up and walked the length of the platform again, just to keep moving. This time, as I neared the edge to read a Samaritans poster, I saw two parallel horizontal lights rounding the bend.

Mum had hunched her shoulders and wrapped her arms around herself by the time I reached her again, so she must have been cold too. The train slowed to a stop. She pressed the button for the door and jumped up into the carriage—the floor of the doorway being level with our knees. Then she held out a hand. I grasped it and pulled myself up. Then I panicked for a moment— if she could get the heebie-jeebies just from sitting next to me she must definitely have them after touching me.

"This way." She pushed past me into a carriage which was far less crowded than any of the trains Dad and I had taken in or around London. There were actually seats free, and you could move in the vestibules and up the aisles of the carriages. Nobody crowded the doors.

"Let's get an aeroplane seat," I suggested.

Mum sniffed. "Why would I want to sit in a tiny, pokey little seat when there are proper tables?" I frowned. Did she really not know how un-tiny and un-pokey this train was?

"Well… we could always pretend we're on a transatlantic flight!"

"Pretend away..." She sat at a table. I stood in the aisle and deliberated, but somehow it didn't seem as appealing to play aeroplanes without someone else to play with, and I didn't want to annoy Mum any more. Otherwise it would cost me another point, and I'd been doing well so far today. I sat down opposite her.

The train began to move, and the station disappeared behind us. A long bank of witch elms went past the window. After them came a huge field with blue oil drums, white jump-poles and red wings lying on their sides. In a smaller field adjacent, two horses were grazing. One was large and dark red—like Mum's hair—with rickety, thin legs. The other looked too small for anyone to ride except perhaps a pre-schooler, and was muddy-white and very fat.

"Who do you think rides that one?" I asked, pointing to the small, fat one.

She looked up. "Probably just a companion pony."

"Did you ever ride?"

"Used to, when I was at primary school."

"Is that the same as junior school?"

"Yeah. Sorry, keep forgetting it's all different for you."

"It's OK," I reassured her. "Could I ever have riding lessons?"

She giggled. "Find a horse and I'll take you. Course, you'd fall flat on your bum."

"Why?"

"You're from London!"

Just as we were rounding a right-hand bend a woman's voice shouted "All tickets, please!"

"Two returns. One child." Mum handed her two ten-pound notes without looking. The officer printed the tickets out using the portable machine which hung round her neck, and handed over change from each of her pockets.

"Is there a snacks trolley?" I asked.

The ticket officer craned her neck to look up the

carriage. "Should be along in about fifteen minutes."

Once she had gone, Mum put her book spine-up on the table, making me cringe. "Just so's you know, I'm not spending money on week-old, overpriced junk off a trolley, provided by a governmentally rejected, bureaucratic, shoddy system with no competition to act as quality control."

More houses began to appear amongst the fields, until we were travelling through sparse townland. A small woman with a shapely nose and thin eyebrows, long eyelashes, light brown skin and nearly-black, wavy hair that came down to her shoulders, sat at the table on the opposite side of the aisle. She wore a dark grey raincoat, a red skirt which complimented her lipstick, black tights and boots, and sat back in her seat, one leg crossed lightly over the other. She was reading something off a notebook computer, one hand hovering above the touchpad. She didn't look up when the snacks trolley clanked in the next carriage, but at one point she took a smartphone out her coat pocket and glanced at the screen, before putting it back, tilting her chin, and resuming her reading. I watched her for another minute or so until she caught my eye. Before I could look away she gave me a half smile. I smiled back shyly, and a second later the snacks trolley stopped in the aisle between us.

The train plunged into a tunnel following Haymarket station.

"I know this bit," I exclaimed, "I've been here before!"

"Well, what do you know."

It took me a moment to figure out that this was a rhetorical reply.

"Can we have a go on the Ferris wheel and ice rink?"

"The ice rink's only up in winter."

"Oh."

I pressed my nose to the window. When I was eleven I came up with Dad and stayed overnight to see the castle and dungeons, for History. He tried to scare me by telling me a story about a creature living in the wall of the Haymarket tunnel. His eyes always widened when he was trying to convince me of something untrue—especially when it was something he had made up himself—but just for fun I got down under the table anyway and sat on his feet until we came out the other side. I didn't think Mum would approve of my doing that now.

"We are now approaching—Edinburgh Waverley— where this train will terminate. Please ensure you have all your belongings, and personal items with you, when leaving the train."

The platform was extremely crowded because it was the tail end of the Fringe Festival. Pigeons flapped across the rafters, and there was an echoing mixture of voices—French, German, a bit of Russian, Polish and Chinese too, in amongst the English. Blue Scotrail trains like the one we had arrived on waited in parallel lines at their platforms, looking like runners at the start of a race. Crowds crossed both ways over a green footbridge far ahead and above. Beyond the ticket barriers there was a complex of shops—including a WHSmith and a Boots, with another indoor area across from them. The roof was made of glass, and was criss-crossed with white beams held up by thin, green-based pillars.

"You'll need the 'out' half of your ticket," Mum said.

Long queues of people stretched up the platform to get to the three open ticket barriers, whilst two officials in high-visibility jackets stood either side. When it was my turn I slotted my ticket into the machine. It was pulled from my hand as though someone inside had snatched it from me, and the gate opened.

"Up here," Mum pointed to the right, where the road sloped up and out into the sunshine.

We came out onto a bridge with tour buses parked nose-to-tail. Crowds of people crossed as if they were tidal waves. I could see and hear a piper in full tartan, standing on the corner. Behind him there was a market that was so full the stalls were barely visible. My vision blurred and I felt giddy, but Mum grabbed my arm before I fell, and steered me to the right, walking just in front of me. Her path left a short, temporary channel with nothing in it, like the wake of a boat. I stumbled along in it. After about a minute the world came back into focus, and my balance returned to normal.

We waited at a pedestrian crossing for the green man. It was hard to see because there was a tall, black man standing in front of me. He wore an orange T-shirt and light blue jeans, and his hair underneath his cap was dreadlocked. Mum craned her head to see round him. To the left of me was Scott's Monument, and behind me and to the right there was a red and white frame structure, as big as a house, and shaped like a football. There were children inside it, attached to bungee ropes that hung down from the top. Every time they bounced they flew about fifteen feet into the air.

The people behind me squashed up against my back, and my feet felt light. I focused on planting each one firmly into the empty spaces as they emerged, and we reached the kerb without any mishaps.

"In here." She pulled me into a shop through some sliding doors.

It was cooler inside than out. It was also a lot quieter. I didn't feel like I was being pressed anymore. The crowds seemed to have been left behind at the doorway, and the palpitations had gone too.

"Well," said Mum, with a big sigh. "That's that!" And for a second, she looked as if she might smile.

Beside Mum there was a white mannequin with no arms or legs, impaled on a stand, wearing a purple and blue floral-patterned top and red shorts. Ahead of us an escalator led up to the next floor. There was a desk in front of us, upon which two stands were stacked with different shades of lipstick. I had my ears pierced for my twelfth birthday, and Dad gave me my butterfly hairclip last Christmas, but apart from that I've never felt drawn to accessories or cosmetics. However, as I gazed at all the colours of lipstick, as well as the bottles of nail varnish and the eye pencils, I felt a flutter of curiosity.

Mum approached the desk, which was manned by a woman with copper highlights and lots of eyeliner.

"How do I get to the children's wear?"

"Two floors up."

I followed Mum to the escalators, stepped on, rested my chin on my hand and my hand on the banister, and enjoyed the feeling of travelling forwards without having to move.

The mannequins on this floor wore brown trousers. One had a dark green fleece that reminded me of Jamie's.

"I like this floor," I said.

"It's menswear," said Mum.

"But the patterns and styles are great. Can I have a look around?"

"No. Come on."

I was about to reply when an assistant approached us. "Can I help you?"

We both spoke at the same time. Mum said, "Just passing through," and I said, "Where are the fitting rooms?"

He laughed, and pointed through the racks. "Male fitting rooms on the left, female on the right."

"It can't just be for men if they have female fitting rooms." I had to work hard not to sound too smug.

Mum eyed me, lips twitching. "Five minutes, then."

I wove in and out the shelves. One rack had extremely soft, baggy black trousers hanging from it. They were summer ones and so were discounted, but Mum had said we were there to look for hats and coats, so I doubted she would let me have a pair. There were also dark green and navy denim shorts, and light brown zip-up fleeces, string vests and patterned T-shirts. Right at the back I found waterproof coats and hats. One mannequin wore a navy blue hat that looked waterproof and would not be too big for me. When I took it off, all illusion of character vanished: the outfit in its entirety had been the thing creating it.

The hat felt reasonably waterproof on the outside, and I perched it on my head. Then I ran back to Mum, who was waiting at the escalator.

"How do I look?"

She eyed my head. "Like a flower pot man."

"Can I have it?" I found the price tag. "It's only 99p."

"I'm not surprised. How badly do you want it?"

"Badly. Very badly. It's lovely and funny and it fits me perfectly."

Her lips twitched again. "If…" she said, slowly, "If I let you have it, will you promise to come up to the children's wear with no more dilly-dallying?"

"I promise."

"It's a deal then."

"Thank you!" I hugged her. She stood stiffly and didn't reciprocate, but she didn't push me away either.

After she had paid, we went up the next escalator—me still wearing the hat—and came off the stairs onto a floor full of tiny mannequins wearing brightly coloured matching sets. Mum kept turning to look at me, then biting her lip and looking away again. One little mannequin wore a white pleated skirt and a blue shirt. There was a big photograph on the wall, of a little black boy and a little white girl, both about five years old. They had their arms around each other, and were laughing at the camera. The girl wore a brown, knee-length coat with a floral-patterned dress underneath, and had a yellow flower clip in her hair. The boy wore a white school shirt and smart, black trousers and shoes. They were standing in a frosted field with an oak tree silhouetted in the far background. It seemed the wrong kind of getup for such an outing.

There were other shoppers in this area along with us. One woman was pushing a toddler along in a green, three-wheeler pushchair, as she examined a range of child-sized sunglasses. The far left corner formed a shoe shop area, where an assistant and a woman in blue were squatting side by side. A girl of about seven years old, wearing a red velvety dress, was walking up and down in shiny, red buckle-up shoes.

"Over here." I followed Mum past three rails filled with leggings, until we reached a sort of alcove with racks of coats.

"Stand there and don't move."

I wasn't sure whether she was being literal or not, so I stood as still as I possibly could while she walked up and down looking at the coats.

"Ah," she said aloud, and picked a long, black corduroy coat with floral lining, off the shelf. It didn't look very waterproof, even if it was warm—and there was no hood. All my previous coats had been waterproof with hoods.

Meanwhile the girl had sat back down, and the assistant and the mother were each pulling shoes off her feet. They seemed to be stuck on, because both grown-ups were having to wrench and jerk. All the while the girl hooted with laughter.

"Aaand this one." Mum pulled a horrible brown leather coat with black fur round the rim off a rack. She was more relaxed than I had ever seen her, apart from when she was asleep, of course. She was also holding a stiff, dark red one, and the black corduroy one.

"That'll do," she said. "Hold your arms out to the sides." I did, and she pulled the black corduroy coat sleeves up over my hands. My tracksuit sleeves bunched up round my elbows, but I couldn't pull them back down since I was standing with my arms out. The mother and assistant were now pushing black, shiny lace-up boots onto the girl's feet. The assistant asked her something, and she nodded. Then she got up and started walking up and down again.

"No," said Mum. She pulled at one sleeve, then the other, until the coat came off.

"Can I move?" I badly wanted to sort out my sleeves now that she had finished.

"Hold on, I'm busy." I held my position, even though my arms were now beginning to ache. Mum pulled the brown leather coat on.

"Oh, no, no, no," she exclaimed, to my intense relief.

"Good. I hated that one."

She laughed, and my aching arms didn't matter anymore. She zipped me into the stiff, dark red coat. This one had a fabric belt around the waist, but it didn't have any pockets, which again I thought was a bit silly for a coat. You'd have to carry a bag wherever you went, just for your keys and money, and you might leave it behind. The belt also made it very tight around the waist, which would be hard for playing football in, climbing trees and running.

"Well that one suits you at least. You'll grow into its cut with time."

I considered telling her that I would never wear it, but she had been good enough to buy me the hat, even though she hadn't wanted to, so I thought it was fair to let her get me something of her choice in return. At least I could in theory be happy that it was waterproof—unlike the corduroy one—and that it had a hood, and that it wasn't the horrible brown one. She pulled it off me and started to walk away. I hesitated, in case she was just going to look for more coats, but then she turned and nodded back at me to follow.

"Are we going to the solicitor's now?" I asked, as we rode down the escalators.

"Not yet. After lunch."

"Please can we get a German sausage?"

"A German sausage?"

"Yeah!"

"What makes you think they'll have German sausages in particular?"

"They had them at the market when... when I was here before."

"Really?"

"Yes!"

We both gazed across at the market place. It was swarming with people. "I don't think I could deal with the crowds," she concluded.

Right beside the station there was another complex of

shops situated under a pyramid which read 'Princes Mall'. In it were more clothes shops, a Body Shop, a stairway leading up to a Costa coffee shop, and a railing overlooking a crowd of tables and chairs bordered by several different fast food shops. I leaned out over the railing. It was crowded here too, but at least I could see floor space.

"Go and choose yourself something," said Mum, as we stepped off the escalator into the food court. "I'll be back soon." And before I could ask how long 'soon' was, or where we would meet up, she was washed away in the people.

I walked a short distance and turned around on the spot. There was a KFC behind me. I stood in one of its two queues and hoped it was the right one.

A person in a cap and apron came over.

"If you just move up one to the right," he said, pointing. Then he retreated back behind the counter and opened up a third till. "And what would you like?"

"Can I have some chips, please?" I asked.

"Medium, large or extra-large?"

I would have expected there to be a 'small'.

"How large is medium?"

He measured with his hand, about ten centimetres off the table.

"And extra-large?"

He did the same gesture, this time about ten

centimetres higher. So 'large' meant 'medium', then, and 'medium' meant 'small'.

"Can I have large?"

"Sure. Anything with that?"

I looked at the menu photos. One showed a milkshake with a chocolate swirl on the top, which looked too big to drink, but perhaps Mum could help me finish it. "Can I have a chocolate milkshake?"

"Medium, large or extra-large?" This time he gestured without me asking.

Given that I already had a medium-sized portion of chips, a small one would suffice. "Medium, please."

"Anything else?"

"No thanks, that's all."

"Sitting in or taking away?"

I supposed I would be taking away if I was meeting up with Mum again in the main food court. "Taking away."

"That'll be two-ninety-nine." I gave him my five-pound note, and he handed me back two one-pound coins and a one-penny piece. "Won't be a tick." He went to his colleague in the back of the preparation area to pass my order on. I wasn't sure where I should wait without the risk of making people think I was still in the queue. The man hadn't said anything about how they got the right orders to the right customers, so I stood where I was. After all, there were no other employees to take orders, so the crowd wasn't being held up any more than if I moved aside or went away.

"That's one large chips and one medium chocolate milkshake."

"That's me!" I called out. He winked and put the order down on the counter.

Whilst I had been ordering, the food court had become much busier. I held the chip bag between my teeth and the milkshake in the crook of my arm, unwrapped the straw and stuck it into the lid. Then I held one thing in each hand and scanned the crowds, looking for Mum. The milk was more like ice cream, so it took a lot of sucking to get any of it up through the straw. I left it for a bit and ate some chips. After five minutes I decided to go back to the bottom of the stairs. I tried to steer round people, but knocked into a broad, hurrying man with a moustache, in a red T-shirt. The milkshake fell on the floor.

"Sorry!" he called over his shoulder.

I bent down but was overwhelmed by the mass of legs walking around me, like water flowing round a boulder in a river. A brown leather shoe kicked the container out my reach. I began to feel dizzy again and stood up slowly, hoping nobody would trip over me or the fallen milkshake, and walked towards the stairs. Once there I leaned against the safety rail, calmed myself down, and ate my chips.

Because I was sure that if I just stayed in one place

Mum would find me in the end, I didn't worry about looking for her any more. Instead I concentrated on my lunch, before scrumpling up the empty bag and putting it in my pocket. My hands felt greasy and sweaty, so I wiped them down on my trousers. At one table I saw the mother and little girl from the shop. The little girl was swinging her feet, which were now in navy blue Velcro trainers. Those seemed much more practical than the red buckle-shoes or the black, shiny boots.

The man who had knocked over my milkshake sat two tables away, reading a copy of the Metro. Then there was a woman with a teenage boy in an electric wheelchair. Intermittently, she broke off bits of burger and put them into his mouth. He was jerkily manipulating what looked like a gearstick on a laptop where the keyboard would usually be. The laptop was mounted on a stand which looked a bit like a robot's arm.

"Hey!" It was Mum. She was eating a wrap.

I gave her my change.

"I waited where you'd go to get out."

"Good. Let's go."

We made our way back through Princes Mall together, onto the road, straight across the street and up a sloping road with lots of traffic islands. I saw a copper monument to our right, with a fountain surrounded by a shallow pool and grass. A pathway ran through the middle to some more shops, and a green building on the far side.

"Left here," said Mum. We turned onto a small street, and then right again onto a bigger one with a long, fenced-off garden filled with purple and yellow pansies. On either side of the street were old tenement buildings.

"Cross over." After checking the traffic we ran across, and approached one of the tenements with a sign above the door that read 'McCauliff & Co'. There was an intercom system with twelve labelled buttons. Mum pressed a button and waited.

After about three seconds there was a crackling sound, then a female voice said, "Hello?"

"Patricia Harrington to see Peter Reid."

The door unlocked, and we were in a concrete corridor with stone steps spiralling up to the left. I followed Mum up and through a door on the right, into a reception area with potted trees either side of the entrance, and a shiny wooden desk in the centre of the room. There were soft, low chairs upholstered in red fabric, and coffee tables with magazines. In the background I could hear a nocturne by Chopin. It reminded me of life back in London.

"You wait here." Mum waved a hand in the direction of the chairs. "And please, please be sensible." She went up to the desk, and I heard her say her name again, but didn't hear what the person at reception said in response. She looked round briefly and bit her lip. Then she jiggled one leg and shifted her weight.

"Miss Harrington?" A short, chubby man had emerged from an office on the right.

"That's me," said Mum.

"Come in." She followed him through a side door.

I sat down and gathered my thoughts. The music playing now had the atonal quality of Debussy. I could just see the top of the receptionist's head, bent over behind the desk and covered with curly white hair. On a small trolley immediately in front of the desk sat a tea and coffee machine, like the one in the hotel Dad and I stayed in during our trip. Beside it was a stack of disposable paper cups and three wicker baskets; one with miniature pots of milk, one with sticks of white and brown sugar, and one with teabags and sachets of instant coffee. I went over to it. It had a schematic of a coffee cup with three wisps of steam coming off it.

"Excuse me," I said to the woman behind the desk.

She straightened up. She wore thick, crimson-rimmed glasses. "Yes?"

"How does this thing work?"

"You just hold the cup under the nozzle."

"The nozzle in the alcove?"

"Yes."

I did as she said. The machine gave a splutter, and a tiny trickle of water spurted out. Then it stopped.

"Not to worry," she said. "I'll get a refill." She got up and went out through a door on the left, staggering back a minute later with a large, plastic container full of water, with a tap at the bottom for decanting.

"Do you want some help?" I put my hands under the bottom of the container. We lugged it across the room.

"Dump it here." We plonked it down heavily. The desk shook.

"Are we going to turn the tap on and make a waterfall down into the machine?"

She laughed. "Hmm… that could make quite a mess!"

"Then what are we going to do?"

"Not sure. Alan's usually here to manage this sort of thing, but he's off today."

"We could always pour the water in using paper cups," I suggested.

"Good lateral thinking." She pushed two buttons either side of the top of the machine. The top half came off, revealing a reservoir which glistened wetly.

The tap of the water container only admitted a tiny trickle, and it took nearly a minute to fill one paper cup. When I tipped the water into the machine it made a rumbly sound and a vibrating sensation, which lessened and turned into a sploshing once the bottom had been covered.

"What's your name?" I asked.

"Anna," she replied.

"Snap!" I grinned.

"There you go, then," said Anna-The-Receptionist,

"Good to meet a fellow Anna!" We paused in our water-pouring to shake hands. She rested a hand on the tea and coffee machine. "Do you think it needs a name too?"

"You mean the tea and coffee machine?"

"Yes. I mean, people name their cars. Why not their tea and coffee machines?"

This was clearly a rather strange Anna, but a good kind of strange. "How about Gary?" I suggested.

"Gary. I like it. Yes, it suits it. Good call."

"What kind of solicitors are you?" In Social Education I had learned that most lawyers and solicitors specialise in one area, such as commercial, family, employment or criminal things.

"We cover family matters."

"So that means you deal with things like divorce and custody?"

"Smart girl."

We carried on pouring in silence until the tank was almost full. Dad wasn't here anymore, so why would Mum need a custody solicitor?

"Anna!"

Both of us looked round. Mum and the man had come back into the foyer. Mum looked as if someone had stuck a pin into her and let all the air out. I wanted to hug her, but I knew from looking at her that doing so would almost certainly result in a points-fine, or at the very least, would not be welcome.

"Sorry," said Mum, addressing Anna-The-Receptionist. I waved to Anna and followed Mum out through the main door.

"Had to, didn't you?" she said, as soon as we were out on the spiral staircase.

"Had to what?"

"Meddle."

"I was only helping her refill Gary!"

The coat was stiff, scratchy and hard to walk in because it restricted movement around my torso and upper hips. Mum kept giving me glances as I made my way carefully down the remaining stairs.

"How's the coat?" she asked at last.

I could tell that in terms of the answer I gave, I would be caught between a shouting fine and a lie. My courage failed me. "It's fine," I said, "What were you and that man doing?"

"Going over some forms."

"Is it something to do with me coming to live with you?"

She looked at me for a long time, then turned away and was silent for a few seconds. "Yes."

My cheeks tingled and my throat tightened. "Am I going to be sent away?" We had reached the bottom of the staircase.

Mum looked at me hard, and then, turning abruptly away, she squeezed my shoulder. "Not if I can help it," she said.

In Dad's flat my window was always open a crack during summer. This made the curtains ripple in the breeze. I would lie in bed at night and pretend I was watching the aurora. You could hear cats singing to each other in the street. I don't know whether the council pulled down what was left of our flat. Perhaps the lower floors could stay—it was only ours and the one above that sustained really serious damage. Everyone escaped from the one above. If they did pull it down, the street would look like the only comb that never hurt my scalp. One of its teeth was chipped in the middle, breaking the perfect row.

At seven o'clock on Sunday morning I dressed, went downstairs and raised the blinds on the kitchen window. A magazine called For Real lay spine-up on the table. I pulled it towards me and turned it round. The page was completely taken up by a huge picture of an extremely shiny, muscly man wearing nothing but a pair of Y-fronts with 'Tiger' written across the waistband.

"Paws off." Mum looked me up and down. "Should've got you some smarter clothes in town."

"Oh, these are fine!"

"Not for church they're not. After breakfast we'll see if we can get you sorted."

As soon as I had swallowed my last mouthful we went upstairs. Once in the bedroom Mum narrowed her eyes and put her hands on my shoulders, as if I were a balloon that might float away.

"Not much difference in it. You can wear one of mine."

She opened both doors of the wardrobe. A row of coat hangers dangled from the rail, each with a full outfit on it.

"How about this?" She held up a blue denim jacket and skirt.

"I've never worn denim before," I said, "Except once, and that was jeans. They made me sweaty and itchy, and the flies unzipped whenever I breathed."

Mum's mouth twitched. "Well if you really can't cope or you keep busting out of them we'll try something else. Take the strappy black sandals too, bottom right. Oh, and you'll need..." She opened the top left drawer of one of the chests of drawers, and tossed some balled-up, black tights over to me. "See you downstairs."

The denim jacket was slightly too big, and the buttons were slightly too tight. The armpits bunched when my hands were down at my sides, and when I bent to do up the shoes I had to hold my breath. Once dressed I wobbled downstairs, gripping the banister with both hands.

It was very windy when we stepped outside. I wore my new coat and hat, and although Mum gave the hat a long stare when I put it on, she didn't try to make me leave it behind.

"Are we taking the car?"

"Nope. It's only just up the road." Her hair was blowing everywhere. She attempted to fix it, but that only made it worse.

"May I?" I reached round by way of indicating my intentions. "I'm good at doing hair."

"OK, then. Thanks."

Her hair was extremely thick and glossy, and flowed through my hands like water. I stood behind her and gathered it into a ponytail.

"Ow! Careful!"

"Have you got a hair clip?"

"Hang on." She fumbled in her bag, then put something into my hand. It was the butterfly hairclip. "I found it in the pocket of the old coat. Forgot to say." She held my gaze. I bit my lip, bent my head and fumbled with her hair.

"All done!" I stepped back to take a look. Mum seemed taller, and her eyes and cheekbones were highlighted. "If only you had a mirror!"

"There's no time…"

"Oh, but you have to see! Just turn and look in the reflection of the window."

She turned, and started. "Dear God, what have you done to me?" She reached a hand up. "I look… I look…" We regarded our reflections, standing side by side. She had a freckle on the side of her nose in exactly the same place as I did. She nodded, and rested a hand on my shoulder. "Not bad. Well, come on then."

We turned right at the junction leading out the car park. The curtains were closed in all the houses on the left. Even the curtains on the downstairs floors. All the people I have ever known open their downstairs curtains once they get up. Except for the people next door. And the man who tried to skin me alive. Hardly anyone here must go to church.

At the main road we turned left, past the house of the man who skins people alive. His garden was hidden from view by a red brick wall, over which grew a tangle of ivy. The top branches of a tree were visible over the wall, with an overgrown bush in the foreground. Mum slowed her pace to look as well. Suddenly the door opened, and the man strode out into the street. This time he was dressed in a smart suit, and when he saw us he started a hobbly run across the drive.

"Hey! HEY!"

"Quick!" Mum grabbed my hand.

It was almost impossible to run in high heels and a skirt. My balance was precarious and I didn't have the range of leg motion that I would have done in a tracksuit. I kept nearly falling, but Mum held me up, and we hurried down a side-street to the left. In the distance I saw the play park near Joanne's house.

"In here." She pulled me down another alley—this one cobbled—and pressed herself flat against the wall.

I copied her.

"What are we doing?"

"Waiting… Shhh."

"For what?" She held up a finger. "Why aren't the church bells ringing?"

"There aren't any. Hush."

"Why not?"

"It wasn't originally a church. Now shut up, he's coming!"

I heard footsteps approaching, and wheezy, rapid breathing. The man passed by close to us down the main street, but he didn't stop or look in our direction.

After another minute Mum let her breath out. "OK. I think the coast's clear." We tiptoed out, checked again that he was a good distance away, and passed a pub called 'Farmer's Rest'. "You stay away from him, Anna."

"Why?"

"You wouldn't believe the number of skeletons in his closet."

The Skeleton Man. It all made a horrible kind of sense now. The skeletons must be the people he skinned alive—the ones who wandered into his garden. Perhaps the dog chased them down for him. I had been lucky to get away with my life.

The church had a thatched roof. It looked like the replica of the Globe Theatre in London. There were half-barrels of red and blue petunias either side of the door, and a row of wooden steps up to the entrance. The wheelchair ramp must have been round the back.

"Don't worry," I said, "We're not the last ones." I pointed up the road to a woman pushing a double buggy with one hand, and holding the hand of a small boy in another. She waved.

"Does she know you?" Mum asked. She kept darting glances at the church door, and as they approached she edged up a step.

I looked again, and recognised Joanne and her children. The angry pinstriped man wasn't with them. "Sort of," I said.

"Guess what!" said Skylar, as the family reached us.

"What?"

"Dad got us a trampoline! How cool is that?"

Joanne tried to take Skylar's hand again, but he jumped away and stuck his tongue out.

Mum shifted her weight from one leg to the other. She was leaning well back from the buggy, never taking her eyes off it. Her face looked pale and she seemed shivery, as she had done with the bat. Joanne smiled at her.

"I've a lot to thank Anna for, you know. She pulled Emily off the road. My husband… well…" she waved a hand, but didn't say anything else.

"I'm happy I was there to help," I said.

"Told me she loved children," Joanne continued, "She's welcome to come over and play any time."

"Well… thanks. Let's see," said Mum. She was now at the top of the steps, and seemed to be trying and failing to turn her back on us.

Joanne squatted down in front of the double buggy and undid the straps.

"Skylar, hold onto Emily for me."

At that moment the baby woke up and began to cry. Mum clapped her hands over her ears, shrank back and crouched against the church wall, eyes closed. I ran up the steps and knelt in front of her.

"Mum! Mum, are you all right?" I turned and looked behind me. "They've gone—it's just us."

Very slowly she uncovered her ears. Her face relaxed, and she breathed in deeply. "Sorry," she said.

Our flat block in London was right next to a street with a church on it. Every Sunday at nine o'clock the bells would start ringing. They would go on until ten o'clock, when the service began. It was the only thing that ever seemed to annoy Dad. I once asked him if we might go to one of the services. His face went red, and he growled something that ended with: "…up to you when you're older." I concluded that they probably served alcohol, and that minors like me were therefore inadmissible. After all, that was why Dad always got Mrs Taylor to babysit me whenever he went to the pub with Miss Corrigan. Then again I was still a minor now, and so were Joanne's children, yet the grown-ups were taking us along with them.

The hall immediately inside the building had a worn, brown carpet. There was a row of coat pegs next to the door. I hung my coat on one, glad to get rid of it. A royal blue curtain hung down from the right-hand wall. The door that led into the main room was propped open with a brick. Mum kept looking around with wide eyes. Every now and then she would crane back to look out the door. I could see Joanne and her children a little way ahead, separated from us by a group of people standing in a queue. A man of about sixty was holding a pile of dark blue, cotton-bound books. He had thick, grey hair, and wore a black suit.

"The Adamson clan!" he said to them. He approached Joanne and started talking to her, but I couldn't hear what he said. Emily reached out from Skylar's arms and took one of his ears very gently.

"Ow, my ear! You've got my ear!" He pretended to struggle and yell while she squealed with delight. Finally he broke free, and they passed on into the main hall. "I haven't seen you before," he said to me, when we got to him. He offered me a book, which I accepted.

"I've never been to church before," I told him.

"Well I hope you'll be a regular now."

From time to time I'd seen glimpses of churches on television, before Dad invariably changed the channel.

This one had a high ceiling, and a platform in the centre like a stage. The chairs were arranged in rows, and at the far end of the room a flight of steps led up to an area that looked a bit like a box seat.

"Near the back, on the edge," Mum muttered.

As we took our seats, I leaned my mouth to her ear. "Is this going to be something like a show?"

She raised an eyebrow. "No, not exactly."

"Sorry. It's just, I don't know much about religion. D—I mean—I was never raised with it. And it was never discussed. I've read some books which had vicars as minor characters, though."

"Oh gosh…" She passed a hand over her face, then held up an index finger. "Right. First, some terminology. A church service is sort of like a pre-arranged programme centred mainly around the Bible, with the minister in the twin roles of commentator and continuity announcer. The congregation—that's us—sing and pray with him, and listen to what he has to say. Sometimes we take communion, but we're not having that today. Prayers are where the minister says some words to God, and if you want to make them your words too you whisper 'Amen' afterwards. A sermon is a sort of lecture given by the minister, designed to help people see what God means and wants. Halfway through the service we have offerings, which is where people have a chance to donate money, though they don't have to. Hymns are songs praising God. The children's address is a little, short, simple talk for the children of the congregation. They usually go off to Sunday school during offerings, before the main sermon."

"What's Sunday School?"

"It's a way of learning about God which is easier and more fun for children than a big, long sermon."

"And when we pray, you said we speak to God?"

"Yes."

"Does he speak back?"

She considered. "Well, I know he speaks to me…"

Interesting. It hadn't occurred to me that she might believe in God. I didn't know any other believers. At least, not ones who openly professed or spoke about their beliefs. She'd never mentioned it before, and again, there had been no indication of it that I could see within her house. Perhaps I would try mentioning classical music to her after all, in case I had been wrong about that too.

"Does he speak to you face to face, like we're speaking now?"

"Something like that. Others might not say the same thing. Sometimes he speaks through people."

"You mean he interrupts them?"

Mum laughed. Bonus points. "Well… that's not exactly what I meant. More like he sends his spirit to communicate the Word directly into some individuals' minds, so that they can share it for him. He makes them his ambassadors."

She turned over the pages of her hymn book. Every time she did so, she licked her index finger. If everyone who used that book did the same thing, they must end up eating billions of germs.

"What is the Word? Is it like a password?"

"More like His essence."

"Oh, right. A perfume!" This time I was making a joke.

Mum laughed again—this was surely my lucky day! Then she breathed in deeply, and straightened her back, looking ahead. "See that board?" She pointed at a wooden board that looked like a bookshelf, except that it had cards on it with numbers, like the letters on Countdown. "Those correspond with the numbers of the hymns we're going to sing."

As she finished speaking, music started playing on what sounded like an organ, but which was actually someone playing a keyboard on a stand in the corner. I strained to see who the keyboard player was over the tops of the people in front, then gaped, then glanced at Mum.

The Skeleton Man didn't look at all angry now. Instead his face was relaxed and solemn. His shoulders sagged, even though the music was cheerful. His eyes were half closed, and as he played he rocked back and forth. His fingers stroked the keys as if they were animals. The melody was quiet, in triple-metre, with an andante tempo, in G major. I was reminded of the music of Bach, but it was more like one of his harmonies than a melody.

The minister walked onto the stage. It wasn't the same man who had greeted us at the door and given us our books. This one was younger, with long, ginger, dreadlocked hair, jeans and a checked shirt. He spoke into a microphone clipped to his clothes.

"Hello everyone." He looked round with a huge smile.

"Hello!" some people called back.

"Right. Indentations. I mean… intimations…"

"He makes that joke practically every week," Mum whispered.

"The latest issue of Alive! will be on the desk outside. Tea and coffee will be served after the service. And now I want to say hello to any newcomers—I have been reliably informed that there is at least one with us today." I grinned, but he didn't look over at me. "And so to business with our theme." He leaned forward, and panned his gaze across the audience.

"We humans seem intent on devising easy, immediate solutions. Instant this, instant that. We simply can't delay gratification!"

I thought of Mum, and of the black and white cat, and of what I wanted for them both. Both were hurting—I was quite sure of that now. Both of them also avoided getting too close to me. Perhaps that would change. It hadn't yet, but perhaps it would. Perhaps it was just going to take a bit of time.

"Not only that, but we want everything to happen on our terms. Well, what if we had to live on somebody else's terms? That is in fact what we have to do all the time, every day, whether we realise it or not. We have to abide by laws set by others and enforced by others, lest we lose our liberty at the hands of others. We have to work for others to make money off others, to buy things off others which we need to live. We have to turn to others when our bodies get ill. In short, none of us are independent. Now, does acceptance of that guarantee our wellbeing? Of course not. There are no guarantees, but we like the illusion of them. Is it any wonder then that today, faith in God, and the ability to engage with him personally, seem to be declining? So often they seem like things we can voluntarily dispense with and suffer no immediate consequences. There are better ways than God to sustain and gratify ourselves, it seems—ways we can see and hear and touch and talk to. But here's the rub: God's larger plan for us does not change just because we are changing, or because the world we live in is changing and the things we want and that make us feel safe are changing. Today's sermon, when the time comes, will explore what it means to trust God and His plan today."

"Hymn book," said Mum, as the Skeleton Man started playing again. I tried to turn the pages in time, but they were thin, like tracing paper, and I couldn't get them to separate. They kept falling back every time I tried to flick them over quickly. She reached across, took my book off me and handed me hers. She pointed at hymn number two-hundred and seventy-three, just as everyone stood up to sing.

"I don't know the melody to this," I whispered.

"Neither do I," she answered. "Just follow along as best you can."

The chord progressions were very predictable, which helped me keep mostly to the tune, coming in as soon as I could on each note. Sometimes I had to stop and re-start when I fell behind, and sometimes I anticipated a note wrongly, which made it hard to concentrate on the words. The four verses felt like they lasted about ten minutes, even though I checked my watch at the end and the total length had only been two and a half minutes.

"Now then," said the minister, directing his words mainly to two children in the front row. "Who here likes sweeties?"

"I do!" they chorused. I heard Skylar's voice say "I do!" as well, but he said it later than the others.

"You do, do you?" He chuckled. "I like sweeties too. I also like biscuits, but who here likes cake?"

The children all shouted "I DO!", and so did I. Mum turned to me, and I couldn't tell if she was angry or amused. The minister glanced in my direction, and I felt my ears go red.

"Oh, that's all of you! I thought so. Well, I like cake too. Especially chocolate cake. Sometimes my wife, Helen, and I make our own. Have any of you ever made your own cake?"

I raised my hand in affirmation. Dad and I used to make my birthday cake together every year—chocolate sponge, with butter-icing in between the layers and crackly, hard icing on top. The minister went up into the box seat and bent down out of sight. I heard a plastic bag rustling, before he returned to the front with a utensil which had a long, wooden handle embedded in a rectangular piece of rubber at one end. He held it up.

"Who knows what this is?"

I put my hand up again. "It's a mixer."

"What's your name?"

I stood up. "Anna." The Skeleton Man was suddenly looking right at me. I turned my head side-on to his gaze.

"Well, Anna," said the minister, "Would you like to explain what it's for?"

"You use it to scoop the cake mixture out of the bowl."

"Top marks for you!" He turned back to the other two children near the front. "Can somebody now tell me please, what you do when you've scooped all the mixture out the bowl and into the cake tins?"

The other children all shouted in unison, "Lick the bowl!"

The minister laughed, along with several of the

audience. "Tell me… does the dough you lick get put in the oven?"

The small children said, "Noooo."

"Does it become a nice, spongey cake?"

"Noooo."

"That's right. It does not. It's the mixture that was created with just as much care, and which started out just the same, but didn't become what it was always intended to become." He paused, and lowered his voice to a serious tone. "God likes to make 'cake' too. But instead of using dough, what do you think he uses?"

Nobody volunteered an answer.

"He uses people. People are like cake mix that hasn't yet been baked. And the world is like the mixing bowl. So right now, the mixture that will become the cake, and the mixture that will stick to the bowl, are all mixed in together. But God already knows who will cling to the world and get left behind. When we feel tempted we should always ask ourselves, "Is this part of God's recipe? Or am I clinging too tightly to what I think and want?"

There was silence.

"Let us pray."

I looked towards Mum. She had put her hands together and closed her eyes, so I did the same.

"Lord, help us to keep thinking of your plans for us as we go through our lives…"

I opened one eye and looked around to see how

everyone was getting on. The man behind me had his head bowed, and was muttering something I couldn't hear. One woman two rows behind and three seats to the right was kneeling, with her head resting on her clasped hands.

"Help us not to get scared when we don't feel in control, and to be patient when we don't get what we want straight away. We are ready to trust you, and to follow your recipe, even if we don't always know what all the ingredients do. And now we offer up our silent prayers."

There was silence, except for a few whispers. Mum was whispering. Once again, she was speaking in that language I didn't know.

"In the name of our Lord Jesus Christ, Amen."

Everyone else said "Amen" too.

I opened my eyes. "Is that the end of the service?"

"No," she whispered, "Now we have offerings, and the children go to Sunday School."

As the children passed us on their way up the aisle towards the back door, Skylar whispered "Come on!"

I looked to Mum. She paused, then nodded. I squeezed out and followed him and the two other children up the aisle. A heavily pregnant woman, with bouncy dark hair, and wearing a red cagoule, was standing in the hall.

"Chop-chop!"

Once in the hall she pulled back the royal blue

curtain and opened a door behind it. A row of wooden steps curved up and round to the right. We followed her up them like ducklings. At the top there was another door, which led into a room that looked like a disused classroom. It had brown plastic chairs arranged in stacks around its edges. Wooden desks lined the walls. At the far end there was a bookshelf, which was filled with children's books. The walls were covered in posters.

The woman took off her cagoule and hung it on a peg on the door. "Right," she said, "Everyone grab a seat. You! Excuse me?" She gestured to me. "Can you get a chair for Kirsty?" She pointed to one of the other children—a chubby little girl of about three, wearing red flip-flops and a navy-blue dress.

"And one for yourself too, of course."

I took two chairs—one over each arm—from a stack next to the bookshelf. Skylar and the other child had already positioned theirs beside each other.

"Right," she said, when everyone was seated. "First I want to welcome our new member." She looked at me. "Anna, wasn't it?"

"Yes."

"Welcome, Anna. I'm Helen. Everyone say 'hello Anna'."

"Hello Anna!"

I waved and said "Hello!" back. Helen went over to the bookshelf and took out a book. I couldn't see the title, but for a second I saw the picture on the front cover—a huge barn stuffed full of hay, with big black birds circling above.

"This is a story Jesus told."

I put my hand up. "Who's Jesus?"

Helen addressed the other children: "Well, there's a question. Who is Jesus? Can anyone tell Anna?"

Everyone answered together: "God's Son."

"And what did he do?"

"Um… um… um he taught things..."

"That's right, Kirsty. And how did he teach them?"

"Stories!"

"Yes. This is a story He told." She opened the book.

"Once there was a farmer. He spent his whole life growing lots of lovely grain and hay."

She turned the book round so that we could see the illustration of the farmer.

"Everything he grew, he stored. Lots of people asked him: "When will you eat what you've grown?" and "Will you sell your crops?" Lots of poor, hungry people begged him for some food."

The next picture showed a woman and child, both in rags, with very dirty faces. They were on their knees with their hands clasped together, looking up at the farmer. He stood over them wagging his finger, eyes closed, head held up, mouth open in mid-speech.

"The man's answer was always the same: "Someday

I shall need it all. Just now there is none to spare." And then, one day, the man died."

Helen paused. "What do you think happened to the crops?"

I put my hand up. "Did the poor people get them?"

"Nope."

"Perhaps he was the only one who knew where the key was..."

"Perhaps. Let me finish reading:

"He never got to eat or sell his crops! Eventually the barns went to ruin and the mice and birds ate all the food up."

She closed the book.

"That makes me sad," I said.

She nodded. "It makes me sad too. Now that was a story Jesus told, to teach us something. What do you think he was trying to tell us?" Nobody moved. Kirsty had drawn her feet up and was hugging her knees. "Have a guess." Nobody answered. "I'll give you a clue. Think about something you love. A possession."

I thought about all my memories of Dad's flat, but chose not to share them because of time and place. That was another concept Dad and my outreach worker had taught me. Still, apart from Mum my memories of Dad were my most special thing. And yet... and yet...

In a moment of insight, I understood how the story connected to the minister's words. I put my hand up.

"Go on…"

"It's like the mixing bowl, isn't it?"

Helen frowned. "I don't quite follow..."

"Well, he tried to cling to his crops instead of following God's plan, didn't he?"

Now she nodded, smiling.

I continued, with gathering confidence: "When he died those things were no use to him anymore, because dead people don't need food, and because he was so anxious about keeping them safe and storing them up forever he made it so they were no use to anyone else either. So he didn't do anything good for anyone."

"Excellent!" Helen clapped her hands. "Jesus wanted us to follow God's plan, to trust that He is in control, and to not let our own fears hold us back, so that we can do His work and help people to understand His love."

"So… what should the man have done then?"

She looked at me with narrowed eyes, then smiled with one corner of her mouth. "That's a very good question, Anna." She turned to the other children. "What do we think? What should the man have done?"

Skylar sat upright. "I'd burn the barn down!"

"Ah, but that would destroy the crops! Kirsty? Any ideas?" Kirsty sucked her thumb and smiled, but said nothing.

The other child put her hand up. "Yes, Mary?"

"I'd… I'd...get a axe and chop it till there was a hole!"

"Yeah," Kirsty squirmed in her seat. "I'd get... I'd get a even bigger axe and go like... like... like... !" She jumped up and mimed, almost losing her balance as she swung her hands around.

"And then what? You've got the food, but what if the rain comes in and makes it soggy? What if the little mice come and nibble on it? What if the birds fly down and peck it all away because there's no door?"

"We could use it all up at once," I suggested. "We could invite all the poor people the farmer said no to before, and cook them a big meal."

"Yeah. Invite all the poor people in the whole, whole wide world!" Kirsty spread her arms and beamed around at all of us.

"And," I added, "At least then the man would be remembered for what he did right, rather than what he did wrong, which is a much better memory."

Helen looked at her watch, and stood up. "Well then," she said. "That was a good chat, wasn't it? Not quite what I had planned, but perhaps it was better. God is in control, after all! I think what we've learned today is that He wants us to be kind, and to use what He provides us with to help people who need it. Right—I have activity sheets for you. Each one has a treasure box on it. I want you to draw some of your own treasures inside it."

"Mum?" I said, after the service had finished and we were walking back home.

"Hmm?"

"You know how the minister said we needed to be patient to walk God's path?"

"Yes…"

"Well, I don't see how that can work when the farmer was supposed to share his food straight away instead of waiting."

"Hmm." She put her head on one side.

"What language were you talking in during the prayer?"

She made eye contact with me, and a little smile played across her face. "Oh—that's a language I use to pray in. Lots of people have a special prayer language."

"Do you think I could get one?"

She smiled again. I was beginning to lose track of bonus points. She also hadn't shouted at me in several days. "Maybe you'd better ask God about that." Then she pinched the bridge of her nose. Perhaps she had a headache. Dad did that when he had a headache.

"Mum?"

"Yes?"

I took a deep breath. I had a funny feeling she wouldn't like the question I was about to ask, though I couldn't say why I felt that. The satellite dish in me could tell me about feelings in the air, but it didn't seem to be much use when it came to working out how other people would react. "If you hate the man so much, why do you keep going to the church where he plays?"

She bit her lip, then smiled, but it looked odd. "They say you should keep your friends close and your enemies closer," she murmured, but then immediately shook her head. "No. I'm not going to let my life be dictated by him. Besides," she cleared her throat, "Someone's got to keep track of the old Grouch."

I tried and failed to figure out what this answer meant. It hadn't been the harsh snap I had been expecting. "Mum?"

"Hmm?"

"Sorry about what happened outside the church."

"That's OK. It wasn't your fault. I'm just not great around babies."

"I understand," I said, and I actually did. I slipped my arm through hers as she bent her head. She didn't pull away.

When we reached the house I saw Jamie dribbling a football in the drive. Ignoring Mum entirely, he addressed me:

"Come on. We're having a game in the park."

"Who is?"

"You and me. I've been here for ages, so you owe me."

His eyebrows looked even thicker than usual, and his mouth turned down at the corners, but his eyes also had shadowy circles around them, and there were red lines staining his cheeks. I didn't ask about these things—I didn't want to put him in an embarrassing situation, especially in front of Mum. "Can I, Mum?"

She clicked her tongue and bounced on the balls of her feet. "Well... all right. But keep out of trouble, OK? And be back at one for lunch."

Because the green was on a slope, every time one of us kicked the ball it would either curve round and roll back down, or travel through the air at high speed. The wind was also blowing downhill. Jamie insisted my goal be on the downward slope, making it much easier for him to score and defend, but I was always in goals with Dad and so had plenty of experience and practice. I was also taller and could run faster. We played three games, two of which Jamie won, but I didn't mind. The wind was warm, and I could smell bonfire smoke. When someone let a Labrador off its lead we decided to stop because Jamie said the football belonged to Jeremy and if it got punctured Jeremy would kick his head in.

"You any good at tree climbing?"

"I've never tried," I answered, "There weren't any near my old flat."

"C'mon, then." He ran down the slope towards the trees by the river. I followed, and by the time we reached the cluster of oaks I had a stitch. He approached the tree in which I had first encountered him.

"This is the easiest one." He gave it a kick. "Right. Here's how you do it."

He jumped and grabbed a thick branch which stuck out. Holding onto it with both hands he walked up the trunk, hooked an ankle over, then wriggled round so he was lying across the branch, and sat up.

"There. Do that."

Jumping up was easy and helped my stitch by stretching my stomach muscles. Walking up the trunk was harder though—my toes kept slipping, and I don't have much strength in my abdomen. My feet fell back down the first time I tried to hook my ankle over, and I had to drop back. My hands were also stinging from the friction of the bark. I rubbed them down my thighs, then put my palms on the grass. The coolness was soothing. Meanwhile Jamie sat on the branch as if it were a horse and watched me.

"Come on then!"

This time when I hooked my ankle over, he grabbed it, which gave me a chance to get a better grip. I could hear the blood pulsing in my head as my heart sped up. "I can't do it!"

"Shut up and concentrate!"

"Let go, I'm going to fall!"

"No, you're not." With his other hand he grabbed my arm and wobbled. His breath hitched, but he regained his balance. I slid my hand forward, hooked my elbow round the trunk, then pulled until I was sitting up.

"There. See?" He stuck out his chest and folded his arms, before taking hold of the tree trunk again. "This is where I go to be away."

I tipped my head back and looked up at the sunlight filtering through the leaves. I learned in art that there were over a hundred different shades of green. Now it seemed like the leaves were scattering them all around. When I levelled my gaze again, Jamie was using a tiny knife to whittle away at the branch.

"Where did you get that?"

"I keep it in my sock. It's my sgian-dubh."

"Your what?"

"Scottish people keep them in their socks." He brandished it: "On guard!" As he continued to whittle his jaw flexed, and he swallowed four times in quick succession.

"You look sad," I said. I poked him in the tummy.

"Ow—get off!"

"Mum was at the solicitor's yesterday," I continued. "She has to sign formal papers. Anna the receptionist thought it might be to do with custody. That means who takes care of me."

"Tell me about it…"

"I just did."

"Idiot. I meant I know all about it. Some people came round to visit. They asked me lots of questions about school. They said I might have to go into a children's home because of my Truancy Problem."

"You mean because you run away?"

He nodded.

"But a home full of children—how lovely! You can be happy about that, can't you? In fact, that's probably why the park's so empty all the time. I bet there's a soft play centre there, and a swimming pool and everything…"

"There's not." His voice sounded flat. "I was in one before. It's either that or another foster home somewhere else."

"Well… why don't you just not run away from school?"

He stared at me. "You don't know what it's like. I'm not going back."

"Why not?"

"Don't want to talk about it."

"OK." I paused. "I went to school until I was eleven. I tried senior school, but it didn't work out."

"Did they put you in a children's home?"

I shook my head. "Dad taught me."

"Well bully for you." He leaned over and spat onto the grass below. Suddenly his head jerked up. "Wait—I know!" He lowered his voice. "We could live here - just you and me."

"You mean run away?"

"Yeah. We could eat berries and birds' eggs and drink

out the stream!"

"That sounds good. But I read Lord of the Flies and it all went wrong for them."

"That's because they were stupid. We'll get it right."

I checked my watch. "Actually, I'd better go home to Mum—it's nearly one."

"But you're Away now. All that stuff doesn't matter anymore! And you never know—you might never be Away again."

"She'd worry if I didn't come home."

"So what?"

"Well, I don't want her to be worried."

"They don't care. Not really."

"That's not true!" I glared at him, willing myself not to believe it. But even if it was so, Dad had taught me that honesty is an ethical obligation, and ethical obligations don't depend on other people behaving well. "I don't feel comfortable breaking my word."

"Well, that's that then." Something fluttered in the leaves above us. We both looked up. "There's a bird's nest in there. Eggs for tea. Yummy."

"How do I get down?"

He stared straight ahead and tried to whistle a tune, but his lips were pursed incorrectly.

I lay across the branch and swung myself upside down, before letting my legs dangle and dropping to the floor. As I hit the ground I had an incredible thought.

"Jamie!"

No answer.

"Jamie, it's important!"

"What?"

"Come down and I'll tell you!" There was a pause, then a rustle of leaves, then a thunk as he hit the grass.

"Follow me!" Together we ran up the slope towards the house.

The kitchen smelled of potatoes. A pan of baked beans was steaming on the hob. The TV was on in the living room.

"Take your shoes off..." I put my head round the living room door. Mum was watching The Chase.

"Hello," I said.

"Hi."

"Can Jamie stay for lunch?"

"There's only two potatoes."

"That's all right. He can have toast."

"Well if he's sure..."

She got up from the sofa and we followed her through to the kitchen.

"You get plates. They're in that kitchen unit." It was then that I remembered we had run out of bread.

Jamie sipped a glass of juice, watching the two of us as we ate. Mum sat hunched forward. I considered telling her that sitting like that would lead to back pain and internal problems later in life, but decided against it.

"Do you like Jamie?"

She stiffened. She and Jamie looked at each other and averted their eyes. "I... I... well, I've nothing against him, particularly... Don't know him enough to say, really."

"He says Carol doesn't want him anymore. Can he live here?"

Jamie choked on a mouthful of juice. I hit him on the back and it sprayed across the table.

Mum put her fork down. "You have got to be joking."

"He can have my bed. I could sleep in the loft." I thought back to the bat—would I mind sharing a room with it? More to the point, would it mind sharing a room with me? We'd both just have to lump it, I supposed.

"Anna, I work full time at a stupid wage just to keep you. Anyway, you're my daughter. I don't just snatch random children off the street!"

"I've got to go." Jamie jumped up.

"No—wait!" Feeling a growing panic inside I reached out and tried to pull him back, but he shook me off, sprang across the room, wrenched open the door and ran out. I started after him.

"Don't you dare!"

I turned to face Mum, who was trembling. All my bonus points gone in one go.

"Get back here. Sit down. Finish your meal."

My cheeks tingled. I wondered whether Jamie would

ever talk to me again—and what Dad would do and say. The hot poker feeling surged up inside me like water behind a dam, until suddenly it burst.

"Why can't you take him in like you took me in?" I yelled.

Mum's mouth dropped open and her eyebrows rose.

"How come he's so different to you? You didn't know me either!"

"I'm your mother! Anna, I made you, I lo... that is, of course I'm going to take you in... I..." She broke off and clasped a hand to her mouth before staring at me, looking all spindly again. But I was too angry and disappointed to give this sudden transition much thought. It was as if all the times she had answered me shortly or snapped at me or pushed me away had joined forces in my head now, pushing me over an edge that no technique any outreach worker had taught me could forestall any more. On top of that, all the care Dad had given me—and out of that, the full force of all I had lost with him—met with my sense of what Mum was failing to give me—and all the hope I had had for how things would be. It was like two opposing winds meeting each other and forming a tornado strong enough to destroy everything in its path.

"You don't care about me! Jamie was right!" I hurled the words with all the bitterness and disappointment I could muster. Then I ran out of the kitchen and upstairs to the bedroom, where I picked up a pillow and smashed it several times hard against the wall.

I stayed in the bedroom for the rest of the day. As I calmed down my anger was replaced by tears, which I wept whilst looking out the window. Some were for Jamie, but most were for Dad—for how his jumpers smelt and his hugs felt, for our walks, for playing backgammon together, and for the flat. As memories crashed against each other like rocks in Saturn's rings, I felt as if I was being pummelled on the inside. After a long time I sat limply on the edge of the double bed. The side of the bed nearest the window was perfectly made. The one nearest the bedside table was crumpled, and the duvet had not been pulled back. I pulled it straight, and Mum's book—Her Eyes—dropped onto the floor. I picked it up and turned it over:

"In this harrowing but charming memoir, Marion Carson describes life with her autistic foster child, Jenny. Wry, honest, often funny and sometimes heart-wrenching, Her Eyes tells of an initially strained relationship which—bit by bit—transformed into a lifelong love."

My mind stilled as I turned to the first page. It described a scene where Marion is talking to her friends, with twelve-year-old Jenny curled up quietly in her lap playing with some Lego. As I was reading about how long it took to get to this point, pale fingers gently reached over the top of the page and eased the book out my hand.

"Best get an early night," Mum said softly, "It's been a tiring day."

It was warm and bright the next morning, but I felt like I'd swallowed a bucket of ice water. If I hadn't shared my idea with Mum I would have misled Jamie in calling him down from the tree, and he might have stopped being friends with me for that reason; but if I hadn't then I wouldn't feel such a mess today. I wondered if we had ever been friends in the first place, and whether there were any reasons left for him to want to be friends now.

"Anna?"

I jumped. The voice was not Mum's. I sat up quickly and saw Molly standing in the doorway. "Your mum's away to work," she said. "Someone cancelled on me this morning, so I'm a free agent. What would you like to do?"

I shrugged. Over the lip of the window there came a blinding point of sunlight. It felt warm on my cheek.

"We could go for a walk, or you could come and see my flat?"

"What do people like to eat when they're stuck indoors?"

"Come again?"

"The next-door neighbour," I said. "The one stuck in bed."

"Mrs No, you mean?"

"I didn't know her name. But the woman who looks after her—"

"That's her daughter, Susan.– "

"Well, she says that if anyone tries to cheer her up or bring her things, Mrs No just wants something else, or tells them to leave her alone. So I thought maybe we could do something different—something to help her feel better, so she'll be happy and Susan won't be irritated."

I got up and started to take off my pyjama top. Then I remembered how Jamie had reacted when I undressed at his house, and began once more to go over things I could have done differently.

"Do you mind if I change?"

"Go ahead. All girls together! So, what did you have in mind?"

"I'm not sure," I said, pulling on a sock. "Is there a particular food that's good for ill people?"

"Off the top of my head I'd say some kind of broth. That's the traditional cure-all, anyway."

"Could we get a recipe book?"

"Well, we could always look in the library in the next town. You finish getting ready and come downstairs. No need to get breakfast—I've made us a picnic."

I couldn't be bothered putting my earrings in today, or clipping my hair back, or brushing my teeth, or washing my face, so once I had finished dressing and gone to the bathroom I joined Molly.

"I don't have a coat," I said. "Well actually I have two, but one's in the dump, and the other's all scratchy and hard to walk in."

"Not to worry. I have the car. We'll just run in very quickly, then run out again. Come on."

Molly's car was pulled into the kerb on the road at the end of the courtyard. It was a small, maroon Peugeot. The bumper was dented on the right-hand side, as though it had been driven into a tree or lamppost.

"Hop in."

I got into the navigator's seat and moved some crumpled road maps onto the floor. The car smelled musty, like the inside of the cupboard under the stairs; a blue pompom dangled on a tassel above the dashboard. It swung back and forth as Molly started the engine. I thought it was ironic that a cleaner's car should be so messy and smelly.

"So," she said, "How's… everything?"

I gathered my thoughts. "I thought it was all going well. I was on my own, and then I met Jamie and I liked him, but—"

"Carol's Jamie?"

"Yeah. But then I made a mistake, and now I'm scared I'll never see him again."

"Why?"

"I asked Mum if he could live with us. She said no. Then he ran away."

Molly laughed. "I wouldn't worry if I were you. It'll blow over with time."

"But what if it doesn't?"

"It will. You meant well. If he's a good friend he'll see that. And if you're a good friend he'll miss you."

"I'm not sure if I am a good friend," I muttered.

"You tried to help someone you cared a lot about when he was upset. That sounds like a pretty good friend to me." She reached over and squeezed my right knee. "Anyway, until he sees sense, you've got me." I felt something which I had to work very hard to control, but this time I didn't know what it was.

The grassy field, the play park, the river and the banking were on our right as we drove away from the Skeleton Man's house. A bizarre mental image came into my head of him standing in a green-lit, flag-stoned room which looked a bit like a witch's cavern, next to a table, with flaming torches in the corners of the ceiling, holding a gigantic carving knife and skinning someone alive, whilst listening to gothic choral music on an old-fashioned stereo system. It seemed like something Edgar Allen Poe might write. The ridiculousness of it made me laugh. Still, I didn't want to get too close.

We passed an empty bus stop and came to a junction

where we turned left, back round almost in a circle. There were silver birch saplings evenly spaced along either side of this road, and their branches extended above us. Their leaves shivered as we passed underneath. The road gave way to roadworks up ahead. A man wearing a blue boiler suit, high visibility vest and green wellingtons stepped out into our path, holding a 'STOP' sign. His skin was black, his face was round, and he had a red button nose. He was wearing a hard hat.

"Open your window," Molly said. I wound it down. She leaned across. "Oi! Kenny!"

Kenny smiled and stooped down to window-height. "Hi-aye!" His Scottish accent was the broadest I'd heard since coming here. "It's yourself. How's tricks?"

"Same old. You still OK for tomorrow?"

"I am indeed." He nodded at me. "Who's this then?"

"This is Anna, Patty's daughter."

"So, you're she," he said to me. "It's an honour indeed." He shook my hand, and my whole body bounced up and down. "Nice to meet you." He stepped back. "Well, best not keep the traffic waiting." He turned his sign round so that it was green with the word "GO" written in white capitals.

"He seems nice," I said.

Molly smiled broadly, and her neck coloured. "Glad you think so!"

"Does he have a girlfriend?"

"Um..."

"Would you like to be his girlfriend?"

Now she went unambiguously scarlet: "I..."

"Oh, that reminds me. I met Ben again. He works at the doctor's surgery."

"Oh… that Ben!"

"Yes. You could come along with me when I get my stitches out. He says you're lovely, so he obviously likes you."

"Oh no, I couldn't."

"Don't be shy! You just have to say hello."

"Seriously, no!" She broke into sudden laughter. I laughed because she was laughing. "Thanks for the offer, though."

The sun had gone behind a cloud, but the rest of the sky was blue. For some reason I felt as if I was four and was just setting off on a weeklong summer holiday to the Cornish seaside, but I hadn't the faintest idea why. The wind had picked up and was ruffling a dark green yew tree and a shrub with pink flowers on, both of which formed part of a public garden area bordered by a wooden fence.

"Kenny put that fence up," Molly said, nodding at it and drawing her spine up straight.

"Perhaps he could sort out the garden for the Skeleton Man," I suggested, "It's all tangled inside, but you can't see much because of the wall."

"The what-man?"

"The man with all the skeletons in his closet. Lives in that huge house up the road."

"Oh, him."

"What's he like?"

"Stubborn, high minded and judgemental. Inherited all his money so never had to learn to be nice to anyone. Don't you go anywhere near him, Anna."

We turned left onto the main road. "Doesn't anybody read here?" I asked.

"Hmm?"

"Well, if there's no library…"

"Oh, they read. It's the council. Won't put the money aside for a library. And nobody's lobbying them."

"Lobbying?"

"Yeah. Badgering. Pestering them till they've done their job."

"I'm good at badgering people," I said.

She glanced at me sideways, and one corner of her mouth twitched.

We ended up on a narrow two-lane road with a stone wall on the right-hand side and an electricity power plant with pylons all clustered together. These looked like huge versions of children's climbing frames, except for not being dome-shaped. To the left a hill sloped upwards, upon which a herd of brown and white cows grazed. Molly pulled the car up next to a wooden gate.

"Breakfast," she said. She peered up through the windscreen into the sky. "Should be OK. Follow me."

We got out, and she pulled a rucksack off the back seat. "One of the neighbours was asking about you yesterday. Said she'd seen you out her window, sitting outside in the garden. Here—I did us sandwiches."

"Thank you!"

We climbed over a gate. Molly was wearing a skirt and therefore had to go slowly, putting one leg over so that she was half-straddling it. Then she lifted the other leg over too and jumped down onto the other side. I climbed up so I was sitting astride the top, then pushed my bottom forward and pinged down in an arc onto the ground.

"ThreetwooneGO!" Molly shouted—a joyful shout. And suddenly we were laughing again and racing each other to the top.

It wasn't a long hill, but it was steep, so by the time we stopped we were both gasping for breath. Above me the electricity lines stretched, and the moon was out behind them against the blue sky. It made me think of a poem by Seamus Heaney, in which some children climb to the top of a hill to look down on 'the telegraph poles and the sizzling wires'. About a quarter of a mile down the hill behind me there was a gigantic pylon, upon which I could just see the 'DANGER OF DEATH' sign. That warning always seemed comically tautological to me—surely what defines danger is its connection to death. The grass was dry, so I sat down and waited for Molly. I realised I hadn't thought of Jamie for over an hour, and then that in thinking that, I had thought of him. But, like the fields below, the worry seemed to have shrunk for now.

Molly looked out over the view too. "Wow," was all she said.

We ate our sandwiches in companionable silence.

"Do you like Queen?" Molly asked.

"Dad and I used to sing 'We Are the Champions'," I replied.

"Ah. Well if it would make you sad…"

"Oh no, I'd like to hear them again!"

"You would? Well, it just so happens I have a CD in the glove compartment of the car. You can put it on when we get back down if you like."

Once we were back in the car, I prised the glove compartment open. It was very stiff and opened grittily. Inside I found a pile of CDs. Some seemed to be home compilations, and there was a Bob Marley one, as well as Ian MacDonald, and the Spice Girls.

"Sorry about the mess," she said. "Don't think anyone's cleaned in there since the nineties. The CDs were in it when I got it."

I found the Queen one and stuck it in the player. For

a second nothing happened, then 'Bohemian Rhapsody' came on.

"Fast forward if you like."

"It's OK, I like this one too," I said.

We were coming into town again now, past more houses and a 'thirty' speed limit. The road had widened. 'We Are the Champions' came on next. It made me feel sad, and yet for some reason I didn't want it to ever end.

"Everyone can sing," I said, because I had studied singing in Music. "You just need to produce your voice properly—open up the back of your throat and breathe deeply, all the way down to your diaphragm." I took a breath, opened up the back of my throat and sang the first chorus. "Now you try."

But she shook her head. "I've got no sense of rhythm and I can't hold a tune."

"Just try. I won't mind if it comes out rubbish."

"Here we are!" She pulled in past two red brick buildings. I ejected the cassette and put it back in the glove compartment in its case.

The library made me think of Dorothy's house in Kansas, with its brown walls and its veranda. It had large windows, steps up to the door, and a concrete wheelchair ramp zigzagging up beside them. There was a wooden bench in the space in front of the building, with a border collie tied to it by a leather lead. It looked up and wagged its tail as we passed.

Inside there was a long, curving reception desk made of smooth wood, with four silver computer monitors spaced evenly around it. Two members of staff were on duty: a middle-aged, Asian woman with a pink cashmere top and sparkly hair slides; and an oldish man with fine, grey hair and glasses.

"Shall we split up, look around and then reconvene?" I suggested. I wanted to see if they had a telephone directory with Carol's number in it, but decided against sharing this.

"Yeah, might as well," Molly agreed. "If I don't see you shall we meet outside the door in half an hour?"

"OK."

I wandered through the biography and non-fiction sections, and even a section with outdated sales brochures. One of them had a smartphone on the cover. Jamie would have liked that. I clenched and unclenched my hands, trying to stay focused. Now I was standing next to a gateway formed by two smaller bookshelves, beyond which was what looked like another smaller bookshelf shaped like a train. Near it was a red and yellow play tent with round, fluffy cushions inside, and a toddler-sized table with an old man—much older than the one behind the front desk—kneeling beside it. He had a book in front of him and was pushing one wrinkly hand over the pages to turn them, like a child who hasn't yet learnt how to use their fingers properly. I peered over his shoulder at the book and saw a picture of Little Red Riding Hood. He was whispering to himself: "I'll huff and I'll puff and I'll BLOW your house down."

I coughed. "Hello."

He stared at me. His eyes struggled to focus on mine, and his pupils were cloudy.

"I'm Anna."

He didn't answer.

"You've got the wrong wolf," I said. "The Three Little Pigs' wolf was the one that huffed and puffed. Yours is the 'All the better to see you with' wolf. Do you want me to find you The Three Little Pigs?"

"I have a doggie," he replied.

"Is that your border collie outside?"

He cringed and hesitated before answering. "I left him there?"

"Well, there's a dog tied to the bench outside…"

"Yes. Yes—that'll be Hops." He nodded to himself, turned his head in the direction of the reception desk and clicked his tongue. "Ridiculous. I've been waiting for over an hour. Ruddy doctors!"

"But this is a library."

He looked even more confused and waved a hand at a father and pre-schooler who were eyeing the area we were in from a distance. "But then, who are all these people?"

"They're people who like books."

"Ah. Well, I'd best be away." He stood up, and his knees crackled as he straightened them. I watched him take tiny steps all the way through the biography and non-fiction sections, and out through the main door, which slid shut behind him.

A spiral metal staircase led up to the first floor. I ascended it and found lots more, higher, older, metal bookshelves. Interspersed between them were coffee tables and purple armchairs. Molly was sitting in one, with a large book in front of her.

"What's that?"

She held it up. The cover showed a photograph of a stainless-steel saucepan on a gas hob, with clouds of steam coming out a vent hole in the lid. The title read Cooking and Curing: Sixteen Nourishing and Healing Recipes.

"Any good ones?"

"Lots," she confirmed. "They've got one for lamb broth. We could easily make that. What do you think?"

"Sounds good."

Once we had checked the book out at the reception we left. I went through the library's exit gate with my fingers in my ears, in case the alarm went off. It didn't. As soon as we were outside, I looked towards the bench, and saw the dog still curled up beside it.

"He forgot," I said. Leaving Molly at the base of the steps, I went up to it. It licked my hand. It had soft fur that felt like plush and rolled over when I rubbed its tummy. I felt around its collar until I found the metal name disc, then pulled it round so I could read the inscription: "32 Fentonpark Avenue. My name is Hops."

"What are you doing?" Molly called. "It might bite!"

"There's an address!" I replied over my shoulder. "We could take him back!"

"Back where?"

"There was a man in the children's section. He was really old and wobbly. He thought we were in a doctor's surgery. He said his dog was tied up outside. We could take him back!"

"Or we could just call the SSPCA..."

"We could drop him at the door and run," I suggested, "His owner wouldn't be able to catch us—he was over a hundred years old."

She chewed on her bottom lip. "Well... All right then. Put him in the back and we'll feed it into the satnav."

I opened the navigator's door and folded the front seat down. Then I put my arms around Hops's tummy and slotted him, wriggling, headfirst into the back. He pushed his head forwards in between Molly and me and stayed like that as we drove. His breath was hot on my ear, and smelled sweet and tangy, like tangerines. I'd never met a dog with breath that smelled like tangerines before.

We turned right, up a junction bordered by a clump

of red and yellow marigolds, onto an uphill street with a multi-storey community building, a church on our left and a row of detached, white bungalow cottages.

"Keep an eye out," Molly said. Some houses didn't have numbers, but I kept count mentally. "Thirty-two." I pointed, then reached back and stroked Hops on the head. "Nearly home."

We parked outside the church. I lifted Hops out and held him by the collar. The house was made of white stone and had two main windows with yellow frames. The paint was peeling off, leaving patches of grey. The front door was ajar. I could hear Schubert, but couldn't place where it was coming from. Molly knocked and we waited. Hops strained forward.

"Hello?" Molly called.

The pressure from the collar was hurting the inside of my fingers, so I let go. Hops disappeared into the house.

I looked to Molly, she nodded, and we followed. A horrible smell—like old roadkill—filled the hall.

"Should we run?"

She didn't move.

She was looking ahead with her chin tilted up, eyes watering.

"What if he's dead?" I shivered.

She shook her head. "He wouldn't go off that fast. It's probably just something in the fridge. Come on."

We followed the smell down the hallway, through

a door on the left. As soon as we entered the kitchen it became so bad that Molly went to the sink and dry-retched. I held my nose and opened the window. There was a cord hanging down above a rusty, white electric cooker, which Molly pulled. A fan to the right of the window started up.

"What on earth is making that ungodly stink?" she gasped.

The cupboards were open, the bin was lying on its side and there was rubbish all over the floor. In one corner lay something I didn't recognise at first, but when I got closer I saw that it was the remains of a whole, raw chicken. The carcass had been picked two thirds bare, and the rest of it was swollen and mottled.

"That fits the bill." Molly's voice was muffled—she had pulled her top over her nose and mouth. "See if you can find the man."

I left the kitchen and walked up the hall. The music got louder. There was an open door on the right, which led through to a living room. The floor was wooden, and an electric fire blazed in front of two armchairs. Hops was curled up in one, and the man sat in the other. His head was on one side, and in his left hand he was holding a miniature radio up to his ear. His right hand was on the armrest and his fingers were waving up and down in time to the music.

"You left Hops behind at the library," I said.

He looked up.

"We brought him back for you."

"Who?"

"Hops." I pointed at Hops.

"That's Daisy."

"No it isn't. His name's on the collar."

He closed his eyes and resumed his finger-waving. For some reason I felt sad, but he didn't seem to be unhappy, so I decided instead to be happy about the beautiful music. I would have liked access to a piano at that point. A few seconds later he opened his eyes again. "I went fishing the other day."

I smiled. "That's good."

"Do you know what this music is?"

"It's the Trout Quintet."

"Correct. Listen to how calm it is." The strings undulated in volume and rhythm, like drifting waves. The tempo increased when the piano came in, as if a current were picking up on a river.

"Fishing isn't calm," he continued. "My pike put up a huge fight!"

"Really?"

"I'll have to take the boat out again before summer's through."

As the music played his eyes half-closed, so that I could only see the whites, and his chin dropped so that it rested on his chest. My mind began to lapse back onto the problem of Jamie. He might be at the tree now. It was a nice day, and he had wanted to go and live there. Or he might have been moved by now, possibly to a different town. I thought about Skylar and Emily and the baby, and how Emily and the baby were cute but they were too young to have proper conversations, and as for Skylar, well, he didn't know what it was like. Jamie had been in foster care too. A different type, and longer than me, but it had still been nice to have a friend with that in common. I appreciated that more than I'd realised.

With Dad, whenever I became anxious about things out-with my control, he would always repeat the same mantra, which I had in a text from him, though I had left my phone at the house:

"You don't know what will happen in the future. It could just as easily be good."

Usually he had been right, like when I did my grade six piano, and when I auditioned for the part of Beatrice. Now, however, the mantra seemed irrelevant. This time I had done something real to someone else, which had turned things bad and might even have lost them to me. It would be all my fault if I never saw Jamie again. Had I not acted the way I had done, we would still be in touch. To distract myself I looked around the room. On the wall beside the double windows, opposite the door leading in, there was a framed collage of photographs. One showed two children—a girl of about four with two blonde plaits and wearing a blue dress, and a baby boy of about one, wearing denim dungarees and red shoes. The girl was halfway up the ladder of a baby-slide, and was looking directly at the camera, laughing. The boy was getting up off the end of the slide having just gone down. Another showed the man, younger, with a fat woman who had her arm around his waist. On the other side was a much younger man with thick, shoulder-length blonde hair, exactly the same shade as the hair of the little girl in the first photograph. A third photograph showed Hops as a puppy, lying in some long grass, with daisies and buttercups around him.

My eye was caught by a movement through the window. I peeked out. The blonde-haired man from the photograph was coming up the path. He looked older, and his hair was shorter, but it was definitely him. At that moment he glanced up and our eyes met. His eyebrows pulled down, and a red spot appeared on each of his cheeks. The photograph didn't show how bony his face really was. He broke into a run.

I dashed through to the kitchen as quickly and quietly as I could. Molly had disposed of the chicken carcass and was wiping down surfaces with a dishcloth. When she saw me she hastily threw the cloth back into the sink.

"Sorry, cleaning's kind of a habit." She went pink.

"There's a man outside. He'll come in at any moment!"

"Oh, shoot, bollards!" She darted glances around the

room as the man's footsteps sounded in the hall.

"Just WHAT is going on here?" He strode into the kitchen, stopped when he saw us, then swept a hand round. "Who the heck are you two?"

"We're really sorry," said Molly. "The gentleman who lives here left his dog at the library. We just dropped him off."

He surveyed the clean counters and his breathing seemed to calm, so it came as a horrible shock when he yelled. "Who told you to clean the place? You had no right to break in here like the pair of do-gooders you are!"

I bit back tears, shivering.

"Now listen here," his voice dropped, and he shook a finger at us. "We don't need any 'help'. So get out, and don't you ever bother us again or I'll have you both arrested."

"Well… some gratitude that was," Molly spat, once we had returned to the library car park to recover. When we hadn't immediately pulled away from the kerbside outside number 32 the man had come after us, rolling up his sleeves. She took a deep breath. She was shaking too.

"Oh well," I countered, "We've got the book now. That's something to be happy about."

She made a small noise in reply. A muscle in her jaw flexed and relaxed rhythmically.

"Are you all right?"

She nodded.

"What's going to happen to the dog?"

"I'm tempted to make a note of the address and call the SSPCA." She took a notepad and pen out of a pocket in her door and scribbled the house number and street down.

"Why is it that the more you try and be kind, the more people shout?"

"Because they don't like charity."

"Charity? Do you mean like the place where Mum works?"

"No, I mean like people who come in with intentions of 'bettering' others in order to make themselves feel good, or so as to look good in the eyes of people they want to impress."

"But we weren't doing either of those things. We were just cleaning the kitchen."

"I know."

"Is charity a bad thing, then?"

She sighed. "No, not bad. Just sometimes it can be a sore spot for people. It was my fault—I should have known better."

"It wasn't your fault. I said we should take Hops back." I put a hand on her knee. "So then, how do I tell if I'm doing charity or kindness?"

"It isn't always easy," she admitted. "I suppose you have to give people space. That and recognise where your responsibility stops." She changed gear. "Whatever happens, Anna, don't you give up your kindness. OK?"

"OK," I said, and I looked out the window at the marigolds on the junction corner.

Once again I got very little sleep fretting about Jamie, and woke up with a head cold. To my surprise Mum took the day off work. She spent most of the morning upstairs on her computer, but we ate lunch together watching Bargain!. I lay on the living room sofa with my notebook and pen, dozing. My mind was fuzzy, and most of my energy was gone. Mum spoke to a doctor over the phone in the afternoon, but it wasn't Ben—I asked. Every now and then she asked if there was anything I needed. Every time I longed to say that I just wanted to be held, but I thought that probably wasn't the kind of thing she meant, so I didn't.

I felt somewhat better the following morning, got a bit of writing done and read some of Mum's Bible which she lent me. Like the hymn book, its pages were thin. It was bound in brown leather, with 'The Holy Bible' engraved on the front in silver letters. I read all of Genesis and most of Exodus. At bedtime I pretended to be asleep. I heard Mum go to the bathroom and brush her teeth before returning to the bedroom, where I felt her brush the foot of my sleeping bag. She must have stayed there for about five minutes, because during that time there were no footfalls, and the only sounds I could hear were the ventilation system, my sleeping bag shifting as I breathed, and two men shouting outside. Then there was the creak of bed-springs, before the light was turned off.

Once Mum's breathing deepened, I sat up, my head clear now, my body full of adrenaline. I had made a decision about Jamie. Since the thing that had upset our friendship had come from me, the reconciliation was my responsibility too. Perhaps he was spending the night in his tree like he'd said. Perhaps he was there right now. Even if he wasn't, I might find a clue as to where he had gone—he had been wearing football boots with studs at the time, and the ground was wet. It would be quiet and deserted, and if he wasn't there I could just check for clues, then come back before Mum woke up.

I quietly wriggled out of my sleeping bag. It didn't seem like a good idea to dress in the bedroom—the more disturbance, the thinner a person's sleep becomes. I gathered my clothes into a bundle and tiptoed through to the bathroom. Even if she did wake up now, she would probably just think I was using the toilet. The thought of putting on used socks and knickers was a bit icky, so I just put my tracksuit top and bottoms on and left my feet bare because my trainers were still in the bedroom. Then I tiptoed downstairs, avoiding all the creaky bits. I found a new one on the third lowest step. The sound made me flinch, but it stayed quiet when I lifted my foot off it very slowly.

Once in the kitchen I turned the door handle gently, pulling inwards, then pushing outwards. It was locked. I looked in the drawers, then under the mat and on top of the fridge but found no key. The windows in the living room were closed. It was dark, but the drawn blinds were thin, and orange street light shone through them. The empty furniture and long shadows gave me a strange feeling, somewhere between haunted and melancholy. There were two large window panes set side by side in the wall, which looked out across the lawn. They were split down the middle, with one shared wooden edge. At the bottom of each was a catch. I pulled one up, then pushed the frame out as far as it would go. A gust of wind blew, and the curtains billowed silently into the living room.

The gap was no wider than about thirty centimetres. Putting my head on one side and sucking in my tummy I squeezed my body through horizontally, until I was lying astride the window frame. Then I groped around with my foot until my toes touched the grass. It felt soft and cold and wet with dew. After wriggling around and bruising my hips a bit I slithered out to stand on the lawn. The street looked very different at night. Everything dark looked more prominent, and I noticed things I hadn't before, such as the two metal skips at the end of the street, the dark spaces around the sides of the garages, and the puddle at the junction onto the main road. Now its ripples broke the reflection of the lamplight into fragments, which glittered when I looked at them out the corner of my eye. In the daytime it had just been a small pool which I had jumped over or stepped around without thinking.

A few drops of rain blew into my face. My arm came out in goose-pimples, partly because of the damp and wind, and partly because I was keeping a watch out for burglars. At one point I thought I was going to faint when something rustled in the hedge until, with a quiet 'meow', the black and white cat emerged. I stroked it and whispered my apologies that I had been unable to meet it and share my breakfast ham. It rubbed against my hand as if to forgive me, then trotted off towards an open wheelie-bin.

The green was silent and peaceful, with few street lamps on the road running alongside it. I could hear the quiet, collective swish of wind in the trees down by the river. Clouds hurried across the sky. A waxing gibbous moon kept showing itself momentarily before being obscured again. A tawny owl hooted, a twig skittered across the road, and a bat fluttered overhead in a wide circle. I wondered if it was my bat. Probably not, but perhaps they were acquainted. This thought made me smile. I listened hard, imagining I could hear high-pitched chirruping, but bats' echolocation usually occurs at supersonic frequency, so it was more likely that I was hearing wingbeats. Running over the green felt different to how it did in the day. The shadows made it look as if I was moving much faster, and maybe I was—I had more adrenaline in me than I would have done had it been day. Without the weight of my shoes my body felt very light. When I reached Jamie's tree, I leaned against it and let my breathing get back to normal. Then I glanced up at the first branch.

"Jamie?" I called in a loud whisper.

There was no answer, but that might have been because he was asleep. I poised, leapt and grabbed with both hands. It hurt to walk up the trunk without shoes on—all the deep ridges cut into the soles of my feet. At least the grain lay the same way as my feet, although that made it harder to keep a grip. Despite grazing my skin in the process, slotting my ankle over the branch was easier than it had been the first time. I wriggled round and sat astride the branch, then looked up into the leaves. Jamie was not there. With that realisation all the worry I had hoped to get rid of by seeing him again came back. I took four deep breaths and clenched and unclenched my hands.

I was about to jump down and start for home when there was a snap—like a twig underfoot—from somewhere below. I went completely still and rigid, and waited. Another snap, then multiple crackling footsteps over dead wood and grass, coming nearer. A figure came into sight from the direction of the river—a figure I knew that Molly disliked and that Mum—well, I wasn't sure what Mum felt, really. A figure much taller and broader than Jamie, with dark hair, and clad in a red dressing gown. The Skeleton Man walked slowly and carefully. When he reached the bottom of my tree he leaned against the trunk. I saw the flame of a lighter like Dad's, and the orange glow the end of a cigarette makes when someone takes a puff. Wisps of smoke rose up towards me. The smell triggered faint gusts of memories. Memories of being held in arms whilst wrapped in a soft, warm blanket; being irresistibly sleepy; of the accompanying smell of beer; and of the sounds of voices and a fiddle.

My breath hitched, and I put a hand over my mouth and nose to muffle the sound. In doing so, I wobbled and grasped a nearby hanging branch. The shaking leaves sounded like a rain stick. The Skeleton Man looked up. I didn't see his face, because it was as if something had burst inside me. I scrambled to stand up, forgetting any previous senses of danger and vertigo, and began to climb faster than I ever imagined I could. I must have only climbed about a metre higher (although it felt like more) when I grabbed what I thought was a strong branch. It snapped, and I flung my arms out, trying to balance myself or else find an alternative handhold. I found nothing. I fell, struck the main branch and carried on down, presumably knocking my head on the ground below because I don't remember the actual impact.

It was warm. I was lying on a soft surface. Through my eyelids I could see that something was moving back and forth across the light. I opened my eyes and saw the dark red upholstery of a sofa. A face came into focus, peering down at me. I tried to leap up and run, but the Skeleton Man put a hand on my upper chest and gently pushed me back down.

"Shh, Anna. Lie back." His voice was scratchy and whispery.

"You know my name?"

"Are you in pain?"

I frowned, trying to work out if any particular part of me hurt. "Only my back. And my feet. And my head. And my hands. Where am I?"

"I carried you in. I know that was a risk, but I don't own a mobile telephone. It would have been just as bad leaving you where you were. Now then, can you wiggle your toes on your right foot?" Although it stretched the skin on the soles of my feet and made them sting, I was able to do so. "And your left?" I did. He nodded, looking at my feet with half-closed eyes.

"Are you going to skin me alive?"

He looked right into my eyes with his narrowed, pale-blue ones. His pupils were very small. I felt as if

I was a mauled mouse that had been adopted by a cat. "Hmmm… No. I think not. Not tonight anyway. What did you…?" He pointed at his lip. I realised he was asking about my stitches.

"Oh… a friend kicked me."

"As friends do."

"I'm not sure if he is my friend any more though. He… we… I made a mistake. I asked him to come and live with me. Then he ran away. I haven't seen him since."

"I see. So, he kicks you in the lip and you stay his friend. You make one mistake and you're persona non grata. Yep, sounds like pretty typical human behaviour to me."

"What does 'persona non grata' mean?"

"It's Latin. Literally translates as: 'person not welcome.'"

"Oh. Well, I don't want to be persona non grata. And I don't know where he is. I thought he might be…"

"In the tree?"

I nodded. "It's his secret hideout." My eyes filled up and overflowed. My nose started to run. I sniffed.

"You went to look for him?"

"Yes."

He reached down his dressing-gown sleeve and brought out a blue cloth handkerchief, which he handed to me.

"He used to live with Carol—that's his foster mum— but now he says he might have to live in a children's home. Or in a different foster-home. It's because of his truancy problem—he keeps running away from school, but he won't say why. His name's Jamie. Do you know him?"

"People!" There was a hard emphasis on the 'p' so that a bit of saliva flew out his mouth. Then he curled his upper lip, like a wolf, and shook his head vigorously. It was then that I saw the Alsatian sleeping by the open fire. I backed away.

"Hot chocolate?" Soft, scratchy voice again.

"OK."

He stood up and went through another door to the right. I sat back down and drew my knees up, keeping my eyes on the dog. There was the sound of a gas ring being lit, and of a pot of some kind being pulled out of a cupboard. The room was spacious, gently lit by standard lamps in the corners, with a large fireplace, a book shelf, a sheepskin rug and several wooden cabinets, some of them the height of a person. I wondered where all the skeletons were stored. Dad told me ghosts were nothing to be afraid of—they didn't exist and even if they did, they were dead and couldn't hurt anyone. Skeletons were just the same—piles of bones. I put my hand up and cupped the outline of my jaw. The wide grin of my skull was both familiar and unfamiliar. I shuddered, but it helped make the thought of the skeletons—wherever they were hidden—not quite so eerie. I stood up and took a few steps forward. My feet held my weight and I didn't have a limp. The Alsatian opened its eyes, lifted an ear and growled.

"Quiet, Jen," the Skeleton Man called through. I blinked. I hadn't imagined the dog to be female. "All bark and no bite," he added.

"That's what Joanne said about you."

"Well, there you go then. A perfect team." There was the sound of liquid being poured, and a teaspoon clinked three times against the edge of a mug. "I don't like people pestering me. Especially children." I tried to tidy my tracksuit, hold myself erect and make sure there was nothing childish about me. "Since you don't seem to be seriously hurt, put another log on the fire."

Two wicker baskets sat on the floor either side of the fireplace. One had small sticks in it, and the other was filled with big logs. Jen heaved herself up and walked away as I approached, giving a half-hearted snap at my hand when I reached out to touch her back. I picked a log off the top of the pile, held it in both hands and darted forwards to drop it on the fire. The Skeleton Man came through with two mugs—one with blue stripes, like pyjamas, and one which looked hand-painted. He gave the hand-painted one to me. I put it on the arm of the sofa.

"Oi! Mug. Coaster. Side-table." He indicated a small, square, wooden table covered with a Chinese silk drape, with a lamp and a plain blue cork mat on it.

The painting on the mug was faded and showed a barn owl with a star above it. Someone had painted them with black outlines, then filled them in with colours which had run a bit and dried in drips. Bits of the ceramic were chipped.

"Did you make this?"

He shook his head. "My daughter. Years ago."

"She's a good artist."

"Was."

"Is she dead?"

"Oh, no. No, we just don't speak now."

"Not ever?"

"Well… one or two words in about fourteen years."

"That's awful."

"Her choice."

I sipped my hot chocolate. It left a light, creamy foam on my upper lip.

"So—this Jamie," he continued, after a few seconds, "You say he lives at Carol's?"

I nodded.

"Have you tried ringing there?"

"I don't know the number."

"She's his foster mother, you say?"

I nodded again.

"Maybe we can find out." He stood up. "Bring your drink."

We went through to a hall with a floor and staircase

carpeted over with wicker matting. He climbed the stairs like a toddler, stepping up with his right foot, then bringing his left onto the same step as the first, before stepping up with his right foot again. His left hand gripped the banister. The bones under his skin looked like a spider as they flexed. Once at the top of the stairs he led the way through to what looked like a study. There was a flat-screened, black and silver PC—a newer model like the ones in the library—and a rotating desk-chair on casters. The rest of the room was covered in chest-high piles of books, with sheaves of blue, crumpled A4 paper between the pages. A light brown, upright piano with yellowed keys stood in the corner with its lid open, the stool pulled out. Some music sat on the stand, falling sideways: 'Jesu, Joy of Man's Desiring'. Thinking through the notes as I scanned the first lines, I recognised the melody from church.

I sat down and played three nocturnes by Chopin. Those were the last pieces I had learnt before the fire broke out in the flat. Music—transient combinations of twelve tones at varying octaves, rising up for a moment and then falling away again until next time, like flowering plants, or the sun and the seasons. It can't be contained, but neither can it be fully destroyed—even when composers crumble to dust and manuscripts burn to ashes, the tunes still exist in peoples' memories and fingertips.

When I finished I turned around. The Skeleton Man was watching me. His eyes were all shiny.

"You have a hand for Chopin."

I said, "His music makes me feel calm when I'm stressed."

"Are you stressed now?"

"Not now that I've played some Chopin. I've never played a nocturne in the middle of the night before."

"Something everyone should do before they die." He half-smiled. "Come on. You can kneel here. Let's check for this Carol."

I squeezed in and rested my elbows on the desk while he booted up the computer. It took a while, but not nearly as long as the one we had in the flat, which had a cube-shaped screen. As we waited I reflected on what Mum and Molly had told me. He didn't seem remotely scary or dangerous. Fierce, perhaps, but some people are, and it doesn't always mean they're bad inside. If anything, he seemed subdued. If he had been dangerous, he could have done something to me when I was knocked out, but instead he made sure I hadn't been hurt and gave me hot chocolate. I thought back to his saying 'people' and wondered if he had been—Dad used the word once and afterwards I looked it up in The Oxford English Dictionary—'maligned'. Maybe that was why he owned an Alsatian, hated people and kept his curtains closed all day.

"Now then, some keywords..." He hesitated, his fingers hovering above the keys. He typed in 'Carol', and 'foster', and 'West Lothian'.

"Why are you searching for Carol?" I asked. "Jamie said he might not be living with her anymore."

"On the other hand, he might be. Best start with what we know."

He clicked 'search'. The first page came up, with the keywords highlighted in the preview lines:

"Carol singers face a curfew after sleepy residents complain..."

"How to foster good oxygen and harness positive quantum wellbeing..."

"Carol Evans grew up in foster care in Winchester..."

"West Lothian fostering agency..."

"Click on that—click on that!"

"Yes, all right, I know!" he shoved my hand away and clicked. A flower-bordered yellow page came up, with a black and white photograph of four older women. Along the top of the page were different headings: 'Who are we?' 'Want to foster?' 'Fostering in Scotland and West Lothian' and 'The Fostering Process'.

"Is that them?"

"Let's find out..." He clicked on 'Who Are We?':

"We are a group of dedicated foster parents. Our job is to provide temporary, home-like environments to children who, for many possible reasons, cannot be cared for by their parents or relatives. We have all been through specialised training and undergone thorough background checks. We are passionate about children and their welfare. To learn more about each of us, please click on our photographs."

I peered at Carol's photograph. It was an outdoors, head-and-shoulders, greyscale shot. She had a weathered face but was smiling. Her blonde hair was pulled back in a ponytail, and she wore a raincoat. The Skeleton Man clicked on her name, and a telephone number came up. I jumped up and twirled, banging my left knee against the corner of the desk. Pain shot through it, but it didn't matter.

"Best not ring it at…" He glanced at his watch, "Half three in the morning. Infuriating, the conventions of normal people. Still, there you have it." He got up. "You'd better get back home. How are your feet?"

"Fine now." The stinging had almost completely gone, and though the base of my back felt tender, the tenderness was in a more definite area and was therefore easier to avoid provoking.

"How's your head?"

"It's OK."

"That's good." He nodded. "You fell from the tree a while ago. If you were in any danger it would be showing by now. You'd be slurring your words and getting sleepy. Certainly not spinning and conversing. I'll phone your mother."

"You know her number?"

"Yes." He held the door.

"It's OK though," I said. "I left the window open to get back in."

"In that case I'll just walk with you. Make sure you get in safely."

The night seemed darker as we stepped out onto the concrete drive, partly because the clouds had thickened and covered the whole sky, and partly because of the comparative brightness inside the Skeleton Man's house. We walked in silence, side by side. After several minutes he spoke:

"So. What did you think of the house?"

"It's different to… to what I imagined."

"Good-different, bad-different or neutral-different?"

I considered. "Good-different, I think. Except for the skeletons, of course."

He stopped. "The what?"

"The skeletons. In your closet. Or was Mum wrong about that?"

He lifted his chin, opened his mouth and gave a grating laugh. "Ahhhh! I see," he murmured, "Those skeletons. Yes, they're all the rage."

"You mean other people have them too? Like a fashion?"

"Oh yes. You'd be hard-pushed to find anyone here who doesn't have at least one." I stared. Nobody told me the Scots hoarded skeletons. But then, nobody told me they kept knives in their socks either. I desperately wanted to know more, but as we drew level with sixteen McCallish Court I saw, to my horror, that the lights were on and the curtains were open.

"Quick," he muttered. We ran through the gate. He knocked hard on the door. When Mum answered it was obvious that she'd been crying. When she saw us her cheeks grew pale.

"Safe and sound," said the Skeleton Man.

Mum glared at him. He gazed back, eyes all shiny again.

"Goodbye Anna—for now." His shoulders seemed to sag. Then he turned and receded into the night.

My laundry was hanging on the kitchen pulley.

"Are you OK?" I asked Mum.

She sniffled and wiped her eyes on her sleeve. "Does it look like I'm OK?" Then she shook her head. "From now on, you're sleeping in my bed. That way I'll know if you try and go wandering off again."

Her parenting methods were so unusual. Dad's punishments had always been fair but were never very nice. Once when I threw his shoes out the window because he wouldn't buy me a book that I wanted, he confiscated my entire Agatha Christie collection. Another time, when I'd stolen all the baking chocolate after we'd had a supermarket delivery, he fined me five pounds of pocket money and made me spend the rest of the afternoon doing his tax returns. He'd said that it was never too early to learn.

Here it was different: when I misbehaved by going over to Jamie's, Mum ran me a bath, as though I was ill and being tenderly cared for. And now she was letting me sleep in the big bed—like a tiny baby who needs to feel safe and not-alone—because I had run away in the middle of the night and talked to someone she hated. It was really confusing. Despite the confusion, though, I couldn't stop grinning as we went upstairs, and I changed back into my nightie.

Just before Mum switched off the light I rolled onto my tummy, rested my chin on my knuckles, and turned to face her.

"I'm glad you don't shout at me so much any more," I told her.

"Don't push it," she answered.

"Why are you so scared of the Skeleton Man?"

"I'm not scared of him. It's… complicated. A lot of things happened a long time ago, and now we don't talk."

"Not ever?"

"Well, one or two words in about fourteen years. Now go to sleep. And don't sleepwalk."

And she leaned over and kissed me on the forehead.

When I was little, Dad sometimes took me to see Nanna

and Granddad, who lived in Cornwall. I remember climbing through the cat flap and out into the garden aged two. The house was near a footpath above the sea. The waves crashed below and the seagulls, black against the sky, looped and shrieked. The grass came up to my armpits and was full of little blue flowers. When I peered down over the cliff, I could see foamy-white water splashing and swirling around the rocks. The wind blew my hair into my eyes and mouth, making me stagger. I sat with my legs sticking over the edge, and pretended I was flying home to my nest. Suddenly I heard someone shout my name. I turned and saw Granddad running across the grass. When he reached me, he put his hands under my armpits, and for a second I thought I really was flying as I swung through the air. Then I was over his shoulder, and all I could see were flowers.

Now whenever I hear the word 'Granddad', that's what I think of—blue flowers, long grass, sea salt and waves.

The sky through the curtains turned lighter and lighter blue, and a thrush began to sing. Mum had faced away from me all night. She'd been breathing deeply so I'd assumed she was asleep, but when she turned around at seven o'clock she was fully awake. "Did you sleep well?" she asked, when she saw that I was awake.

"Yes thank you. Why didn't you tell me before that he was your dad?"

"Because."

"Because what?"

"Just because."

"All right. Why don't you and he speak?"

"Many reasons. It's very complicated." She threw back the duvet, got out the bed and stretched. Then she dressed, opened the curtains and went downstairs. I lay still for a bit longer, then washed, put on a clean tracksuit and went down too.

The front door was open. It was a balmy, sunny day, with a slight haze. Mum put ham on two slices of toast, filled a glass with orange juice and put everything on a tray, exactly like when I made breakfast for her on my first morning.

"Molly says you like to eat outside."

"Yes. I learned about the calls of most garden birds when I was eight. And Molly and I had a picnic on a hill a few days ago—it was lovely."

"Hmm."

I sat on the grass, but Mum took a chair out. She chewed, looking straight ahead with her face, but somewhere down and off to the right with her eyes.

"I phoned work," she said. "I'm going in a bit late today."

"Why?"

"Need to get those stitches removed." She nodded at my mouth.

"I thought your doctor was in Livingston. I could just come to work with you."

"Kind of stupid to register you in Livingston when you're going to be here most of the time. Besides, like I said—I can't be ruled by fear. Anyway, they run a drop-in clinic today. It'll be ok. Just..." She cleared her throat: "Just don't make me come in with you."

"You don't have to come along with me if you don't want to. I can manage."

"No, I'll come." She paused and looked away. Then she smiled. "Right. Teeth, and then we'll walk to the clinic."

"So," she said, as we made our way up the road, "You met him."

"You mean my... your... the Skeleton Man?"

"Skeleton Man?"

"Yes."

She laughed quietly and repeated the term. "It suits him. Anyway—what did you think of him?"

"I drank from your cup."

An expression I couldn't decipher flickered across her face.

"The one with the owl," I added, for clarification.

She smiled. "Oh, that. He kept it?"

"Yes."

We walked on. "There are things I regret," she said. "I could have handled them differently. I was... I was very raw at the time."

I waited.

"Look, Anna," she continued, after about a minute, "You're a teenager. Before you came here did you get, like, pocket money?"

"Yes. One pound fifty a week." I fought back a feeling of disappointment that she had not elaborated on what had happened between her and the Skeleton Man.

"What did you spend it on?"

"Books, mostly. From the second-hand bookshop. I saved up. I got others from the library too."

Her mouth worked, but not in the angry way I had seen before. I thought of her bookshelf—all the books filling it and piled on top. "What do you like to read?"

"Well, I went through an Agatha Christie stage when I was ten. And Seamus Heaney. I quite liked some Auden. And I started reading The Lion, the Witch and the Wardrobe, but Dad stopped me. And photograph books. I had one about bats—sorry..." She shuddered. "One Christmas I read my height in fiction."

"Really?"

"Yes. And I love to read aloud. I used to read to... well... to a lot of people. Except that now I don't have any of them. The books, I mean. But also the people."

She nodded, brow furrowed.

"Anyway," I went on quickly, "I'm happy I had them. I write a lot too. Alison gave me a notebook and pen. It's nearly full now."

"What sort of things do you write about?"

"Just things I do. And things that make me happy."

"What makes you happy?"

I stuttered—my mind went blank. It was the kindest thing she'd said to me since I'd arrived, and I was caught completely off guard.

She laughed again. "Well like I said, I don't have much to spare, but I could probably manage three pounds a week. How does that sound? At least then you can save for more books. And if you want to read C.S. Lewis go ahead. Fiction, theology, it's all fine with me."

"Oh, thank you!" I slipped my arm through hers. "I'm going to build my own collection here."

When we got to the clinic Mum sat on the wall and told me to go on in. I hadn't realised she was being quite that literal when she asked me not to make her go in with me.

"Oh, don't forget this…" She handed me the doctor's form. It was very crumpled and stained, and still had blood from my lip smeared across part of it, but she had filled in the sections I hadn't known.

Once inside, I realised that what with all that had gone on, I hadn't thought about Jamie all morning— Mum's sudden change in behaviour and the rare chance to chat casually with her had overshadowed it. Now though it all came surging back, as though a dam had burst in my mind. I couldn't ring him now—we were out the house and Mum was outside. I clenched and unclenched my fists a few times. A sign was propped up on the reception desk. It read: "Drop in, 9:30-11:00am." It was a different receptionist this time—another woman with long, blonde hair, and nails painted with purple and silver swirls.

"This is for you," I said, handing her the form.

She hesitated, then took it between her finger and thumb and dropped it somewhere under the counter, lip curled.

"Also, I need to get my stiches taken out." I pointed at my lip. "Can I see Doctor Strachan? I saw him last time."

"You'll see whoever is ready for you first. Now take a seat."

The waiting room was occupied by a woman in a black suit looking at a pink smartphone, an old man with wispy white hair, brown trousers and an oilskin coat like my old one, a black woman in jeans and a summery blouse, and a girl with lilac hair who couldn't have been much older than me. She was sitting in a chair in the far right-hand corner, leaning against the wall and crying quietly. The one spare seat was between her and the old man.

I sat down. "Hello. What's the matter?" Getting no reply, I repeated the question.

She lifted her head. "Nothing." Then she sank back down against the wall.

On the coffee table in front of the chairs there was a National Geographic magazine, and a round wooden plate full of indentations, each with a green marble on it, forming the shape of a cross. The central indentation was empty. I picked the plate up.

"Been trying to solve that thing for years," said a voice to my right. The old man pointed at it.

"What is it?"

"Solitaire." He reached over, jumped one marble over another into the central indentation, and removed the one that had been jumped over, placing it in a groove around the rim of the plate.

"You do that until there are no more marbles left beside each other. Should be able to get it down to just one in the middle, but I've never managed it. The wife knows how."

I got all the way down to four in a square, before the man was called away by Doctor Warren. Then I played three more games, but on each occasion I ran out of pairs of marbles. Two, three or four were always left isolated. A third of the way through my fourth game the girl with the lilac hair pointed wordlessly to a marble on the arm of the cross nearest me.

"Jump over this one?" She nodded. I did, and she pointed to another one. We went on like this until there were just two left—one in the centre and one beside it.

"Why were you crying?" I asked again.

She opened her mouth.

"Anna!" Ben Strachan was standing in the corridor from which the doctors' offices led off.

"Good luck," I said. The girl smiled, shifted in her seat and leaned her head back against the wall.

"How's things?" Ben asked, as I sat down at his desk.

"OK, thanks. I also met my… my Mum's dad."

"You met John?"

"That's his name?"

"Yes. Though now most people I've talked to just call him The Man. What's he like these days? One hears so many rumours…"

"I played Chopin on his piano. It was the middle of the night. He's still got the mug Mum painted when she was little. I drank hot chocolate from it."

He searched in a drawer and pulled out a packet of surgical scissors.

"I told Molly you thought she was lovely," I added.

He dropped the scissors. "You… what… I hope you didn't… just… !" He spluttered something else I couldn't understand.

"I thought you two could meet and get to know each other. Didn't you want someone to marry you? Or was I wrong about that?"

"N-no, you weren't wrong…" He looked a bit pale.

"I asked her to come with me to the surgery. She said no."

He laughed for several seconds. "Did she?"

"Yes."

"Mum came with me instead. She took a few hours off this morning."

"She did?" His voice dropped. He put his hands on the desk and leaned forward. "Is she here now? I didn't see her in the waiting room."

"She's outside. She wouldn't come in."

He stood up again, all expression leaving his face. "Ah."

"Also, I think Jamie's not my friend anymore. I asked him to come and live with me and Mum got all cross. Then he ran away." I clenched again as he put a hand on my shoulder, then worked the scissors up and under the loop of my stitch.

He snipped. "Ow!"

"Done!" He picked at the loose threads, then wet a cotton ball and dabbed. A tiny smear of blood came away, but it wasn't nearly as bad as the bleeding had been when the stitch was put in. "Well, that's you discharged. Give your mum my regards... if she'll take them, that is. I would say hope to catch up soon, but..." He sighed.

"But that would mean I'd have to hurt myself again or else get ill?"

He cocked his head. "Y-yes. Well. Anyway, best of luck with... with everything."

"Thanks."

I found Mum sitting on the low stone wall bordering the clinic's lawn.

"All done!" I called.

She gathered up her bag. "Good. Let's go. I said I'd be in by eleven."

As we departed, I saw a shadowy figure draw back from one of the surgery's windows.

Molly's car was parked in the road outside McCallish Court. Molly herself was leaning against it, eating a banana. She waved when she saw us approaching.

"I've brought you your charge!" Mum called, waving back.

Molly chuckled.

As we reached the car, Mum took a twenty-pound note out her purse and tried to give it to Molly, but she wouldn't take it.

"I'll be back around six, ok?"

"Fairy-nuff."

Molly and I watched Mum go. Just as she was opening the door of her car she straightened and turned round again. "Text if you need anything," she said to me.

After we had waved her car out of sight and settled ourselves into Molly's car, Molly seemed to go all quiet and strange. Then she sucked in a breath:

"You know, you really can't go sneaking out at night."

I didn't answer. We drove back up the road.

"It isn't fair on your mum, it scared the life out of me

and it wasted police time. Did you know she called the police? Again?"

"No." My stomach hurt. "Where are we going?"

"Hmm. I've half a mind to forego all the fun plans I'd devised."

"I said I was sorry!" Tears threatened. I seemed to have made everyone unhappy since coming here.

"Hmm. Yes, I suppose you did. Oh well. Do you still want to make the broth?"

"Of course!"

"Thought so. Then we'll go to the shop first and pick up a few things. After that we'll go to mine."

"All right."

"And we'll talk more about this later."

It wasn't until we were back in the car, having picked up two packets of lamb chops, a clove of garlic, two onions, some carrots, some celery and a bunch of fresh basil and rosemary, that either of us spoke again. I spent most of the time in the shop trailing round after Molly, clenching and unclenching my hands.

"I thought we could invite your mum round," she said, as we set off again.

"Oh, good. She can try some of the broth."

"That's what I had in mind." She suddenly giggled: "She can be our guinea pig!"

"What do you mean?"

"To check it's worked. Before we risk it on Mrs No…"

That made me laugh too. "I don't think she'd like to know that!"

We drove past the Skeleton Man's house, turning left into the road with the church, then right at the T-junction at the end of it, and came out onto a street lined with modern, concrete-walled flats. One had an elm tree growing near enough for the branches to almost touch a jutting out complex of three windows two floors up. Molly pulled into the kerb, behind a green Volkswagen.

"Here." She pointed. We went down a gravel path which cut through the middle of a small lawn, and up some steps to a communal door with a Yale lock and a series of push-buttons, each of which had numbers engraved on plaques beside them. She unlocked the door, and I followed her up four short flights of linoleum-covered steps.

"One of these days," she panted, as we reached the top, "I'm going... to move... to a place... with a lift!"

The door to her flat was tall, painted shiny black, and had a plaque with 'McLean' engraved on it. She used another large, silver key to unlock the lower lock, then opened the door using the Yale key again. The first thing I saw when I entered the hallway was a huge, black coat hanging on a peg beside the door.

"That's Kenny's." She gestured in its direction. "He came round for lunch yesterday. I suppose I should take it back sometime." She picked at a sleeve. Then she gave it a quick pat and continued on through a door to the right.

The kitchen had a wooden floor, a wooden table and chairs, wooden counters and cupboards, and wooden shelves. It reminded me of an old farmhouse Dad and I once visited in Charlwood.

On Molly's table were two muddy potatoes, and a handful of cherry tomatoes.

"He left those, too," she said. "I mentioned making broth and he brought them round. They're home-grown. Aren't they great?" She rolled up her sleeves, went over to the sink and turned on the tap. "Wish I could grow my own food, but I've not got room for anything bigger than those." She nodded towards the windows, each of which had a herb box on its ledge—thyme, parsley and sage. "How are you with a knife?"

We sat opposite each other at the table. The onions were extremely strong. I cut a good amount off the tops and bottoms, like Dad showed me, and soon found myself sniffing repeatedly, my eyes tearing up and overflowing.

"You OK?"

"Yes," I answered, blinking. "I'm a bit stressed, though."

At once she put down her knife. She pulled a chair up and sat down beside me. "Want to talk about it?"

I told her all about Jamie.

"Oh, Anna." She put a hand on my forearm, then fetched me a tissue. "You know, my mum always tells me the same thing whenever I get stressed out about anything."

"What does she tell you?"

"'Never make a sticking point out of anything that isn't glue.'"

I thought about this. It sounded like something Dad might say.

"It means you shouldn't worry about something unless you're sure you've good reason to do so. OK, so Jamie ran off. Sure, he might have decided not to be friends with you. Then again, he might not have. All I'm trying to say is, you don't know that you have anything to worry about here, so why act like it's a foregone conclusion? You've certainly not got anything to cry about..."

"I wasn't crying."

She scrunched her eyebrows. "But you..." She indicated the tears on my face.

"Oh—that's just the onions!"

"Tell you what..." She refilled the sink and tipped the peeled, diced potatoes into it, "You finish those onions, if you're up to it, and we'll ring Carol."

I managed not to cut my hands, then washed them and fetched the cordless phone from a small table in the hallway. I took it into Molly's living room, sat on the sofa and dialled the number. If Jamie were out, Carol, or perhaps Joe or Jeremy or Alasdair might answer the phone. That would be strange because I'd never met or talked to any of them, so to me they felt like characters in a book. At the same time part of me was intrigued at the idea of a story turning into real life.

The phone rang three times before someone picked it up.

"Hello?" said a woman's voice. It sounded a bit like Mrs Langton, whom we used to see smoking in the next-door garden. She would always stub out her cigarettes in the bird bath, which eventually became so full the butt ends started dropping onto the grass below. The main difference was that this voice had a thick Scottish accent. Thicker than Molly's, and slightly thicker than Mum's.

I swallowed: "Hi, my name's Anna. Is Jamie there?"

"Hiya, Anna. He's no' in the now. He's in school."

"What about his Truancy Problem…?"

"Aye, well, we're working on it. Shouldn't you be in school?"

"I'm home educated. At least, I was when I was with Dad. I'm sure Mum'll sort out a teacher here soon. So, Jamie's not going to a children's home?" I concentrated on staying relaxed as I said this last bit.

"We'll see. Anyway, I'll get him to gie ye a quick ring when he gets in."

"Thanks."

"No problem, hen. Bye, now. Bye."

It was just before one o'clock. I had been so sure that phoning Carol would immediately make everything all right. Half past three seemed like an impossibly long time to wait—and he might not go straight home.

Molly was frying some of the lamb with a few vegetables when I returned to the kitchen. I slumped in a chair and scuffed my right foot back and forth over the floor. My trainers had lights along their outer sides which were supposed to flash when I stamped, but they were second-hand and the batteries had already run out by the time I got them.

"Oi! Don't get skid marks on my floor!" I stopped and rested my chin on my arms instead. "No joy?"

"He's out."

"Well, we'd better get this broth on to cook down. It'll take a good few hours. Once it's simmering, we'll have lunch." She fiddled with a dial on what looked like a ceramic pot with an electric cable and plug coming out. "Gotta love a slow cooker!"

I didn't have much of an appetite, but it would have been bad manners not to eat what she had made for me. If I hadn't upset her earlier then I didn't want to do so now.

"I texted your mum. Didn't tell her the bit about being a guinea pig, but she does want to come round, so we'll have to do things properly. Making bread's good when you're angry or stressed. All that mixing. And soda bread goes well with soup. What d'you say?"

I shrugged.

"Oh, come on! That's got to be something to be happy about!"

After lunch we skimmed the top of the broth using two slotted spoons. Molly put the scraps in a small, blue bowl, and set them to one side.

"What are you going to do with those?" I asked.

She shrugged. "Dunno. I might put it out for the birds when it cools down. They need lots of fat right now to put on weight for the winter. Or I could just give it to Jesus."

"What?"

"Talk of the devil. There he is now!"

I was about to ask what on Earth she was talking about when there was a muffled meow. I turned to see the black and white cat sitting on the outside middle windowsill. It must have climbed up the tree and jumped across. It looked cleaner and less bony in daylight.

"He's yours!" I exclaimed.

She opened the window. "Well, he's not really mine. Like I said, he's sort of common. But I feed him, so he keeps coming back. Kenny wants to call him Rorschach because of his black splodges, but I've settled on Jesus, and that's that."

"Why?"

"Because Jesus supposedly travelled from house to house. Kenny says I'm daft—that one day he'll show up when I've got posh guests and I'll scare them all silly shouting 'Jesus! Get down!' Do you believe in God?" As she was talking, she had fetched a tin of cat food from one of the cupboards. She was in the process of opening it but turned round to look at me as she asked this.

I put my head on one side. "I… I don't know. I think I might."

She turned away again, scooped the cat food into the same bowl as the scraps from the lamb, and placed it on the floor. "Well perhaps you should pray to him about Jamie, then."

Jesus jumped off the work counter, hunched into a ball, curled his tail around himself and began to eat, growling "Nyam-nyam-nyam-nyam."

In church they knelt on the floor on special pads. Not all of them, but perhaps the ones that did were more likely to get the answer they wanted. There weren't any pads like the ones in church in the kitchen, so I went back through to the living room, took a cushion off the sofa and knelt on that instead. Then I clasped my hands, bent my head and closed my eyes.

"Please make Jamie and me friends again. Amen."

I felt like I ought to wave a wand and say 'Abracadabra' to finish it off, but I didn't have a wand, and if Abracadabra could make everything OK then Mum wouldn't cry at night, and Mrs No would be well, and Dad… and Dad… and Dad…

There was another meow. Jesus peeked round the door and trotted towards me. I stroked the top of his head with the back of my hand. He stepped into my lap and curled up. There we sat, listening to Molly walking around the kitchen, then up and down the hall. Later she went to the bathroom, then finally she was quiet for about half an hour in the one remaining room which must have been her bedroom.

A loud buzz on the intercom made me start. Jesus leaped up and darted through the door.

"That'll be your mum!" Molly clattered up the hallway.

The broth smelled strong now and was mingled with the biscuit-y smell of fresh soda bread. My stomach rumbled. I opened a drawer under the sink and found some cutlery, just as Mum and Molly came in.

"You got things in hand here, Anna?" Molly asked.

I nodded, counting spoons, and the two of them went through to the living room. Once they had gone, I laid the table, looked through the cupboards and found glasses and napkins. I folded the napkins into standing-up fan-shapes, like the ones in the restaurant Dad and I sometimes went to at the start of the month. Then, because I couldn't resist it, I crossed to the slow cooker and lifted the lid. The broth was brown, with soft chunks of vegetables shifting around in it. The steam wet my face. The smell made me want to get a straw and suck it all up, straight from the pan.

As I approached the living room to call Mum and Molly I overheard Mum's voice:

"I'm scared… I'm just so scared…"

I poked my head round the door. They were sitting on the sofa. Mum had been crying again. Molly's hand was outstretched, touching Mum's outer left forearm like she had done when she'd thought I was crying.

"Why are you scared?"

Both looked up. Mum shoved a folded blue piece of A4 paper into her cardigan pocket. Molly withdrew her hand and stood up.

"Nothing you need to worry about, Anna."

"Smells good," said Mum. She took a two-pound coin and a one-pound coin out of her purse, and thrust them at me. "Here. First week of pocket money, as promised."

I ladled the broth into three bowls, then cut the soda bread. The first slice went sort of wonky, until I learned not to press down at the same time as slicing back and forth. I cut two pieces for each person, then put the butter dish—which was on top of the microwave—in the middle of the table. Mum spread some butter on her bread and dipped one end into the broth. She took a bite and chewed.

"How is it?"

She didn't answer straight away. Then she swallowed:

"It's good. I'd say eight."

"Out of ten?"

"Yes."

"Hooray!" Molly and I high fived.

I ate all my bread before starting on my broth. Then I sipped it from the spoon, rolling each mouthful around before swallowing it. It had a sweetness from the carrots, a tang from the tomatoes and onions, a saltiness from the lamb, and a buttery background. The only thing I'd ever seen Mum scared of was a bat. Perhaps another one had got into the bedroom. If so, that was no problem—I had removed the first one, after all.

"You look very pensive," Molly said.

"Oh… I was just thinking."

"Penny for them?"

"I'm sorry?"

"It's an expression. It just means, care to share your thoughts?"

I drew breath. The phone rang.

"That'll be Jamie!" I yelled. In my haste I knocked my chair backwards as I jumped up. Carol must simply have taken down the number I had called from to call me back. I dashed into the hall, picked up the receiver and pressed the green button.

"Hello?"

"Hi." Jamie's voice sounded higher on the phone than it did in real life, and more staccato.

We were both quiet for a few seconds. Then I cleared my throat. "Sorry."

"For what?"

All the stress I'd been feeling fell away like a receding tide. If he didn't even know why I was sorry he couldn't possibly have been avoiding me because of Sunday. I hadn't realised my lungs were that big. "It doesn't matter."

"Ah."

Each silence seemed to go on for ages, but I knew he was there on the other end of the phone, and that everything was fine. It felt like we were together again.

"It's nice to hear you," I said.

"You been smoking something?"

I didn't know how to answer this question—it didn't sound like any of the figurative expressions I knew, and yet no child I'd ever met had smoked. Except two of my friends at school, outside the gates, at the end of the day. Perhaps it was rhetorical.

"Look," he continued, "We'll meet up soon. OK? For football or… or something."

"OK then."

"Yeah." Another silence. "All right, bye."

"Bye."

Though my throat was painfully twisted up, my mind was filled with light. There was a pause, then a click, then the continuous buzz which sounds when the person on the other end has rung off.

When we got home, I checked the bedroom for bats. If one had somehow got in the window it might be tangled up in the curtains, like a moth. I shook them but found nothing. Then I opened the wardrobe and rattled the coat hangers. Lastly, I flapped the bedclothes and my sleeping bag around. As I was doing so, Mum came in. I straightened the duvet hastily.

"There aren't any bats," I said.

Mum put her head on one side as she gave me a long look, then started forward. I had a mad thought for a second that she was going to give me a hug, but she stopped and shuffled her feet. Then she smiled and shook her head slightly. "That's good then."

I slept late and was woken the next morning by Molly. She was wearing a blue sash over her shirt, with a schematic of a house with a smiley face on it.

"Come on, Sleepy Head!" she said, "It's Mrs No Day!"

We ate boiled eggs and soldiers in the garden. Jesus came and joined us, so I fetched him some ham. Molly stroked him, and he rolled over onto his back, tail twitching.

"Why are you wearing that?" I pointed at her sash.

"Well, when I clean for your mum, for example, I'm doing it privately. But I also do work for the council as part of their Home Help scheme. It's for those dealing with Complex Issues.

"What sorts of Complex Issues?"

"It varies. Some people have mobility problems. Some are carers. Between them Mrs No and Susan tick both those boxes."

She tickled Jesus's tummy. He flattened his ears, hissed and swiped at her, eyes dark.

"OW!" She sucked the back of her hand, which was bleeding. He darted under the gate and away. "Fine, so it's one of those days."

"What days?"

"Not-Molly's-Cat Days, that's what."

We washed up, then made our way next door. The curtains were closed in the room on the ground floor, but all the others were open.

"Is that Mrs No's room?" I asked.

Molly nodded. It seemed odd that a person who couldn't leave the house would voluntarily shut out the sunshine and view too. She rang the bell. My hands grew clammy, like when I was standing on Mum's doorstep for the first time. I heard brisk footsteps, then a lock being turned. The door opened.

"We don't want... Oh, it's you." Susan pointed at me. "And you!" She turned to Molly. "She's with you?"

"She's in my care. And she has something for Mrs No."

Susan glared at me. "Oh, a do-gooder, now, are we?"

I hadn't thought of the broth in that way, but now Susan mentioned it I realised it could be construed as

Charity. I wasn't sure how to answer. If I said 'yes' then I'd be admitting the charge of do-goodery. And yet literally-speaking I do like to do good, so 'no' was a lie.

"It's just one neighbour saying hi to another," I settled upon.

"It was my idea, really," Molly added. "I apologise if we caused offence. We were acting with the best of intentions."

Susan sniffed. "You always did have a habit of putting your foot in it, Molly McLean."

"It wasn't your idea…" I whispered, as we stepped inside and wiped our feet on the mat.

"I know," she mouthed, and put a finger to her lips.

The doorway led into a very narrow corridor, which opened out into a hallway with a staircase to one side, and two doors leading off. One of them had a yellow sign on it with the words "CAUTION! Miserable birch inside" (the word 'birch' is a substitute). Tiptoeing through the hall to the kitchen, I noticed this was another house devoid of photographs.

"She takes a couple of hours to get started in the mornings," explained Molly, after we had shut the kitchen door behind us and all let our breath out. "You can go in and see her when she wakes up. If you dare."

"I wouldn't recommend it." Susan pulled on her coat. "Right. I'm going to the supermarket. There's plenty for you two to be getting on with—washing, ironing, floor needs mopped and hoovered too. And this time, try not to leave the sink in such a tip. See you later." She turned her back on us and closed the door.

We didn't talk for some time, except for a few fragments of sentences such as: "Ironing board's in there", and: "Where are the clothes pegs?" The muscle in Molly's jaw was flexing again, like when we delivered Hops back to the old man.

"Are you all right?"

She shook herself. "Yeah, I'm fine. She just... they both... I try and let it slide off, but..." She waved a hand at the door.

"What's actually wrong with Mrs No?"

"Arthritis. In her hip."

"But that's great! Mrs Taylor's mum had arthritis in her hip, and she got surgery. They replaced it with a steel one."

"It's not as simple as that with Mrs No—here, hold this." I took two corners of a double duvet cover and folded them in half, as Molly did the same with her two corners. "She had a lump here..." She laid a hand over her left breast, "Six years ago. They operated on it, but she had a reaction to the anaesthetic. They managed to pull her back, but it was a close call. After that she vowed she would never have surgery again. In fact, she said she would never go to hospital again. Anyway, her hip started playing up a couple of years later. She didn't want to tell anyone as she was only forty-four. She went to see Ben Strachan. Or rather, Susan bundled her into the car and drove her down to North Hill. He said she'd need surgery, and that was it—she wouldn't listen to a word more. Now if anyone mentions the 'S' word around her she won't have anything more to do with them. Trouble is, that was six years ago and since then it's just got worse and worse. These days she's in so much pain she can hardly walk and has a lot of trouble sleeping. The tiredness brings on migraines. That's why the curtains are always closed, and why we all have to be so quiet."

"I had migraines when I was practising for my grade six piano," I said, "They're horrible."

"Yeah, they are," agreed Molly. "That's the trouble with this job. Some of the folks treat you like dirt, but there's always a blooming good reason!" She banged the ironing board legs together so that it snapped flat. The noise rang out, and we both cringed. There was a thump from the other room, then the sound of a voice:

"Who's that? Susan! SUSAN!"

"Oh, crumbs." We looked at each other. "Well I don't want to confront her—I probably just woke her up! She'll skin me alive!"

"Is that an expression?"

"Yes. You go!"

"I don't want to go! She doesn't even know me!"

"You wanted to make the broth—at least you have a

peace-offering."

I opened my mouth to retort, but found I had nothing to say.

"It's in the fridge door. In a jam-jar."

"SUSAAAAN!"

"Quickly, quickly!"

I hurried to the fridge, extracted the jar and tiptoed to the bedroom door. Then I turned the handle and pushed it open just wide enough to squeeze through.

"Shut the door! You're letting in daggers of light!" said a strident voice from the dark.

The room was about the same size as Mum's bedroom. Beside the door was an upright piano, with laundry and dirty plates piled on it. Against the opposite wall, under the window, was a sofa. If the curtains hadn't been shut, you could have sat on it with a book and the light would have fallen perfectly across the page. But it was far too dark for reading.

"Well? What have you got to say for yourself?" The voice had lost some of its edge and sounded like Mum's at the end of a working day.

"Sorry we woke you, Mrs No." I approached the far side of the room where she sat in a riser-recliner chair, wrapped in a fleece blanket, with a trolley-table next to her that had an empty bowl on it. Her hair was shoulder-length and mostly black, but with a few bright silver streaks which made it look like a horse's tail. It was too dark to see the colour of her eyes, but her cheeks were parcel-paper-crinkly, and her cheekbones were pronounced, like Susan's. Her hands lay curled on her lap.

"What's that you've got there?" she demanded, nodding at the jar.

I pulled the trolley-table towards me, then manhandled it so that it formed a bridge over her legs. Then I put the jar on it for her to see. She picked it up and squinted at it.

"What is this muck?"

"It's broth. Lamb broth."

"Ah, so I'm some kind of helpless Victorian invalid now, am I? Well at least it isn't grapes. Do you know how many grapes I ate in the four years after…" her breath hitched, "Over the first four years?"

"No. How many?"

"I'll give you a clue. 2004 was a leap year."

"Are you asking me to calculate the number?"

"You've got brains, haven't you?"

"Yes, but I can't do that in my head!"

"Didn't you ever learn how to multiply big numbers?"

"Of course I did. I could do the sum on paper, but it's far too dark to write in here."

"Is it, now?" She leaned forwards, moaning as she did so, and pushed her table to one side. Then she stood up, gripping the back of her chair with both hands, before edging round the room holding onto the walls. She had a bad limp and leaned heavily on her left leg. Every time she stood on her right foot, she huffed out a breath with a squeak at the end. After about a minute she reached the windowsill and opened the curtains a crack. A shaft of light fell across the room, illuminating an old yogurt pot with the spoon still in it, as well as a cobweb in the corner to the left of the piano.

"There. Is that better? There's paper and a pen on the desk." I crossed the room and fetched a biro and an envelope. Then I cleared the rubbish off the piano stool, sat down, crossed one leg over the other and started to write. It took a bit of scribbling to get the biro working. Meanwhile, Mrs No traversed back round again and lowered herself into her chair.

"Right, it's not hard. What's three hundred and sixty-five times two?"

"Seven hundred and twenty."

"And three hundred and sixty-five times ten?"

"Three thousand six hundred and fifty."

"Good. Now add the two together and multiply the total by four. Have you done that yet?"

"No."

"Well after that you just add another twelve to account for the extra day."

"So, nothing plus nothing is nothing, and five plus two is seven, and…"

"Oh, for shame. Look, it's the product of twelve and three hundred and sixty-five, multiplied by four, plus another twelve to account for the extra day in 2004. Since I'm already halfway through my life and can't afford to waste any more of it, I'll tell you. Eighteen thousand, seven hundred and seventy-two grapes. Or about six hundred and twenty-two bunches." She peered at me. "Speaking of maths, shouldn't you be in school right now?"

"I don't go to school," I replied. "I used to. Then Dad took me out and taught me at home."

"Hmm. It shows."

"Now I'm back with Mum, though. She spends all day at work."

"Who is your mother, then?"

"Patty next door."

One of her eyebrows arched, and her eyes gleamed in the half-light from the window. "Indeed? Well, she won't have time for that kind of thing, will she? She's far too busy burying herself in her work."

"Oh, that's not her fault. I know she wants to be there, but she works full time at a stupid wage just to keep me."

"I'm sure she does. That woman has no soul. She wouldn't know love if it flung its arms around her and told her she could never fall out of its light."

"Oh, she loves me—I know it! She must do. She's been so good to me."

"How?"

"She does my washing and buys my food. That's two things…"

"A prison guard throws food in to her prisoner every day. Is that prison guard acting out of love?"

"Well… no. Duty, I suppose. But she bought me a new coat and hat too."

"The prisoner's lawyer brings him a brand-new suit to wear to the trial. Is that love or an attempt to grow a career?"

"She also gives me pocket money. That is, she does now…"

"Give a dog a bone and it'll be quiet for hours. Do you think Susan looks after me because she loves me? Ha!"

"I…" I didn't want to presume anything bad about Susan, but at the same time she had said nothing but bad things about Mrs No during all the times we had talked.

"Oh, she probably loved me once. I was a loveable thing a long time ago. Not anymore. But the point is, as long as people can win your unwavering allegiance and good faith by fulfilling basic duties, you'll always be neglected and exploited. Do you know how much your grandfather suffered because of what your mother did?"

"No. What did she do?"

"She cut him out of her life, is what. Told him she wanted nothing more to do with him. All because he was concerned about her marriage."

My chest gave a jolt. "Why was he concerned?" I wasn't sure I wanted to know the answer—another crack in Dad's memory—but I had to ask. Breathe... I told myself. Breathe...

"Well, because it was so sudden. One day she was off to the Glasgow School of Art. Next day she was married. No wedding ceremony—just in at the church door, down to the registrar's and that was it."

Well, that wasn't as difficult to hear as I had imagined it would be. "I think he worried she'd been pressured into it." She glanced towards the door. "He'd have you in a heartbeat, you know."

"Who?"

"Your grandfather. In his care. I'm surprised you aren't in it already."

"Why?"

"Out of him or your mother who's got more money, time and experience?"

"But... but I belong to Mum..."

"You belong to you, Anna. Don't ever forget that."

We sat in silence for about a minute, me clenching and unclenching my hands. "How many cakes have you eaten?" I asked at last.

"Eh?"

"When I first talked to Susan, she said you always wanted cake when you were given bread, and soup when you were given cake."

"Did she?"

"Yes."

"Cheeky madam!"

"Molly helped me choose the recipe book and make the muck… I mean… the broth."

"Oh, Molly. She's got two left feet and a soft-boiled alarm clock." While I was trying to picture this, the sound of a vacuum cleaner drifted through from the direction of the kitchen. "There you go! I rest my case!" She pressed her index fingers to her temples. "Well, then. I suppose I'd better sample a bit of this. Heat me up some, would you?"

"Can I use the microwave?" I breezed through the kitchen door. Molly had stopped vacuuming now, and was winding up the cable.

"I suppose so, why?"

"Mrs No wants me to heat her up some m… broth."

"Really?"

"Yes."

"Really?"

"Yes!"

"Now?"

"Yes. And she opened the curtains a tiny bit."

Molly leapt in the air and punched upwards with her fist. "Result!"

"Well, she hasn't tried it yet."

"Even so!" She pointed me to a cupboard in which

bowls were stacked. With a dishcloth wrapped around my hands I prised open the lid of the jar, then poured some broth into one of them.

"Pour yourself one too," she added, looking at her watch. "It's nearly lunchtime and you deserve it."

"But then there'll be none left for you or Susan."

"Who cares? It's Mrs No that matters!"

I brought the two bowls of broth through on a tray, with some bread on the side, which Mrs No pushed away. "Now, let's see what damage this does…" She sipped some from the spoon. "Not half bad."

I started on mine too. "I used to like eating syrup sponge cake dipped in tomato soup when I was seven," I told her.

"How original."

"Then my friend Beth said it was gross, so I stopped doing it. But you could always try it."

She peered at me. "Now there's an idea… There's a very interesting idea."

"I could go and get you some sponge cake now, if you have any. I know it's not tomato soup, but…"

"I don't mean that! I mean being gross. That seems like an excellent idea. Shake things up a bit."

"Oh, I see."

"Can you burp on cue?"

"No. Can you?"

"Haven't done it since I was eight, but…" She

swallowed, then gave a long, deep belch which sounded like a motorbike going by. "Now you try."

I sucked in my stomach and managed a tiny burp that sounded like a pop.

"No, no, no—that won't do at all!" She shook her head. "You have to really gulp, then sit up straight, huff in without breathing, and let fly when you feel it coming up your throat. It's like loading a gun and shooting, except without all the mess."

I gulped several times. "It just keeps escaping out my nose."

"Try swallowing a bit of muck at the same time."

I gulped enough air—along with several spoonfuls of broth—to make my stomach feel full, then huffed out. This time it sounded like a motorbike that has tried and failed to start.

"WHAT is going on in there?" Molly's voice was muffled, as though her lips were pressed to the edge of the door.

"None of your business!" Mrs No called back.

"Well, it's time for us to go. Come on, Anna."

"So soon? But we were just getting started." Mrs No grabbed my wrist and leaned forward, wincing again. "Will you come back?"

"Of course," I told her, feeling surprised but elated. "And I promise to practise my burping."

"And think about your grandfather, too. There's a

loving home for you there," she whispered.

I drew back without answering and opened the door. As I did, the sign fell off.

"Oh, sorry—I knocked this down." I picked it up and dropped it into her lap.

"I can't believe it… I can't believe it… she let you in! You're a witch!" Molly bounced along next to me, down the drive and through the gate. "Mind you, what was all that burping? I mean, I know garlic repeats on some people but…"

"She was teaching me how to burp on cue." I demonstrated. This time it sounded like a motorbike engine that has started successfully, sputtered and then cut out.

"Charming."

"You try—it's fun."

"No, you're all right."

"Where are we going now?"

"Back to yours. We'll eat our lunch there, then take Kenny back his coat."

Molly had made sandwiches, so we sat outside on the lawn to eat them. My sandwiches were mixed salad with cucumber and cream cheese, on brown bread. She had also packed us each a can of lemonade, a packet of salt and vinegar crisps, a tangerine and a chocolate-covered wafer.

I nibbled my sandwich. "Molly?"

"Hmmm?"

"Why did my mum cut the Skeleton Man out of her life?"

"Who told you that?" The muscle in her jaw flexed again.

"Mrs No. She said he suffered a lot because of it. But she didn't say why she did it."

Molly put a cherry tomato into her mouth, chewed it thoroughly, swallowed and moistened her lips. "The thing you have to understand about your mother—and I wish others would too," she said, "is that she's very, very harsh on herself. I mean look at her—she isolated herself for twelve and a half years!"

"What do you mean?"

"Most people, when they make mistakes or react to something in ways they later regret—they're able to get to a point where they can see it as that and face up to it. Might take them a while but they get there. And then they're able to make amends and let it go."

"Are you talking about her marriage to Dad?"

She stiffened. "What do you know about that?"

"Nothing. Only, Mrs No said it was very sudden."

"Well, how would I know? It was in Glasgow." Molly's voice was tight.

I hoped I hadn't made her cross again. When I was in London my outreach worker once talked to me about the need for discretion and finesse in delicate situations, after I phoned up our neighbour, Mr Langton, to ask him what Mrs Langton had died of. That was the day after she had died, and I can see now why that was probably a bit inconsiderate. Now I seemed to be inadvertently hitting all the delicate spots in both Molly and Mum.

"The important thing is, your mum can't just forgive herself like that, plus she hasn't had anyone to bounce things off, so they either radiate out of her or get bottled up. When she makes mistakes or when bad things happen, she puts all the blame on herself. Whether it's deserved or not. Even when there's no-one to blame."

"Is that why she cried so much when I went over to Carol's? And when I got back the night before last?"

She dipped her head sideways. "Well, partly. She blamed herself for letting you get into potential danger."

"But I was fine."

"Yes, but she didn't know that, did she?" I was relieved to hear the tightness go out of her voice, as she smiled gently. "All she knew was that you'd gone walk-about, on your own, in a strange neighbourhood. In the middle of the night!"

I thought about this as I drank some lemonade and opened my packet of crisps. "What did the Skeleton Man do to make her cut him off?"

"Well, I don't know the whole story. There was some kind of scandal years back when she was a teenager, involving a rogue relationship. She was still in secondary school at the time. The neighbourhood was... is... religious. VERY religious. Blooming religion. Well, somehow it all got a bit too involved—at least, I think that's what happened. Do you know what a miscarriage is?"

"It's when you're pregnant but you lose the baby in the early stages."

"That's right. Well, I think it was something like that."

"Oh. That's sad. I can understand why she would have been upset."

"Well... it wasn't so much that, I don't think. Anyway, my mum was the caretaker at that school—she tried to be friendly to your mum in passing, but your mum dropped out soon after that and then ran off to the Glasgow School of Art. Came back a few years later, married and pregnant and no longer on speaking terms with your granddad."

I was deep in thought as we finished our lunch, cleared the rubbish away and drove down the road towards North Hill clinic. My temples pulsed. I shut my eyes and pinched the bridge of my nose. We turned left up a small hill with identical, new, semi-detached bungalows either side. Each one had a small, square lawn in front of it, like the one in front of Hops's owner's house.

"Kenny's house is round the next corner," said Molly, slowing the car down to walking speed. I shook myself out of my thoughts. "Anna, what I told you..."

"Yes?"

"Don't go spreading it around, will you? And don't go worrying yourself. People'll try and drag you in and fix your colours to their masts, but you have to decide for yourself. You're not a pawn."

Kenny's house was bigger than the ones on the hill and had two floors. It looked out across the main road onto the countryside, so if it hadn't been for the streetlamps it would have felt as if it was out of town. A low stone wall surrounded a medium-sized lawn, with a wooden picnic table in the middle of it. The lawn was covered in pots of all different sizes. Some were made of plastic and some of ceramic. There was even a mixing bowl. Each one had a plant in it. There were two that looked like broom— one with white flowers and one with yellow. Then there were three irises, a red-leafed shrub, a green-leafed shrub, some flowers that looked like giant daisies, some pampas grass, some purple, blue and yellow lupins, some forget-me-nots and several heathers. In one corner there stood a stone bird bath, and a nut feeder for the birds hung from one of the downstairs windows.

"Wow," said Molly, taking in the garden. She parked the car and we got out. She opened the boot and extracted the coat, along with a large, round, papered package.

"Hi-aye!" Kenny weaved his way between the plant pots towards us. He wasn't wearing his hard hat or high visibility jacket this time. Instead he wore black tracksuit bottoms like mine (but without the line of pink down the sides), and a yellow T-shirt which read "I'm allergic to cats…" Below the writing there was a black silhouette of a cat lying on its back.

"Coat!" Molly threw it over the wall at him. It landed on his head, and he stepped backwards into a tray of petunias. His arms shot out to the sides and his hands drew circles in the air. She doubled up laughing. Once he had regained his balance, he pulled the coat off his head and slung it over his arm. "Cake!" She threw the parcel in his general direction. He dived, plucking it out the air as if it were a rugby ball, and tucked it under his left arm.

"Come and have a cuppa," He turned and walked up the path. The back of his T-shirt read: "But I eat them anyway."

"So, what did you do this morning—rob a garden centre?" Molly cut the cake as Kenny made a pot of tea.

"Har har. They're flattening the garden at number 45. The Macks got moved out."

"What?" Molly's mouth and eyes formed o-shapes. "But… they can't do that!"

"Aye, they can. And they have. They've sent them across town. A flat, apparently. More size-appropriate, that's the story. It's a young family they've put in that house now, and they've no time for all the work."

"So you rescued the resident plants?"

"No other takers."

Kenny carried the sliced cake outside on a plate. I fetched three small plates—one for each of us. Molly followed, carrying a tray with a pint bottle of milk, two mugs, a sugar bowl and a tea pot with a red tartan cosy on it. She'd poured a glass of orange juice for me.

"I got as many as I could. They're in holding here till I find homes for them."

"I just can't believe they'd do something like that. After he broke his rib and all."

"Well, you know. They were looking for an excuse. That was the clincher, I reckon. It was going to happen sooner or later." He took a huge bite. "Magic," he declared thickly, spraying crumbs onto the table. I picked up my slice and nibbled the narrow end. It was sweet and crumbly, with a lemon tang and an almond background taste. There was a thin line of soft icing in the middle.

Molly took out her phone and tapped on it, then put it back in her pocket. "Did the badger come back?" she asked.

"Yep, three nights in a row now. I put out scraps but I've nae idea what the beggars eat. It was just a couple a bits o stale bread, some pepper cores, bit of old fruit, some leftover rice…"

"We could go to the library and find out," I suggested.

He swallowed and turned to me. "We could."

Molly sipped her tea, then looked out across the road.

"You can sometimes see aeroplanes coming into land from here. Edinburgh airport's not that far away." She pointed to the hedge along the opposite verge. "Mind the time we went bramble-picking? I still have one pot of jam left."

After tea we helped 'whip the plants into shape', lining them up in rows along the bottom of the wall and dead heading them. Once there was space, we had a game of tag. It started with Molly picking up a watering can and trying to water Kenny; ended with her tripping over her skirt and dragging him down by the arm. I tagged them both, and we all took a few moments to laugh. I wished Jamie had been there—he would have enjoyed it, though he might have pretended not to, since grown-ups were involved.

We talked on the lawn for a few more minutes, and Molly fell asleep. Kenny and I left her, quietly gathered up the cups and plates and took them inside.

"Ah, sweet Molly McLean…" He craned to look out the window. Then he turned back towards the sink. "Do you think she likes me, Anna?"

I considered. "Well, she patted your coat when you left it at hers. And she made you a cake. But Mum makes me food and gives me clothes, and Mrs No says that's like a prison guard throwing food to a prisoner, or a lawyer furthering their career."

"Sounds like a right barrel of laughs, this Mrs No."

"She lives next door to us."

"I don't know the woman."

"She's got arthritis in her hip. You can't blame her."

"I had back pain for years till they fixed it. Disnae mean you have to pull others down with you."

"She said if people could win my unwavering allegiance and good will just by fulfilling basic duties, I'd always be vulnerable to neglect and exploitation. What do you think?"

He scratched the back of his neck. "Well I know I don't think that. And I know Molly doesn't either. And who's happier—us or her?"

"You, I suppose."

"There you are then." He put the last cup away and went to lean on the windowsill, looking out at Molly. She was beginning to wake up. We watched her sit up slowly and rub her face. Then she looked at her watch, out towards her car, and back at the house.

"Aye," he concluded, as she got to her feet and began walking up the path towards the front door, "If it's real, and it's the right kind, and you've got the right way of showing it, you cannae love a person too much."

"Anna, wake up—Anna." Mum was shaking my shoulder. It was early the next morning.

"What? What?" I rubbed my eyes and sat up.

"Put on your church clothes." She threw them onto

my side of the bed. Then she started to dress herself.

"But it's not Sunday…"

"Well, duh!"

I tried to imagine why else I might have to dress smartly. "Are we going somewhere special?"

She chivvied me off the bed, before straightening the pillows and duvet. She was talking very fast. "You know there's been some major cock-ups with the social services, right?"

"What cock-ups?"

She counted on her fingers: "You were posted off a day early. Should have been a social worker travelling with you. Should have had regular visits from the Livingston branch ever since you arrived."

"But we're fine." I tried to keep my voice calm, but the things Dad's lawyer had said about Mum when she lost custody of me as a baby now weighed heavily on my mind. Perhaps the only reason I was still with Mum now, and not with someone judged better suited to ensuring that I would thrive physically and emotionally, was because of those cock-ups. So far they had meant that nobody had been able to check up, develop concerns and take me away.

"I know!" Her voice rose to an almost falsetto pitch. She closed her eyes and breathed a couple of breaths through her nose. When she next spoke, her voice was at a more normal pitch. "Anyway, someone's coming out today. They'll be here at nine. So, two rules. One, whatever anyone's told you about me, forget it. And two, they'll probably try and wheedle information out of you with casual conversation and stuff. You've got to say the right things."

"Why?"

"Because otherwise they might try and take you away."

"Why would they do that?"

"Because they're social workers! That's what they do!"

I shivered and glanced out the window across the lawn. Dad had always advocated a Total Honesty Rule. He'd warned me that there would be a few exceptions—mainly things like not telling someone they looked lovely despite their warts or evading a question by offering a different but related positive answer if the direct answer was negative. Now, given what various people had said, I wondered if he had been being entirely sincere in his professing to advocate those things. Now I couldn't ask. Nevertheless, I mentally added social workers as another exception to the Total Honesty Rule. I bit down a tiny bit of hot poker feeling—I had been planning to get up the courage to ask Mum outright about the things Molly and Mrs No had said.

"So, what should I say?"

"Just… tell them everything's fine and that you're very happy. OK?"

"OK."

After breakfast I had a shower and brushed my teeth. Mum insisted on checking they were clean afterwards, which she had never done before. She dressed in a black skirt and tights, along with a knitted cream top which had to be kept wrapped in plastic when it was on its peg in the wardrobe. I clipped my hair up and put in my earrings, one of which had rolled off the bedside table and under the dresser. Mum spent fifteen minutes plucking her eyebrows, then doing her make-up. Then we made the bed, hoovered the floor, dusted the surfaces, folded the laundry, mopped the kitchen and wiped the surfaces—even though Molly normally did all those things. Sometimes Mum crossed to the window of whichever room we were in and peered out, like a dog waiting for its owner to come home. She tensed at the sound of every car. At ten to nine she made a pot of tea.

"Molly's so much better at this kind of thing than I am."

"You mean at cleaning and tidying?"

"No, this." She waved a hand at the teapot and pulled a tin of biscuits from one of the cupboards. There was a gentle knock on the door. "Oh God. Now remember, everything's fine, and you're very happy."

The social worker was female, with a soft, low voice. I didn't hear their exchange at the door, but after a few seconds Mum moved aside, and she stepped in. She was about fifty, with curly grey hair, and wore a black windcheater which Mum took from her and hung up in the hall. Underneath it she was dressed in a pink polo-neck and grey suit trousers, with brown woolly socks and black lace-up shoes.

"Tea?" Mum offered.

"Please. I'm parched. Been driving since seven. Got caught in the rush-hour."

"Milk? Sugar?"

"No sugar thanks. And pardon my manners. I'm Gayle Henderson. Good to meet you, Mrs Harrington." She held out her hand. Mum shook it by the fingertips. "And Anna." I shook her hand too. It was a firm handshake, but not vigorous.

"It's very nice to meet you," I said. Mum counted out three sugar lumps and dropped them into her own tea. Her hands were shaking.

Gayle's voice dropped in pitch and volume as she made eye contact with me. "I'm sorry for your loss, Anna."

I clenched my hands and jaw. I was sure Gayle hadn't meant to show a lack of discretion and finesse, but she had hit a delicate spot for me. The image I had been fighting to keep away ever since I arrived came into my mind; a hospital bed, with a prostrate figure so bandaged he looked like he'd been mummified. And Mrs Taylor's hand on my shoulder as they turned the life support machine off...

"Anna, don't draw blood, darling," said Mum's voice, and I felt her prise my fingers open.

"I apologise," Gayle said, quietly.

"It's OK," I forced out, "I've got Mum. That's something to be happy about."

"Indeed," Gayle took a sip of tea. "And it seems like a lovely house. That's another thing to be happy about."

"I've made lots of friends—Molly and Kenny and Ben and Jamie and Skylar."

"Friends from school?"

Mum stopped stirring. "We're still in the process of sorting that out," she said, sounding a bit snappy. "I spoke to the local yesterday and they've agreed to take her once the formalities are in place."

I felt like I'd been hit in the face by a Boeing 747.

"Good, good."

Now my mind was stuck on memories of the electric school bell which rang at 150 decibels every fifty-five minutes, and clocks which were all a few minutes different from each other, and teachers who made so much more sense than pupils but who weren't allowed to be your friends, and corridors which went round in circles, branching off to classrooms which all looked the same, and people ramming me in P.E. while the teacher pretended not to notice, and older pupils queue-jumping in the canteen so I never got any lunch.

Gayle put down her cup. "I wonder if one of you might show me to the bathroom?"

I started to get up, but Mum put a hand on my shoulder. "You wash up, Anna. Then you can go and play if you like."

The two of them disappeared upstairs. I heard low voices which were drowned out when I turned on the hot tap. As I scrubbed, I glanced out of the window and saw Jesus padding across the lawn. I joined him outside. A few minutes later Gayle came and squatted beside us. She stroked Jesus's back. His tail lifted up and shivered as her fingers reached the base.

"You know your mother and your grandfather both love you very much, don't you?"

My throat tightened. I stroked Jesus harder.

"And you know that I care about you too and want to help in any way I can."

Jesus wound his way round Gayle's legs, leaving white hairs on her trousers.

"We're just doing our job, you know—checking you're in the right place."

I nodded.

"Is there anything you'd like to tell me, Anna?"

I rewound all the way back to when I had first arrived—the shouting, the feeling that Mum hated me, the isolation, the disorientation, the not speaking, the hug-drought. But in the end she was still my mother. "No," I said at last. "No—I'm fine. Everything's fine. I'm very happy."

I squatted on the path with Jesus for some time after Gayle had gone. Then Mum crouched beside us both.

"I'm not going to school," I said, not looking up.

"You've got no choice." My lungs felt as small as table tennis balls. "Believe me, Anna, I know school can be... well... unbearable. Especially if you're a bit different. And I'm sorry I have to put you through it, but did you seriously think you could just carry on reading and playing football and wandering round the neighbourhood?"

"I can't go back to school." I clenched my teeth. I began to tremble.

"If you don't, they'll take you away!"

I jumped up and ran out of the garden, ignoring Mum as she shouted after me.

I ran all the way to the Skeleton Man's house and through his gate. Jen barked from inside, but I wasn't scared of either of them anymore. The curtains were closed, as always, but I banged on the door.

"What on earth is that racket?" grumbled a muffled voice. The lock turned and the door opened. I didn't look at his face, so I don't know if he was as cross as he sounded. I flung my arms around his waist and buried my face in his dressing gown. "What the-?" He flinched. Then he relaxed. "Ah. Anna." He put his arms around me lightly, as if I were a treasure chest that had been thrust at him in the middle of a supermarket aisle.

"I don't want to go. I don't want to go..." I sobbed.

"For heaven's sake, woman!" He prised me off, frogmarched me into the living room and sat me down on the sofa before going through to the kitchen, where I heard his voice but not the words. After about a minute I managed to stop crying enough to breathe properly and reflect. It felt strange to be called a woman. A mixture of thrill and fear. Soon he returned, drew up a chair and sat opposite me. "Now talk sense, slowly and calmly."

I wiped my face on my sleeve. He handed me a red checked handkerchief. I told him all about Gayle's visit, and about Mum's insistence that I attend school.

"So, it's school that's bothering you."

"Yes."

"Ah." He sat quietly, fingers pressed together under his chin. "If you didn't have to go to school, yet still got an education, would that suffice?"

"I don't know," I scrunched the handkerchief in my hand. "Gayle says it's a big transition and Mum says if I don't go they'll take me away, and not to believe Gayle. But it makes no difference because Mum has to work so she can't teach me at home anyway."

"But we can surmise then that this Gayle did not

explicitly tell your mother that you would be taken away if you did not attend a school in the area?"

"Yes." For some reason I had the urge to ask the Skeleton Man about what Mrs No and Molly had said. "Do you think Mum loves me?"

His head jerked. "What?"

I repeated the question.

An unreadable expression came onto his face. It reminded me of Jamie when he told me he might have to go to the children's home. "Sometimes people are afraid of love," he said.

"Why?"

"Lots of reasons. Some people feel like they're not good enough. Some feel scared of what they might have to give in return. Some are scared of being ridiculed. Some are afraid of getting their hearts broken. Of course, it can go the opposite way too. Some people try too hard to hold on to what they love. I learned that the hard way."

"What happened between you two?"

His eyes took on their shiny quality again. "She had a boyfriend in school. Not usually a problem, but he was a good bit older—three years, and that's a lot when you're thirteen."

"That's how old I am!"

"Yes. I didn't know about this boyfriend for about a year. Well, I knew of his family—his father ran the best butchery in West Lothian. I just didn't know about him and Patty. It was all far too big for them. She was just a little girl. I tried to stop them seeing each other. She rebelled, of course, so I let it go a bit. I hoped they'd both move on, but they didn't."

"She had a miscarriage," I interjected.

His eyebrows went right up. "Who told you that?"

"Molly." I hunched, feeling my ears going red. "At least, she says that's the rumour that went round."

He nodded, slowly. "Y-yees. Yes, she did, although I wouldn't have told you that if you hadn't already known. You're going to rip that."

I stopped twisting the handkerchief.

"Well as you can imagine, that was a huge shock to me. She was so young. I had no idea their relationship was so… intimate. It all seemed a bit much."

"Was the baby a boy or a girl?" I had trouble getting the words out. After thirteen years as an only child the idea of a brother or sister was almost inconceivable.

"Too early to tell. Anyway, after that she also point blank refused to go back to school."

"Molly said she dropped out."

"That's right. She felt judged."

"Just like me!" I felt a sudden rush of relief, mixed with profound compassion.

"Well, not quite like you. Luckily I found a different school which she agreed to attend, so the situation was defused. But she was never quite the same again after that." He shook himself. "She thought I was judging her too."

"Were you?"

He eyed me strangely. "No. It hurt me, but only because she's my daughter." With that, he stood up abruptly. "Now then. When you and I first crossed paths, you were dumping rubbish into my bin. Correct?"

"Yes." The conversation was clearly over for now.

"In that case, I have just the job for you."

I followed him out the living room and into the room where he had made the cocoa the night I fell out of the tree. My mind felt like how your eyes feel when you've watched a long firework display, and suddenly the darkness closes back in—the after-visions were still popping and fizzing in my brain. I now no longer knew who was owed my allegiance, and I doubted if any of Dad's texts or any amount of chat with Molly could help me with that.

The room I found myself in was a kitchen—a long, narrow one, too small for a table or chairs. A strip of fluorescent lighting ran the length of the ceiling, and I could see the outlines of several insects which had become trapped inside. A wooden pulley like the one in Mum's house hung down. Along the length of the wall in front of us ran a work surface, and the wall nearest me was lined with wooden shelves and hooks, which had cooking ingredients and equipment stacked on them and hanging off them. The floor was made of cracked linoleum. In comparison to such a lavish living room it seemed strangely cluttered and derelict.

"This way." He indicated for me to follow him into a porch in which there was a deep freeze, a doormat, a frosted, glass-panelled door, and a couple of brown, ceramic dog bowls—one empty and one half-filled with water. The Skeleton Man opened the frosted glass door, and I got my first look at the garden.

It would have been a beautiful space, but the grass had grown waist-high and was dry, dead and tangled. Raspberry bushes had grown over the high brick wall outlining the perimeter and had encroached onto the lawn. There was already a thick layer of ivy climbing up the brickwork. In the far left corner, a rose bush poked through the tangle, but it was shaded by the cherry tree I had seen from the road when walking to church with Mum. In the middle of the lawn sat the frame of a deckchair, its canvas broken and flapping. A white plastic chair with one leg broken off rested on its back along the right-hand edge of the wall. I stepped off the porch and felt uneven flagstones under my feet, invisible among the weeds. The Skeleton Man stood in the middle of the overgrown lawn, surveying the surroundings as if he wasn't quite sure where to begin. He waved a hand, made to speak, and then stopped. Then he tried again.

"After your mother left I sort of let my organisation

slip." His head drooped. Then his chin snapped up.
"Still, I've got to do it some time, and perhaps another
person being there would be helpful. And I'd rather have
family than any old stranger. If you love clearing rubbish
so much let's see you clear that lot." He gestured to a
collection of milk bottles, plastic wrapping, polystyrene
cups, dented cans and old newspapers that had been
thrown over the wall. "I'm something of a celebrity
among the charming children of this town."

While I picked my way around the edges of the garden,
the Skeleton Man began to strim back the long grass. The
sound was loud, but not unpleasant. It reminded me of
Thames boat rides and vanilla ice cream, Mr Langton's
sprinkler and picnics at Regent's Park. For a second, I
felt autumn again on the wind, like a herald running to
deliver a message prior to an attack. Except autumn isn't
a battlefield. Autumn is warm air hitting your face as you
come in from outside, and pale-yellow windows against
darkening blue skies, and street lamps, and amber leaves
tumbling across the pavement. If Mum got her way, by
the time all that came in I would be in school.

Having gone one third of the way round the garden,
my bin bag was full. My arms and face were scratched
from picking paper out the raspberry bushes. "SHALL I
JUST PUT THIS IN THE BIN IN THE DRIVE?" I had
to yell it twice before the Skeleton Man heard me over
the strimmer. He gave me a thumbs up with his right

hand. I tramped through the living room and into the hall, before opening the front door and dumping the bag in the bin. Then I straightened up, letting the lid drop back down, and gazed out across the road. There, slouching along towards North Hill on the far pavement, was Jamie.

"Jamie! JAMIE!" He glanced up, and his jaw dropped. He craned his neck, then darted across the road to meet me. I couldn't quite hug him over the low wall, but I managed to grab both his forearms.

He wriggled away and jabbed a finger at the front door. "You're in… what… He'll KILL you!"

"No he won't. Come on—I'll prove it." I grabbed his sleeve and opened the gate. Jen started barking as he tiptoed through.

"Quiet, Jen!" I called. The barking stopped.

"Woah…" Jamie's mouth hung open. "You just…"

"Oh, she's no worse than him." I felt rather smug at having earned Jamie's admiration.

At that moment the door opened, and the Skeleton Man came striding towards us, eyebrows down, seeming to increase in size as he approached.

"Who's this then?" He glared down at Jamie as though he was a hawk and Jamie was a rabbit. Jamie shrank back.

"This is my best friend," I told him.

"Ah. One of the bottle-throwers, no doubt."

"No-o…" Jamie's face went pink.

"You'd better not be. Well, if you're a friend of Anna's you can't be all bad. Do you know how to work secateurs?"

"What are they?"

"Hedge clippers. Ever used them?"

"Carol showed me once."

"Then come round the back. There are some old flower beds somewhere under all the tangle."

I finished clearing the rubbish and Jamie clipped back the bushes along the short far wall towards the cherry tree. Just as I was filling my second bin liner, he gave a cry and held something up. The Skeleton Man put down the strimmer, I put down my bin liner and we went to see what he had found. It looked a bit like a wind chime but it was not designed to make a noise. Rather, it was a series of small, cracked, circular mirrors, suspended from what looked like tangled fishing line attached to an X made out of wooden dowelling. One end had a hook on it.

"I'd forgotten about those." The Skeleton Man stepped into Jamie's personal space and took the mobile from his hand, holding it up. Jamie didn't move away but squinted up at it flashing in the light.

"Was it Mum's?" I asked.

"Yes. A stocking filler when she was ten, meant to decorate her bedroom. She thought it would look nice hanging from the cherry tree. It must have come down in a storm or something."

"Can we try it out inside?" Jamie asked. "If we hang it near a window it might catch the light."

"Yes, let's. Come on."

We had hot chocolate, and I let Jamie have Mum's owl mug to drink from. He turned it round and shrugged: "It's just a mug. Big deal."

"You two come with me." We followed the Skeleton Man up the stairs and through a door into a part of the house I hadn't seen the previous time I'd been there. The corridor was wide, bare, also wicker-matted, and a window at the far end illuminated dust particles swirling in a beam of sunlight. "Wait here." He disappeared into a room off to the right. A few seconds later he beckoned to us to follow.

It was a small, single bedroom with pale-blue walls. The curtains were white and patterned with dark blue stars. A small chest of drawers stood on one side of the window, and a desk and chair stood on the other. A white sheepskin rug lay alongside the bed, which was covered by a dark blue cellular blanket. It was lined with cuddly toys—worn and discoloured. There was a beaver with a toy Sonic beside it, then a knitted blue elephant with pink felt ears, then a lamb with a body covered in what looked like real sheep's wool, then a monkey in a nappy, with a hole in its face for a mouth, and a half-peeled banana stitched to one hand. Jamie picked the monkey up and stuffed the end of the banana into its mouth, before putting it back in its place. The wall on the right had shelves all up it, like the kitchen. These were filled with fiction and poetry books. I saw Roger McGough, Allan Ahlberg, Jo Shapcott, the Harry Potter series, several Famous Five titles and a book by Salman Rushdie. There were posters on the walls—Fleetwood Mac, and one about the solar system.

"Were these Mum's things?" I asked.

The Skeleton Man nodded. "I got them out when she fell pregnant again, after marrying your..." He gestured in my direction. "This was going to be the... the grandchildren's room." His voice was husky. He gripped both my shoulders, not quite so hard that they hurt, but so that his fingers dug into my collar bones. "You know you're always welcome here, don't you?"

I opened my mouth to thank him, but he swept on:

"Might you consider living here? I've been noticing the quiet ever since you played the piano."

My face grew hot. Jamie was suddenly fully occupied tying the mobile to the top of the window frame. "But... I live down the road. With Mum. I can't leave her—not now."

He closed his eyes, bit his lower lip and nodded once. "I thought you would say that. I understand. But I will say that if you did live here, you'd never have to go to school. I'd teach you. We could design the curriculum ourselves. It could be very piano and music based."

I stared at him, trying to work out what I should say next.

"There!" Jamie cut in, saving me. The mobile was successfully strung up, and points of light played on the walls like hundreds of eyes winking at us. For about thirty seconds none of us said anything. Jamie tilted his head and swayed along with them.

The Skeleton Man addressed him: "Speaking of school, hasn't term started?"

"Er, well…" He shuffled his feet, eyes averted.

"Ah. So, it's like that, then."

Now Jamie was looking at the floor. His face was going redder and redder.

"Well, I'm disgusted. Does Carol know you're here? I've got her telephone number. I can call her now."

"No! Wait!" Jamie slowly bent down and rolled up his right trouser leg to reveal a gigantic green and blue bruise stretching over his knee and up to his lower thigh. Then he rolled up his top, and there, in the middle of his chest, was another huge bruise with a small scab off to one side.

The Skeleton Man caught his breath. "What… who… which person did this to you?" he snarled.

Jamie shrugged. "Some kids. At school."

"Where do you go to school?"

"St. Eleanor's." He shifted his feet again. "You can't say

anything. They'd kill me."

"I don't think that's going to happen." He looked at his watch. "Come with me, both of you."

We walked back up the road, past the junction to Mum's house, past the Premier shop and the sweet shop, towards the centre of town. Before we got as far as North Hill clinic we turned right, up a long road which led back down towards the river and the green. Normally I don't mind silence but that time I wished someone would talk. The Skeleton Man's eyebrows were all frowny. Jamie was biting his nails.

"It's at the end of this street." He pointed ahead. "We've got about ten minutes until the bell goes."

Through the houses in front of us I saw a low, flat complex of rectangular buildings, surrounded by tarmac paths and green grass on either side. We followed the road down to a high fence made of dark green posts embedded at intervals of about six feet, spanned by green, diamond-shaped metal grids. On our side the road curved into a small roundabout, with a blue sign above it that read 'drop-off and pick-up point only'. From inside the grounds came laughter and a few squeals. All the children wore yellow tops, and on the ones playing closer to the gate I could see a circle printed in the top right corner of each, with the fullness of a picture in the centre.

"Now then," said the Skeleton Man, "Which ones are

the problem?"

Jamie squinted at the figures, then pointed at two boys and one girl leaning against a picnic bench. One boy was tall and thin, with shaggy blonde hair. The other was tiny, with ginger hair. The girl was tall and chunky, with black hair down to her shoulders. She was eating something, but I couldn't tell what it was.

"Good. Now go in there, and if they bother you, just you tell them Grandpa John has got your back. See what they do."

"Good luck," I said.

Jamie sucked in a breath, then let it out through puckered lips before taking a small plastic disc out of his pocket and pressing it against a box on the school gate. It beeped, and a light turned green. He slipped through. The Skeleton Man saluted him, and I waved.

"That's what they call me—they shout it over the wall," he muttered.

We watched Jamie walk up the playground, until the gang of bullies thronged around him. They seemed to engage in some kind of exchange, before Jamie pointed back towards us. They all turned to look. The Skeleton Man stood ramrod straight, glaring ahead, before saluting him. The gang appeared to pull back and talk to each other. Then they walked away.

I had lunch at the Skeleton Man's house and gardened for the afternoon. With the Skeleton Man strimming and mowing, and me clearing, we soon got a good chunk of the lawn looking presentable.

The Skeleton Man dragged an un-broken deckchair over. "Strange boy," he remarked out of nowhere.

"He's my friend," I replied.

"Good."

When I got back home, I slipped into the bedroom and sat on the bed while Mum typed. Soon she stopped and came over to sit beside me.

"Hi," she said.

"Hi," I answered.

"So, did you have a good time at... over there?"

I gathered my courage. "He asked me if I wanted to go and live with him."

"Ah." Her hands scrunched into fists. "Yes, I thought he would before long."

"Is that why you didn't want me to know him?"

She didn't answer.

"He said he could teach me at home."

"Of course he did. When you came here the first thing he did was challenge me for custody."

So that was what the visits to the solicitor's had been about. "Did he get it?"

"Not yet. But I've not exactly been the model mum."

We both bent our heads. I had no idea what she was thinking, but I was thinking about all the motherly things she had done, especially the little things: sitting with me when she thought I was asleep, praying over me in her special language, pocket money, reading Her Eyes, the coat and hat—even though she didn't like the hat—the crying when she thought I was in danger, looking after me when I had a cold, coaching me for the social worker and pushing me to attend school, lest I be taken away. All despite such painful memories and such fear, and despite being so harsh on herself. My chest seared, but I felt strangely at peace with it this time.

"You're my mum," I said, and I touched her hand. She pulled back.

"And what a mother - what a track record!"

"What do you mean?" She gripped the edge of the bed with both hands. I persisted: "Do you mean the rogue relationship, the miscarriage and not talking to the Skeleton Man?"

She drew a sharp breath in. "So that's what you've been talking about, is it?"

I didn't answer—I didn't think she would appreciate knowing that I had gleaned my information from several sources.

"That 'rogue relationship'", she spat, "Was the last time I was really properly happy. And that was eighteen years ago—we got together in the summer of 1996."

"He said it was all a bit much when you were so young."

"Then he cares more about social conventions than

he does about me being happy."

This made me think. Dad once said that during the process of getting me my Asperger's diagnosis he kept questioning himself as to whether he was doing it to help me, or just to make me 'normal'. It was something he claimed never to have fully resolved within himself.

"If we were too adult in our relationship then it's because we loved each other with an adult love." She went pink. "I told my father I was having sleepovers at my friends' houses. Then we would meet up and just be together. I'm not proud of the lies I told. Once, we went up the hill and slept out and watched the stars. We had to leave before the sun rose, so we didn't get discovered or miss school. We were all dewy. Another time we took a train to St. Andrews and went night swimming on the beach."

She gestured in the direction of the banking across the green. "Tracked the river to its source... Most teenagers think of romance as a flirty night at a bar or club and then a drunken one-night stand. If you string a load of them together like sausages, it's upgraded to a 'relationship'. The trouble is, that kind of dynamic has virtually nothing in common with the dynamics of things like a lasting marriage, or having a settled home, or raising a strong family, or growing old together with peace, so where does it all lead? We weren't like that. We knew each other. At first, we talked and talked, but later we talked very little—we didn't have to. I felt safe with him. I knew he loved me. He's the only person who ever made me feel that way."

"Was that before the miscarriage?"

She looked at me like a songbird looks at a vulture. Then she closed her eyes for a few seconds. "It was an accident. I tried to keep it a secret—I was sixteen, nearly seventeen, and about to start some serious exam revision. But I wasn't going to abort—no question about that. A life's a life. Even so… I lost it."

Her mouth wobbled. Molly had been wrong then— the loss of the baby had mattered to Mum, at least as much as the stigma.

"It may have been early, but it was still a person, and it deserved to be given a gender and a name, so I called her Kayleigh. And then somehow—I don't know what happened—everyone at school found out about it, and about him and me. Anna, you have no idea what it's like to have the air thick with un-whispered rumours and accusations—the world you have to confront every day peppered with strange looks. I'm not strong. I can't just stay true to myself and blaze my own trail through that kind of battering. Not like you…" She gave me a weak smile. "I broke it off. Couldn't cope. He was devastated of course. Kept begging and pleading with me. In the end I blanked him. Refused to go to school. Refused to answer the door or his phone calls. Even refused to go out the house for a while in case I met him on the street. He was the one person who would have stood by me. My dad was no use. He just thought I'd reaped what I'd sown—probably still thinks it. That's the last thing I need—people preaching at me. But essentially, I clamped a pillow over the nose and mouth of the relationship between me and this boy, and pressed down until it stopped struggling. Then I ran away to art school. That's where I met your dad."

My mouth went dry. This was the first time she had mentioned Dad of her own accord. I prepared myself to hear uncomfortable truths. She had been so brave sharing such hard things. The least I could do was listen, even if it felt like being kicked repeatedly in the head.

"The Skeleton Man doesn't think that," I told her quietly, squeezing her hand.

She rocked back and forth slowly a couple of times. The bedsprings creaked. "Well what does he think?"

"He says it hurt, but then you're his daughter."

"Did he tell you the whole thing?"

"Well… he told me about the miscarriage and the relationship. Is there more?"

"Yes. But maybe that's enough. You're only thirteen."

"I want to know. I need to know." There was an edge in my voice which I didn't expect, but I had been holding in so much, in the hope that somehow, I'd discover the truth behind why Mum was the way she was. To face being denied it now, yet to know that there was a reason—that it wasn't just all in my imagination—was an unbearable prospect. "Tell me. What happened with you and Dad?"

"Oh, it was one thing after another," she said. "We got married in a whirl—said our vows in a random church after its Sunday service, then slapped our names on a register in front of one witness pulled in off the street. Not exactly my dream wedding, but I figured it was the vows and signatures that counted more than the frills. Although, not exactly ideal vows either—Thomas wrote them."

"What were they?"

"To promise to look out for each other and to be a friend to the other, as long as time, integrity and compatibility of character allow. Doesn't really bind you in any way at all. Anyway, the whole affair really upset my dad. So right from the get-go there was this horrible atmosphere of tension hanging over us. I couldn't relax into the marriage as I would have done otherwise. I dropped out of my course in the Christmas term of 1998, when I found out I was pregnant again. That's when we moved back here."

"Into this house?"

"Yes." She scrunched her fists, like I do when I'm trying to keep calm. "That one was sort of planned. I mean, I thought having a family would make everything better. I just… I stopped being quite so careful."

I took her hand.

"Thomas was pretty well off at that stage so it wasn't the tight squeeze it could have been. But I went into early labour. They strung things out for two weeks with bed rest and drugs, and got me to the Royal Infirmary in Edinburgh, with all the intensive care baby equipment. But I was only twenty-one weeks along when he was born. A little boy—Archie."

"A big brother," I murmured, and felt an overwhelming swell of sadness. I would have loved a brother.

"His lungs were too premature to work properly, even though they gave him all the help they could. He died in my arms the following morning. It was the hardest thing I have ever been through."

"What did he look like?" I closed my eyes to better picture.

"He had this pink, red, shiny skin, but it was so soft. He had the tiniest fingers and toes, and a layer of downy fuzz all over, like a warm peach. It was the most surreal experience of my life. He looked so other-worldly, moving around and trying to kick and cry, just like any baby. My dad was absolutely destroyed when he died. As far as he was concerned, Archie was his first grandchild. But then he went all preachy on me again—practically made it into a sermon about the virtues of prudence and the penalties of rashness. And that was it. I told him I no longer wished to be associated with him in any way."

So that was what had caused the rift. I made a face. I knew the Skeleton Man loved me—he had asked me to live with him. And the fact he had retained Mum's possessions and cup convinced me that he loved her too, even if he had shown a huge lack of discretion and finesse. But I also knew, having lost the dearest person in my life less than a month ago, that the person from whom I would really have liked to receive support and comfort was my closest surviving family member. Maybe Mum felt the same, deep down inside.

"Didn't expect him to honour my request," she continued, interrupting my thoughts. "I didn't really mean it. Thought I meant it at the time, but now I know I didn't. He was just trying to make sense of it all, I suppose, and he's always been kind of critical in doing that. Doesn't mean he didn't feel it too."

"The grandchild's room is still all set up as it was at the time," I said.

She squeezed her eyes shut, then nodded into her chest.

"Well, then I fell pregnant again."

"With me?"

"With you. Much too soon. We'd been sure we'd try again at some point, but we meant to hold off and just try and let things settle after Archie. That didn't exactly work out. And that's the worst thing—after losing two you want to be happy—you want to with all your heart—but it doesn't feel... safe. You almost feel like you don't have permission. Like being happy will cause something bad to happen."

I thought about the Happy Game, and Dad, and the fire. The Game seemed rather flimsy and trite now. My memories were breaking beyond repair.

"Not being able to celebrate damaged our marriage even more—Thomas wanted to just live in the moment and trust in whatever would happen. Because of my history I was referred immediately to a high-risk pregnancy clinic. He thought we had it made now that we were getting help. But I couldn't take that same leap of faith. He wasn't the one whose body was tasked with carrying the baby and not killing it off or jettisoning it too early. I think he resented me dragging him down like that, so we spent less and less time together. And he started picking on me. Everything I did was unwise. Everything I ate was unhealthy. The types of toiletries I used were 'toxic'. Heck, he even picked on things I was helpless to control—like how many hours of sleep I got! Eventually communications dried up between us. I didn't have many friends; when we got married he told me I didn't need them now I had him. He never hit me or anything—he just had a way of making me feel hideous and shameful if I didn't do what he wanted. I would have loved for my father to step up then. He didn't. Did he tell you that bit?"

I shook my head.

"Thought not. It's just been one massive elephant in the room ever since."

I couldn't have spoken if I'd wanted to now. My body felt cold all over, though my palms were wet.

"When I was seven months along, I got something called HELLP syndrome—it's a condition that happens sometimes when you're pregnant. Organs start to fail and stuff. Anyway, like I said, you were delivered by Caesarean because we were both so ill. And that's the scar you asked about." I nodded, remembering it. Proof of a connection nobody could supplant or take away, whatever else may have happened.

"We'd done it—you were alive. And then I had several big bleeds. Spent weeks in ICU. My milk dried up. So, I didn't give you a good birth, I didn't give you a good start, I couldn't even take care of you... And look at me now. I can't even give you a proper bedroom!"

She said this last bit with a hiccup. By now I could barely breathe. Could the internal satellite dish be turned off?

"I'm happy sleeping in bed with you," I managed, after a few tries.

"Not only that, I work all day so I'm not even there... That's one of the reasons why he got you back then. That - and the fact I wasn't breastfeeding. But I had to do something. So, I worked fourteen hour shifts at the distillery six days a week. Minimum wage, but I did save some money. That's all gone now. Besides, I'd got it into my head that I somehow brought people bad luck, and that if I hung around you too much you might get cot death or something. I know it sounds stupid... Of course, he had charm on his side too. And social smarts. And contacts. And an outside reputation. And a famous smile. And tears on cue. They would believe him."

I bit my tongue—the urge to defend Dad threatened to ruin everything.

"Oh, things weren't easy for him either..." She laughed—that laugh of hers which makes me cringe. "But honestly, I made a mistake taking up with him. I should have stayed with..." She bit her lip so hard it bled. "Oh, you might as well go and live with your granddad! You'd be better off."

"I said no."

I tried hard to pick up a signal from her but couldn't tell what she was thinking or feeling now. But then, knowing that sort of thing can often be difficult—especially since people can think and feel two directly conflicting things simultaneously. A Schrodinger's Cat of emotions. And people often hide or deny their true feelings. "I said no," I repeated. Then I thought of Molly. "You shouldn't be so harsh on yourself."

She gazed over the bed and out the window. "You're

mad," she muttered, through clenched teeth. "Bonkers. Off your head. A dipnut."

"I'd rather be a dipnut than live with anyone else."

She tried several times to say something, but it seemed to get stuck in her throat each time. "When you came back," she managed at last, "I tried to make myself hate you."

I felt a sharp pain in my chest at that. "Why?"

Her eyes seemed very large in their sockets, but they weren't bulging.

"I… I think I was scared."

"What were you scared of?"

She lifted her chin, but her hands clasped and grasped at the bedspread. "What if they'd taken you away again?" The hurt seemed to sputter in her as she said this, like a kettle on a rolling boil. "What then?"

It was raining. The droplets pattered against the outside of the window. Once again, I didn't have an answer. My mind was a jumble of sympathy and compassion and confusion, like a painting palate where all the colours have been swirled together. All my memories of the Dad I had thought I'd known—the character I'd loved—now seemed like crayon pictures drawn on the wall of a paper house. The thought of his texts nauseated me.

"Do you hate me?" I didn't mean to ask aloud, but the question came out of its own accord. I didn't want to know the answer. Had I wanted to know, I could have asked at any point since arriving.

She looked as if I had given her an electric shock. Then she slumped and began to cry, as if the tears had been building up for weeks behind a locked door, which had finally given way.

"So many times…" I heard her say indistinctly, before she managed to stop and breathe. "So many times I would look at you sleeping and just… just want to hold you."

Those words—like water to cracked, dry earth. "You can," I told her gently. "I'm here. And I'm alive. And nobody is ever, ever going to take me away again."

She came towards me. Then she shook her head. "I… I don't think I remember how…"

"I'll show you," I said. And I put my arms around her and held her as a father might have held his daughter after she had gone to school and her friends had beaten her up again.

That night my dreams were filled with satellite dishes, walls of eyes, the Skeleton Man's garden being uprooted, and babies squirming on an open hilltop. I wanted to ask God to stop time and give me a moment to work out what to do with all Mum had told me, and how to make everything all right. That's what family is supposed to do. But time didn't stop. The sun moved through the sky; the earth flew through space. Early in the morning, after

Mum had left but before Molly got there, I snuck out and smashed my phone against the wall of the house. Then I gathered the pieces up and dumped them in one of the skips. False, false, false. All of those messages, all those memories, all that love, all that supposed wisdom, false. If the old oilskin coat and hat had been Dad's, then I understood now why Mum had taken them to the dump.

Molly and I barely spoke that morning. We cleaned the house, had an early lunch and called on Joanne. Skylar came running out to greet us and persuaded me to bounce with him and Emily on their new trampoline. I managed to pretend to be engaged and enthusiastic. After a few minutes the repeated downward pressure of the bouncing made me need the toilet.

"I'll be back in a minute," I shouted, jumped down and ran inside. As I was on my way back out Joanne diverted me through the living room and into the kitchen. She closed the door and motioned me to take a seat.

"Simon, the minister, was in touch with me. His wife, Helen, runs the Sunday school. I gather you've already met."

"Yes, I remember her," I said, "She was very pregnant."

"Mmm. Seven months. Anyway, she thought you might like to read a passage out in church. Not this Sunday, but the following one."

"I… well… ." I really didn't think I could cope with any more things filling up my mind.

"You don't have to make a decision right now," she added. "There's no pressure. If you don't want to do it, I'll do it. The theme is thankfulness. Helen remembered how you found happiness in the farmer story. She suggested you to Simon as a potential reader, and he mentioned it to me in passing. Anyway, the passage is Psalm 100. Do you have a Bible?"

"Mum lent me hers," I said. The farmer story and that attitude of blinkered happiness seemed impossibly long ago now, like it existed on the other side of a deep chasm.

"Well, have a think and give me a ring later on."

I didn't tell Mum anything about the reading because I wanted it to be a surprise. That evening we went for a walk—just her and me. We went past St. Eleanor's and up a single-track road with sheep poo scattered on it, and thick whin bushes on either side dotted with yellow flowers. It wasn't especially sunny, and the sky was covered by a layer of cloud, but it was mild and bright. A cow mooed in a field. The noise of the town slowly fell away to wind and birdsong, and the faraway sound of a tractor. To our left there was a bank of trees. A field sloping down to our right was filled with glossy, half-ripe corn that looked like fur on a giant animal. It reminded me of Winter Hill, just outside London.

Mum cleared her throat. "I want to apologise."

"What for?"

"I was wrong to stop you from talking about him."

"I didn't know about… everything."

Something felt like it was rushing up a beach inside my heart. It felt painful, but once again, it was an OK kind of pain. "I'll go to school on Monday."

Her eyebrows went up. "Are you sure?"

"Yes. It's like you said—I might not like it, but I am strong. I can be true to myself, and I can blaze my own trail. And if anyone tells me I'm annoying or tries to beat me up, I'll just tell them Grandpa John has got my back!"

We walked most of the way back in silence, but just as we approached the first houses on the outskirts of town, Mum spoke again. Her words came in stops and starts, and she looked straight ahead and down as she said them.

"Anna, every time I've bared my soul, I've lost something. So you need to understand it's going to take a very long time before I can learn how to do it naturally again. Maybe I never will. But I can try."

"It's OK." I linked arms with her.

She cleared her throat, her eyebrows pulling together for a moment. "For the longest time I've been Patty-who-behaved-outrageously. Some people smiled at me, but it was always kind of forced, so I stopped looking. Lots of them probed for details—you could tell by the way they talked—so I shut them out. I don't deserve to be forever in the dock."

"No," I agreed, "You shouldn't have to always be defending yourself."

"Exactly. But yeah, that's why I am the way I am." I laughed. She turned to look at me, then realised the irony in her justifying herself like that, and laughed too. "Sorry. Bad habit. Anyway, what I wanted to say was that since you came here people have started smiling at me differently—it's like they can't help it, now. I reckon it's because their first thought isn't 'There's Patty-who-behaved-outrageously' anymore—it's 'There's Patty-Anna's-Mum.'"

I didn't know what to say. Even if I had known, I don't think I would have been able to say it. Luckily, I didn't have to try—as we turned in through the garden gate I heard running feet, and saw Molly charging across the car park.

"What's she doing here?" Mum asked. "She's not due here today!"

Molly didn't greet us with a smile or a 'hello', either. She simply leaned against the gate, her mouth open and her eyes glassy, trying to catch her breath.

"Kenny proposed to me."

"What?"

"Kenny proposed to me! He proposed to me! He proposed to me!"

So Molly wasn't going to end up marrying Ben Strachan! Unless she'd said no to Kenny's proposal, of course, and that didn't seem likely. Molly started to laugh. It reminded me of myself having a panic attack. I hoped she wouldn't end up breaking things and yelling. That's what I used to do before my outreach worker taught me to punch pillows and write in my notebook instead.

"OK, hang on." Mum took her by the arm and steered her to the kitchen. Once in, she made her sit at the table. "You've made me so many cups of tea," she said. "I'm afraid I might have been quite a burden to you."

"Don't be silly!" Molly seemed to be growing calmer now.

"What happened?" Mum asked.

"Well it was quite funny, really…" Molly's cheeks went pink and she fluttered her eyelashes with a small laugh. "I'd spent the morning out at Mum's, and Kenny texted and asked if I'd pop in on my way back. Said he'd made a cake in return for the one I gave him before. Remember, Anna?" I nodded. "He never makes cake! Anyway, he wanted to give it to me properly, so I got there and he met me at the door. He had the curtains closed—said he wanted it to be a surprise. Then he made me close my eyes too—even blindfolded me in case I cheated! I heard him go inside, and when he came back out again he told me I could look. So I pulled off the blindfold…"

"And?" The kettle had boiled, but none of us got up.

"And it was this Victoria sandwich cake, with jam in the middle, white icing on the top, and a marzipan bride and groom that looked like us, surrounded by green question marks."

"And what did you say?"

"I got him to spell it out for me. Sort of took the romance out of it a bit…"

Mum snorted. "But then what?"

"Then I fainted. You know me—I never faint!"

Mum burst out laughing.

"Fainted dead away! Came to lying on the grass. I started to get up. And I was terrified he'd think he'd scared me off, or that he'd made a terrible mistake and go back on it. I was gearing up for this high speed, oh-so-romantic improv speech, and before I could say anything… I fainted again!"

"You're joking!"

"I'm not! Anyway, I came to—again—and this time he was lying on the grass beside me."

"Had he fainted too?"

She wrinkled her nose. "I don't think so… We just lay there for a bit and looked at the clouds. He saw a barn owl. I saw a mountain. Then I turned to him and…"

"Do we want to know this bit?" Mum darted a quick look in my direction.

"Oh yes! I turned to him and told him he had a long way to go as a fiancé. I mean, come on! Any real gentleman should at least be able to catch a swooning maiden! Not just let her drop like her strings have been cut!"

"So then what?"

"Then I asked where the cake was."

"Well naturally," said Mum, "Can't be mixing up our priorities."

"Indeed not. He'd put it on the picnic table. So, I got up really, REALLY slowly, and asked if I could have a slice. And we divvied it up between us."

"Don't tell me you ate it all, you greedy pig!"

"Certainly not! I let him cut it and ate the slice he offered me. Almost broke my teeth on the ring. Then I spat it out and made him do the thing properly, on one knee and everything. Then it all got soppy, 'cause I started crying and he started crying…" Now her eyes filled up. I hoped she wouldn't cry again—I'd had about as many tears as I could take. Mum offered her a tissue. She waved it away and sniffed loudly.

"And then what?" I asked.

"Well then I went in for the snog, didn't I?"

Over the weekend Jamie, the Skeleton Man and I worked in the Skeleton Man's garden, transferring the plants into flower beds as we cleared them. The repetitive digging and clearing, and the hoisting of things across the lawn, acted like a mental anaesthetic. In the absence of sadness, a sort of peace crept back in.

I was too nervous to speak much on Monday morning. When I came out of the shower at quarter past eight I found some new clothes laid out. There was a blue linen shirt, a black skirt, some black tights, some shiny lace-up shoes, and a black cardigan. Mum brushed and clipped back my hair as I buttoned the cardigan as slowly as I could.

"I ordered the clothes when I went to meet the learning support staff on Thursday," she said. This did not reassure me. At my old school one of the learning support workers had informed the new music teacher about my Asperger's and my passion for music. On Monday the teacher opened the lesson by approaching me and saying: "I hear you're quite the music expert. Lots of autistics are, you know. Now, you're not to go on and on or jump in with all the answers. Other people matter too."

"What did you tell them?" I asked.

"I told them you had recently lost your father, that you had just moved here, that you didn't like loud noises, that you needed clear boundaries, and that you were very friendly and thoughtful. They said they have a couple of other children with Asperger's, so they have some specific supports in place already. Such as a sensory room."

"What's a sensory room?" My old school had two part-time learning support workers and one learning support room, which was a repurposed cleaning cupboard.

"It's a room where you can go to relax if you feel too

stressed to work or listen. I blooming wish they had one at work."

Intrigued, I tried and failed to imagine what that would be like. I hoped it wouldn't be like a psychiatrist's office.

Once dressed I went down to the kitchen, where Mum put some pancakes on my plate.

"Keep a move on; I want us driving away by twenty to nine."

"Are you taking the morning off again?"

She nodded, pouring milk into her coffee. "I've had to ask your granddad to bring you back today. Don't know what'll happen in the long run."

"Couldn't Molly help?"

She shook her head. "From now on I expect she'll be spending most of her time helping Kenny with the house he's building for her."

I dropped my pancake. "She's moving?"

"Yes—out of town. Nearer her parents. They'll still be within reach—just further away."

"Will she still clean for us?"

"I don't know."

"Will she look after me while you're away?"

"I don't know." She clenched her teeth and turned away.

It occurred to me that perhaps this had been another reason why Mum was keen to get me into school. And it was all because of Kenny. Why did he have to build a house? And why did it have to be so far away? And what right did he have to take Molly away from so many people for whom she had been such a huge, crucial part of their lives? Perhaps Molly would go off him once she knew him better. He was only a person, after all. And there was always a chance the house would prove structurally unsound or something and they wouldn't be allowed to live in it.

I breathed in, imagining I was an extractor fan, then let it out slowly, imagining all the annoyance leaving with it. "At least she won't be leaving until they get married and the house is done," I concluded.

Mum had also bought me a schoolbag and lunch box. The bag was a large, black rucksack, with a snap fastener, and straps around the waist.

The lunchbox was a plain, clear Tupperware tub, which Mum had already packed for me.

I sat in the navigator's seat. The morning was cold, but the sky was clear and the sun shone over the farmland, glinting off Mum's wing mirror. We turned down the road towards the roundabout leading to the station.

"What are you doing today?" I asked Mum.

"Seeing my solicitor."

"Why? Has something else happened?"

"Don't know."

"If anyone tries to take me away from you, I'll run away and come back here."

She said nothing, and kept her eyes on the road ahead, but her face broke into a beautiful smile. Then she pressed a button on the dashboard. Some music came on. It had a breathy, sweeping quality, a looping base and a syncopated rhythm. The singer was female, with a Nordic-sounding accent.

"Who is this?" I asked.

"Bjork. Do you mind?"

"No, not at all."

We turned left at the roundabout, onto a road that seemed to define the outskirts of the town. The song was an urging for the listener to come to the singer so they could take care of them. When a line came up about jumping out a building that was on fire, a deluge of horrid images came into my mind. Smoke—not like bonfire smoke, but so piping hot, and so thick, that it felt more like, lung-scalding soup than gas. Through the eye-watering haze the only things I could see were the orange, flickering rim of the bedroom door, and a white searchlight backlighting swirling air currents, guiding me towards the window, and a twenty-five foot drop onto a canvas held taut by firemen, police and some neighbours who had seen the fire and rushed to help. And then a mental picture of the pieces of the phone, lying smashed in the skip. Hot poker. This time, instead of trying to drown it out with happiness, I decided to ask a question I had been wanting to ask for a long time but hadn't known if it was appropriate. For some things, though, there's never an easy time or place.

"Mum?"

"Yes?"

"Where's your mum? Does she live somewhere else, like you and Dad?"

I thought she would go stiff and cross, but she didn't. She turned towards me slightly for a second. "Sort of. She got brain cancer when I was five. She's in heaven now, with Kayleigh and Archie."

"We're a bit alike, then," I said. "My dad died, and your mum died. And your mum was the Skeleton Man's wife. So we can all help each other."

"You know, I hadn't thought of that. You're right." She reached over and squeezed my knee. I think it was meant to be like a hug—you can't give a person a hug at the same time as driving—but it tickled so much that I involuntarily squealed and squirmed away.

"Is that why you believe in God?" I asked, "So you can see them again?"

She was quiet for a few seconds. Then: "That's an awfully big question to unpick on a school run, Anna."

The local senior school was situated on the other side of the town from St. Eleanor's junior school, but we still got there in under fifteen minutes, because the main road circumvented most of the morning traffic. There were no children playing outside, but then the clock in Mum's car said it was twenty past nine.

"We're late," I remarked. Not a good start, but at least we made it.

"It's OK," she answered, "They asked me to bring you in a bit late so you wouldn't be caught up in the rush to class. And so's you'd arrive between bells."

We got out the car, and immediately I noticed the sense of peace. We were some way from the main road, and a tractor whirred again in the distance. In the foreground I heard chirping—chaffinches nesting in some crevice within one of the school's buildings. The school was made up of two long, repurposed flagstone barns, each two storeys high, with sloping triangular ceilings—one with its end facing the car park, and one side-on to it. Six portable cabins surrounded a tarmac playground, with eight picnic benches made of a red type of wood. The whole school seemed to be bordered by a low stone wall.

"I remember these." Mum ran over to sit at one of the benches.

"Were you happy here?" I asked.

"Yes, very. For the first four years, at least." She cocked her head. "I thought it would be harder coming back. But it feels… nice." We were silent for a few minutes.

"This isn't a bit like my old school," I told her. "Mine was much, much bigger. And it was all one concrete building which went up four storeys. It looked like an anthill when you viewed it from above. And there weren't any stone walls around it—there were huge metal fences."

"It sounds like a prison," she murmured.

An oak tree encroached on the playground between two cabins. A gust of wind rustled its branches and a group of swallows startled from it, backlit by the bright, mottled clouds.

"Come on then." She pointed in the direction of a cabin to our left, in one window of which grew two sunflower plants. On its door was nailed a sign with an arrow labelled 'Learning support' pointing to the right, and another labelled 'Reception' pointing to the left.

The reception area was more of a hall, with some wooden chairs in a row, each with faux-leather stuffed backs and seats. In one wall there was a glass partition, and through it I could see an office, but there was nobody in it. It looked like the learning support room here would be another repurposed cleaning cupboard. The glass partition didn't reassure me either—the learning support room at my old school had a glass partition looking out onto one of the corridors, so that when people went to the canteen or to their next class, they would stop and peer in.

On our side of the reception there was a silver bell, like the kind in hotel lobbies. Just as Mum went over to it, a man came through the front door. He was tall, looked about forty, and had black, slightly greasy hair and a beaky nose.

"Patty and Anna?" He shook Mum's hand, then held out a hand to me. In surprise I took it and shook it. I wondered how he could possibly keep track of every individual child, much less every individual visitor.

"I'm Gavin Shaw, the Guidance Teacher. Let me show you to the learning support room and Rachel will take you from there."

He indicated a small door in the wall opposite the main entrance. We followed him through, into a room which looked almost like a living room.

Mum whistled. "Well... THIS has changed!"

There was a large, squashy blue sofa against one of the walls, and what looked like a synthetic tent against another, big enough to sit on a chair inside, but not quite big enough to stand up in.

Mr Shaw pointed at the tent: "That's the sensory room." There was a long wooden table in the middle of the room with office chairs pulled up to it, and four PCs at one end. At one of these sat a boy in a winter hat with ear flaps. His neck was stretched forward, his eyes were fixed on the screen and he was clicking repeatedly with the mouse.

"Hi Jess."

Jess looked up, nodded his head and raised a hand.

"What are you playing?"

He reached down and held up a case, which had 'Fun French' written on it, with the colours of the French Flag.

"Good, good!"

At that moment there was a zipping noise, and a hand pushed the flap of the tent back. Out stepped the girl from the GP waiting room—the one with the lilac hair. Now she wore thick, round purple glasses too.

"Oh, hi!" she said. In contrast to how quiet she'd been when we were playing solitaire she now spoke with a loud, abrupt voice, accompanied by a big smile.

"Do you know each other?" Mr Shaw asked.

"Yeah. We played solitaire," explained the girl. "I didn't tell you my name. It's Cal."

"I'm Anna," I replied. Cal thrust out her hand and we shook.

"This is the learning support room." Cal waved a hand around the room as if it were a stage. "This'll be your 'safe base'. You'll work here until they know you're up to speed with what our classmates are doing."

"Thank you for that, Cal," Mr Shaw said, "Saved me the breath!"

"We can work together!" I said.

"Yeah!"

"Now," he continued loudly, as Cal opened her mouth again, "Through here we have the staff office." He stuck his head through a door on the right. "Rachel! I'm gonna leave Anna with you, ok?"

"Right you are," said a female voice, and out came a smiling young woman with curly black hair, full cheeks, high heels and an ankle length skirt.

"See you later, Anna." Mr Shaw waved and stepped out the door.

"Will you be OK?" asked Mum.

"I think so," I said, and suddenly felt like clinging to her coat. I resisted the urge, and she laid a hand on my shoulder. Then she hugged me, turned and left, closing the door.

The rest of my morning was spent sitting at the central table, flicking through second year Maths, Geography, Home Economics and History textbooks, identifying which topics I had already covered. As it turned out I was about a year ahead in most respects, and Rachel had to give me the SQA National 4 and 5 textbooks, of which I had only covered about a quarter. Cal kept peering over from her computer screen and pointing at bits, saying things like: "Oh we did that. That was cool," or "That bit's hard." About every ten minutes Rachel would call through from the staff area, "Cal—less talk, more focus, please!" whereupon Cal would go quiet and concentrate for a few more minutes.

During break time Cal and I both went into the sensory tent. Its interior was lined with huge cushions and a couple of gigantic fleece blankets. It had a mobile hanging from the ceiling, with stars made of mirror material which reflected coloured fairy lights strung up along the tent's seams, casting what looked like shards of light off the walls. It reminded me of Mum's mobile. At the far end there was a bookshelf.

"This is amazing!" I lay down, wrapped myself up in the blanket and rubbed it against my face. I felt like a butterfly in its cocoon, or a dormouse curled up in its lair for the winter.

Cal lay on her back, raised her leg and jangled the stars with her toes. The shards of light leapt back and forth across our faces and hands, like excited fairies. "See? It's just like a disco!" She laughed.

"It's better than a disco!" I said.

It was P.E. in the afternoon. I would have spent it in the learning support room too if I had a choice, but Rachel sat me down.

"You know, Cal goes to P.E."

I couldn't see what that had to do with anything.

"Go this time at least. It's a new block. They're doing circuit training today. You can change here—I'll come with you. I think you'll be pleasantly surprised."

I was surprised. Before we began, the teacher—Miss Marney—sat everyone down at the front of the games hall.

"Now," she said, "What you're going to do is go round

the room in groups of five. You will have three two-minute stints at each station. At the first station you are stepping up and down from the bench, as many times as you can in two minutes. The second one you're doing press-ups—again, as many as you can. The third you're bouncing on the trampolines—as high as you can. And the last…" She jogged over to some hula hoops in a circle on the ground, with a pile of hand-sized bean bags in the middle, "You're standing on one leg in a hula hoop, throwing bean bags to each other in a clockwise manner." Several of the children laughed, and so did I. "You're counting throws you can do in two minutes without losing your balance or dropping the bean bag. If you lose your balance or drop a beanbag you start counting from one all over again. You'll go round in groups of five." She paused and walked up and down in front of us. The room was completely silent. "This is a competition. Competition is key to sport because it connects us in what we do and in what we aspire towards. The person who wins each round will receive points, which we'll tally up at the end. However…" She looked each of us in the eye with a twinkle in her own, but a firm-set mouth, "I expect no cheating and no gloating. The reason you are competing is to prove to yourselves what you can do when you really put your minds to it, and so that you can share the experience. You are not doing this to show everyone else how much better than them you are."

She didn't raise her voice or sound like an army officer, but instead spoke with a strength, softness and clarity of tone. I found myself looking forward to the lesson.

"Told you you'd like it!" Rachel said, as I returned to the learning support room at lunchtime, having come second place, received a Chewit, and chatted to Miss Marney about football as people filed out at the end. She had complimented me on my technical and strategic knowledge and invited me onto the school team—which met from half past three to five o'clock on Thursdays.

"Miss Marney is such a good teacher. And so nice!" I flung my bag onto the sofa and unlaced my shoes in preparation for the sensory tent.

"Ah, she's a good soul isn't she?" replied Rachel.

I was dismissed five minutes before the end of the school day and was halfway across the playground before the bell went. Out in the car park I saw a red Volvo parked on the kerb, and as I approached it the window on the passenger's side slid down.

"Hurry or we'll never get away!" said the Skeleton Man.

I threw my bag in the back and plopped into the navigator's seat.

Before I was even strapped in, he had revved the engine, pulled out and the school was receding into the distance behind us.

"Your mum asked me to pick you up," he said. "I think

you should know that that's the first decent conversation I've had with her in years."

"Did it feel like your mind was filled with light?" I recalled the feeling I'd had after reconciling with Jamie and tried to imagine it ten times bigger.

"You could say that, I suppose." His eyes scrunched at the corners, but they were smile scrunches. "She's much different, you know."

"She is?"

"She is. It must be you, you magic girl. Anyway. How was school?"

"It went really, really well!" I said, my voice growing louder like Cal's as I began to tell him all about my day.

When we got back to his house Jamie was pacing up and down the pavement.

"Hi Jamie!" I called, getting out.

"Oh, hi." He ran over to the Skeleton Man and took hold of each of his hands. I blinked, my mouth falling open. Obviously, he had been a more regular visitor than I had realised. Not only that, but a tactile Jamie registered with me like the moon transforming from a sphere into a cube. "Can we put the shrubs in today?" he asked.

"Have you been to school?" The Skeleton Man loomed over him, but Jamie didn't shrink back—not even a tiny bit.

"Yep."

"ALL day?"

"Yeh."

"Is that the truth?"

"Yes!"

"In that case, certainly we can."

Jen bounded around us as we worked. Occasionally she squeezed in beside me and dug with her paws. I turned over the soil in the remaining beds using a garden fork, picking out stones and weeds and tossing them into a pile behind me. Meanwhile the Skeleton Man and Jamie unwrapped and planted each shrub. There was a small tea bush, which the Skeleton Man said should yield tea leaves in about two years' time. There were two elderberry shrubs and two juniper bushes. Perhaps Molly could come over sometime and make juniper jelly and elderflower cordial. But not Kenny. Then there was a rosehip bush. I remembered hearing something on the radio about rosehips being good for arthritis. It might help Mrs No. I'd have to look in the traditional medicines cookbook again to see what to do with them. Hopefully Molly would be able to help, if she wasn't too busy working on the house with Kenny. Finally, there was a tall climbing rose.

"That'll have to go up the wall," said the Skeleton Man. We surveyed it lying out on the grass.

"I'll go up," Jamie said.

"Good man. I'll fetch a ladder."

"I'm a good climber. I'll just go up the tree and crawl along."

"Don't be idiotic. You'll fall and break a leg."

"He won't," I said, "He's used to climbing trees. He climbed the tree I fell from."

"I can't risk it. I'm fetching a ladder." He stomped off. As soon as the hall door was closed Jamie ran to the tree.

"Don't!" I cried, "He'll skin you alive!"

"Pfft. He's just another grown-up, moaning and groaning. I'm not scared of him. I'll show him!"

As he was speaking, he planted a foot halfway up the cherry tree where two thick branches forked out from one another, and, grasping a branch in each hand, levered himself up. The sound of banging and swearing came from outside the front end of the house. In four scrambled leaps Jamie was up about eight feet. He grabbed an overhanging branch and swung himself feet first onto the wall. I watched in fascinated dread as he balanced his way along, until he was at a spot immediately above where the rose bush was laid out.

"You'll be in such big trouble," I remarked.

"Just dig a hole and plant it! Quick!" I did as I was told. As I stood the rose against the wall, thorns scratched my wrists and stuck to my jumper. Jamie squatted down, took the top of the plant between his right finger and thumb, and I started to tie the branches to the frame.

"Oi! What did I tell you?" The Skeleton Man's voice set Jen barking, and Jamie startled and wobbled. He recovered quickly though.

"It's OK! Look, we've done it!" He waved from his position atop the wall.

"You could have cracked your head open! Come down at once!" The Skeleton Man wrestled the ladder out the door, leaned it against the wall and glared up at him. He stuck his tongue out.

"Can't I tie the high ones? You can tie the low ones!"

"You're a scoundrel, that's what you are." We waited for him to give a yes or no answer, but he didn't. Instead he stooped, picked up a tie, straightened up and secured one of the rose's branches. I dropped my fork and joined him, and for the next ten minutes we worked on securing its branches in place. Then we stepped back and looked at our work.

"Pretty good," said the Skeleton Man. I agreed. "Look," he carried on, "a bud." He reached out a spindly finger and stroked its closed petals.

"GRANDPA JOHN! CATCH ME!"

Both our heads snapped up. Jamie had a huge, wide grin on his face. The Skeleton Man barely had time to step back and hold out his arms before Jamie launched himself off the wall. He landed heavily on the Skeleton Man, who stepped backwards, making contact with my pile of weeds and stones. He fell, and his shin-bone cracked over the fork I had laid down when tying the rose.

For a second, they both just lay there. Then the

Skeleton Man let out a roar, but it wasn't like his other angry noises or Mum's shouting, and it didn't carry any words of admonishment. It was more like a lion's roar when it's been shot. Jamie sprang up, eyes huge, face pale, saying "Sorry, sorry, sorry, sorry..." I dropped down beside the Skeleton Man's head and took it in my lap. For about a minute he did nothing except groan and scrunch his face into expressions that registered on my dish like whenever Mrs Langton's angina took hold. I put my fingers in my ears, even though he was only making squeaks and huffing out breaths between clenched teeth. Finally, he reached up with both hands and pulled my wrists away from my ears. I sang a loud monotone to drown out all noise around me, then saw his face had settled down, his mouth was moving and his eyes were fixed on me. I stopped the note.

"Call the GP," he gasped.

"Shouldn't I just call 999?"

"No. It's probably just a bad sprain. Call the GP. Number's by the phone in the main hall." He lifted his head, cried out, dropped it back, then shouted for Jamie. Jamie looked poised to run. "Get a blanket. No, wait, get my coat. From the hook inside the back door."

Jamie and I ran inside together. I found the phone on what looked like a footstool to the right of the front door. As I searched for the number, I heard Jamie fumbling at the back door, before he ran back outside again, presumably with the coat.

I found a wad of scrap paper underneath the phone, each piece scrawled over with handwriting. My hands were shaking so much I had trouble peeling the papers apart, but eventually I found a tiny slip labelled 'GP'. I dialled the number and tried to keep my breathing calm while the phone rang at the other end.

"Hello, North Hill Clinic, Alice speaking. How can I help?"

"Hello," I took care to speak slowly and to enunciate, as I had learned in drama. "I'm calling to report a broken leg belonging to a Mr John Harrington." I told her the address.

"John Harrington, you say?"

"That's right."

"Right. Hold on a mo…" There was a click, and Vivaldi's 'Spring' came on. I tapped my fingers, growing calmer within its familiarity, so it came as a shock when the music cut off and Alice's voice said, "I've called an ambulance and I've dispatched Doctor Strachan. He's on call a few doors away, so he should only be a few minutes." Even though I was trying not to imagine the Skeleton Man quietly expiring on the lawn I smiled for a second—it seemed that on this occasion, calling the GP was the same as calling the ambulance.

After thanking her, saying goodbye and hanging up, I ran back outside and paced around on the lawn, working off the adrenaline that almost felt as if it was pouring out of me.

"Go and stand in the drive and show them the way," the Skeleton Man told me.

Ben Strachan got there first. I waved him in. He stopped for a moment on the threshold of the hall, then followed me through the living room and kitchen (glancing at the owl mug, which was on the draining rack), and into the back garden.

"It was her fault," Jamie said, pointing at me. "She left the fork and pile of stones on the ground."

"You were the one who jumped off the wall!"

"Well, let's not lay blame," the Skeleton Man cut in. Jamie looked from him, to Ben, then took the Skeleton Man's hand. The Skeleton Man shut his eyes.

"Quite right," agreed Ben. "That won't help us at all. Let's just assess the situation. Now," he squatted by the Skeleton Man's head. "Can you hear me, John?"

"Mmm. Hello." He didn't open his eyes.

"The ambulance is on its way."

I took the Skeleton Man's other hand.

"Please don't die," I said.

He snorted. "Don't be stupid! I've just sprained something."

"We'll see what the X-ray says," said Ben. "I have some painkillers with me. Anna, can you ring your mother and tell her what's happened? She might want to come round."

His face was hard to read. Then he turned back to the Skeleton Man.

"I don't know her number," I said. He recited a mobile number and made me repeat it back three times correctly. "Worth a try at least. She's slow to change". Chanting it to myself and feeling more and more confused, I returned to the hall and dialled.

"Hello?" said Mum's voice.

"Mum," I said.

"Anna! Is everything ok?"

"School was fine. I hope your meeting with the solicitor went well. The Skeleton Man's broken his leg."

There was a long pause. "Well. God." She cleared her throat.

"Ben's with him now. The ambulance is coming."

"Ben…?"

"Ben Strachan. Jamie and I were planting a rose and Jamie jumped off the wall. The Skeleton Man tried to catch him and broke his leg over a garden fork. At least, Ben thinks it's broken. The Skeleton Man thinks it's just sprained, but when I sprained my ankle running in my old school's sports day, I didn't make the faces he's making. I th—"

"But Ben's with him, you say?"

"Yes. He was on call nearby."

Another long pause. "Well, I'm sure you don't need me there as well. Doctor Strachan'll have it all under control."

"He thought you deserved to know."

"Thanks. OK, well, if you can hitch a lift with the ambulance, I'll meet you in A & E. OK?"

"OK."

As I hung up, I couldn't help thinking that since Mum had wanted the Skeleton Man to be with her when she was in distress, she should be with him now, when he was in distress. I heard an engine. I went to the drive and saw the ambulance pulling up. Two paramedics got out—a man and a woman. The man asked if this was the house of John Harrington. I said yes and showed them into the garden.

"Right, lass," the male paramedic said to me, "You'd best come up here and hold your granda's hand this side. And—what's your name?" He directed this second question to Jamie. Jamie told him his name. "You're doing a smashing job, Jamie—keep up the good work. Are you her brother?" he jerked his head in my direction.

"Me? Nope. She's just my friend."

The female paramedic conferred with Ben Strachan, then squatted next to me:"Mr Harrington? We're going to take you to get a wee X-ray up at the hospital in Livingston."

"Why is it always a 'wee' this, and a 'wee' that?" he grumbled. "Why not a huge one? Unleash the gamma rays! Go on—fry me! You never know—I might come out with an extra head and a pair of wings."

I laughed, and so did the female paramedic. "Well you're lucid enough—I'll grant you that! Now, I'm going to place a cannula and give you a shot of something for the pain. Then we're going to get you onto the stretcher."

I watched as the needle slid under his skin and felt my spine tingle. Ben put a hand on my shoulder. "Perhaps I'd better try ringing Patty myself, so you can go home."

I shook my head. "She's going to meet us at the hospital."

"She is?" His eyes widened.

"Yes. It's OK, I'm happy to ride in the ambulance."

Jamie patted the Skeleton Man's shoulder. "Grandpa John, please tell me when you're ready to do the garden again."

"There's not much more to do," replied the Skeleton Man, patting his hand. "But I'll give Carol a ring when I'm out. Shouldn't be too long." He squeezed his eyes shut and smiled. It looked like he was wrenching his mouth into the correct shape. "Good job we got that patio all cleared and levelled in time for the crutches!"

Every time we went over a bump the Skeleton Man scrunched his face up tight like a cabbage, but the drip—which I overheard was an opiate solution—seemed to make him sleepier over time. He was dozing as we pulled in at the back door of A & E, but when they wheeled him off to the X-ray he opened his eyes, looked at me, reached up and brushed my cheek with the back of his hand.

I was led into the waiting room where Mum was already sitting. When she saw me she stood up, and laid a hand on my shoulder.

"Well done, Anna."

I hadn't realised how tired I was before, but now it all seemed to crash in onto me at once. I slumped into a chair. At that moment Ben came running in. He stopped when he saw Mum, and his whole body went tense. Mum's mouth was open in an almond-shape. Then her lips pursed, and her eyes averted.

"Hi, Patty..." Ben said.

"Hello, Ben." Her voice was constricted and sounded like it did just before she shouted. I braced myself. He approached, taking hesitant steps, and sat on the other side of me. He clasped his hands, leaned forward with his elbows on his knees, and looked straight ahead. Mum sat ramrod, hands in her lap, looking straight ahead as well, but every now and then she shot a sideways glance at him.

"Anna—there's a little shop just down that corridor." Mum pointed, then handed me three pounds. "I haven't given you this week's pocket money. You might be here a long time. Get yourself something to eat. Or do. Or both."

I hesitated, confused by the tension my dish was

picking up, coupled with the casual-sounding suggestion, then slowly made my way towards where Mum had indicated. A man was lying on a trolley in the corridor, blood dripping down into his badly swollen right eye from under a bandaged hairline. As I passed, he craned his head up and met my eyes. I edged away and ran the rest of the way through.

The shop had a stationery section with novelty notebooks in it. I bought a blue one patterned with silver moons and gold stars, along with a cheap biro. I still had fifty pence left over, so I bought a bag of butterscotch sweets to share between the three of us.

Now the man in the corridor was shouting at a passing nurse. I edged past quickly and got back to the waiting area to find Ben crouched on the floor, partially shielding Mum from view. One of his elbows was resting on a chair, and the other lay across his knee. Mum was still sitting as she had been when I left, hands in her lap, shoulders and head pointing away from him. As I approached, she held up a hand.

"Just give me time, Ben."

"How much time? It's been sixteen years."

My mind fast forwarded through all I'd been told. I felt as if I was a jigsaw puzzle being torn apart and put back together again—this time in the correct formation. Then they saw me. Ben stood up.

"I think you'll both be all right now," he said. They

nodded at each other—unsmiling. Then he left.

"So, the rogue relationship was with Ben Strachan?" I asked, once it was just us.

She sighed. "Yes. Yes, it was."

I started to say, "That makes me so happy", because in a way it did. Ben and I got on well, which would be important for when he and Mum got married. And he still loved her after all these years and all that had happened, so I was convinced he would be a good and faithful husband. Mum definitely deserved a good, faithful husband. And if she made him happy too so much the better. At the same time, my dish did not detect happiness from Mum, and for me to be happy when she was not felt wrong. "Are you going to get married?" I asked instead.

"Anna, how can I possibly know that after a ten-minute conversation following sixteen years of silence?" She snapped this question at me, but I found I didn't mind her snapping any longer. I knew it was just because she felt raw.

"Sorry," I said. "So, what were you and he talking about, then?"

She pushed some hair behind her ear, a strange look upon her face. "Oh, nothing much."

That Friday I was woken by Mum. She didn't shake me as she had when she woke me for church. Instead she simply tapped my shoulder, calling: "Anna… Anna…"

Sleepily I rolled over to face her. I didn't feel very well. I started to cuddle back down, but she tapped my shoulder again.

"Anna… I need you to wake up."

"Mmmmff… why?" Her voice grated in my ears, even though she was using her soft voice rather than her shouting-at-me one.

"Because I have to go to work, and Molly's ill." Maybe I'd caught something off her.

"That's OK," I mumbled. "I can stay here."

"Hmm…" She wrinkled her nose. "I wouldn't like the social services finding out I'd left you home alone. I mean, I know I did it before but…"

I sat up and started to get dressed, too groggy to bother being modest. Maybe that's how Mum felt on my first morning, when she'd been late for work and had changed in front of me.

"Susan next door says you got on well with her mother, so I thought you could go over there."

"Oh—I'm happy about that!" I said. I tried to bounce out of bed and get ready quickly, but I felt about twice my usual weight.

Mum put a hand to my forehead.

"I'll be fine," I told her. I didn't want to miss spending time with Mrs No.

"Good. Susan says you can have breakfast round

there, so that's one less thing to worry about. Only, my boss just lost half her workforce for the morning—stomach flu—and she says if I don't get in there pretty damn—I mean pretty darn—sharp today, and stay the whole time, it's another point against me, and I've already got one. You only get three."

"You mean if you get three, you'll lose your job?"

She looked down. "Well... let's not go there unless it happens."

"Oh thank Christ," said Susan, as she opened the door to us. "She's been driving me up the wall. 'When's Anna coming', and 'Where's my boiled egg', and 'The tea's not the right temperature'... Here, in you go. Perhaps you can cheer her up while I nip to the shop—I could do with a break." She herded me through the 'Miserable birch inside' door, before hurrying to get her coat on.

Taking care to speak and tread softly, and to let in as little light as possible, I cleared a pile of books and papers off the piano stool and sat down, wincing.

"Looks like you're not so comfortable yourself," remarked Mrs No from her recliner in the corner.

"No, my back hurts. And my stomach hurts. And my head hurts."

"And I thought you were meant to be Little Miss Happy! Now you know how I feel most of the time. Would YOU like a grape?"

"Well…" I couldn't help but smile, because I knew my honest answer would be 'yes', but I also suspected that it wasn't the answer she wanted to hear.

"All right, Mrs Polite. I'll let you off the hook. How's the burping coming on?"

I gulped in some air and let fly. I actually surprised myself at what a good one I managed to generate but then, my stomach and intestines had been rumbling and doing other funny things since I'd woken up, so perhaps that had something to do with it.

"That was a cracker." The pitch of Mrs No's voice went right up at the last word. "I don't think even I could manage one like that—and I've had four years' practice!"

"Do you have any more muck left?" I asked.

"No. Why? Do you want some? Have you not had your breakfast?"

Maybe that was also why my stomach was rumbling, but oddly, I didn't feel hungry. In fact, I felt sick and wobbly. And a bit warm and sticky between my legs. That was odd—it wasn't liquidy as if I'd wet my pants, but it was more substantial than sweat.

"Where's the toilet?" I asked, standing up and clutching my stomach, which felt like it was being drawn down towards the floor with magnets.

"It's basically the cupboard under the stairs. Are you OK?"

I nodded and hobbled out, the stickiness very

obvious now. Had it been there all the time and I'd just not noticed? The light switch was on the wall outside the bathroom door. I switched it on, and a whirring fan started up.

Once I was seated, I had an attack of diarrhoea. After that I felt a lot better. Then I just sat for a while. Sitting in a slightly crouched-forward position, with my arms wrapped tight around my stomach and my head down, seemed to help. It was when my head was down that I caught a glimpse of blood splattered across the gusset of my knickers. Not just a little bit, and not red, runny blood either. A lot of thick, sticky, dark blood, with brown chunks in it, like lumpy gravy. My whole face went numb, and so did my fingers. I felt in my tracksuit pockets for Dad's phone—maybe his texts would tell me what to do, or at least let me dial 999. The phone wasn't there. Then I remembered I had smashed it.

I drew breath and tried to shout to Mrs No for help— but my voice simply stuck in my throat. It felt like the few times I'd woken up in full sleep paralysis and tried to make a sound, but although I could get the air out, my vocal cords wouldn't come together to make that air generate any sound other than the hiss of it escaping from my lungs. The stuff was still dripping out of me, into the toilet. If a slight cut to my lip could put me in danger of shrivelling up, then this would surely do it a lot quicker. My hands seemed pale. Straining to see myself in the mirror my face seemed pale, too. I obviously didn't have much blood, or time, left.

In my mind I rifled through my memories of all Dad had taught me. Everything seemed scrambled together in a useless pile—like rummaging through a box which has just had toys and desk papers and stationery and books and dirty laundry and used cups all thrown into it together in a hasty attempt to tidy up. He actually never taught me anything about that part of my body—Mrs Taylor taught me how to wash down there. And Dad had once mumbled something about babies growing in a woman's tummy from a mixture of Dad's and Mum's genes and later being pushed out through a special hole between the legs. I would have to communicate with Mrs No somehow... unless Susan got back now.

The cupboard under the stairs shared a wall with Mrs No's room—the wall that had the piano against it on her side. Perhaps if I knocked she would hear me. If I knocked SOS she would know there was a problem. The survival book I read said that, like CPR, you're supposed to keep tapping out SOS until help comes. I didn't know if Mrs No knew Morse code, but if she was intelligent enough to calculate how many grapes she'd eaten over the course of four years, she might be able to understand. Having a logical solution, instead of panicking on my own with no way forward, calmed both my fear and the pain in my stomach. So did the rhythmical tapping, even though I didn't know if anyone was coming.

"Hello? Anna? What's wrong?" Mrs No's voice came through the wall, slightly muffled. She knew there was something wrong. That was good—she'd understood my communication. Dad would have been proud. I just kept knocking and knocking. I didn't want her to think the emergency had passed. Then I heard a shifting noise.

After another six minutes of knocking I heard a sort of lopsided rhythmical thumping approaching the door, accompanied by the same squeaks Mrs No had given when she got up to go to the window. She had actually walked all the way round, through the hall, to the bathroom door.

"Can you unlock?"

I stretched forward, trying not to drip even more on my clothes, and pulled the bolt back. My ears were red and my face was hot and my hands were clenchy— it felt terribly wrong letting such a new friend into the bathroom with me, but this was an emergency. Like going to the doctor's, normal rules don't apply in an emergency.

"I'm bleeding out," I whispered, and I sat down and pointed to my knickers.

Mrs No craned forward, one hand against the wall to lean on. Then she did the last thing I would have expected her to do—she smiled.

"Oh, that's nothing to worry about, my darling," she

said, "That's completely normal."

"It is?" I almost didn't dare believe her.

"Oh, yes. It's a change that happens to every girl when they get to about your age. You're one of the club, now!"

"What causes it?"

"Do you know what your womb is?" I nodded. "Well, to use a comparison. A tree grows new leaves and blossoms so that it can seed and grow offspring, and in autumn those leaves fall to the ground. Then in spring, new ones grow. It's just autumn in your womb right now. It's called your period. Didn't your dad or mum warn you about it? Didn't you read about it anywhere?"

I shook my head.

"Tcha! What's the world coming to?"

"Why does it hurt so much?"

"It's just a few cramps that go with it, that's all. Sort of like shrugging off a coat. You can cuddle a hot water bottle or take painkillers if it's unbearable. I have paracetamol. Stretching helps, too."

"So it'll stop on its own?"

Mrs No nodded. "After a few days. You'll probably have it again in about a month. Might take a while for your cycle to settle down—it usually does when you first start. In the meantime, you can just wear a pad in your pants to absorb the blood. Change it every four hours. You mustn't flush it down the toilet—it'll block the drains. Put it in a bin."

"Where do I get the pads from?"

"Just about any shop has them. I'll call Susan on her mobile and see if she can pick you some up."

I smiled to myself as I heard Mrs No on the phone to Susan. She sounded normal now, not soft as she had done when she'd been explaining about my cycle.

"Susan? It's Heather. Your mother. YOUR MOTHER— are you deaf? Yes, I'm on the phone—did you think I was just shouting down a megaphone across the street or something? I'm on the hall phone. I have legs, you know. Listen, could you pick up some sanitary towels? And possibly some cupcakes or something? And get a move on—we're under siege here."

Once she had hung up, she knocked on the bathroom door again. "Here –" she posted a gigantic book round the door. "Greek Myths and Legends. I know you're a fast reader but that should keep even you going till the cavalry arrives."

I had got to the vulture tearing out Prometheus's liver each night, only for it to grow back again, by the time Susan arrived. Mrs No brought me a navy skirt and black tights, and some pink, frilly knickers. They weren't quite the type of bloomers people used to wear in the early 1900s, but they were certainly reminiscent of them. The pad was also a lot bigger and thicker than I expected, and as I stuck it into the gusset I couldn't help but think that my legs would be wedged apart and I would have to waddle around like a duck until the bleeding stopped, and everybody would know. At first it did feel like that, and I was very conscious of it, but Susan had brought some cupcakes and cookies, and as I laid the table for tea, I noticed that the pain had almost completely gone.

When Mum came home, she found us all laughing and chatting round the table—even Susan.

"What's all this?"

"Oh, just pink, frilly knickers," said Mrs No.

On Sunday, Mum and I walked to church arm in arm. Mum tried to make conversation, but my answers were minimal, even curt; I had too much on my mind, what with my upcoming reading.

The minister opened the service by telling a story about Jesus curing ten lepers, who then go away dancing and happy, but only one returns to say thank you. After singing a hymn about thanking God for giving us Jesus and the Holy Spirit, he told the children in the front row another story, about a man who dies and gets a tour round heaven. He sees God's order room, where hundreds of angels are streaming in with requests. Then he sees God's packaging plant, where hundreds of angels are wrapping up gifts and sending them to the mail room. Next, he sees God's shipping room, where hundreds of angels are posting off gifts to people. Finally, he sees God's parcel acknowledgement room, where one angel is dozing with a cup of coffee. He said it's easy to pray to God when we want something, but we often forget to thank him when we find ourselves blessed, and that when difficult times come along, we often forget that we are still blessed. We said a prayer thanking God for all the blessings in our lives. Then we sang another hymn, this time about praising God in different places and in different ways.

My reading was immediately after the offering. The other children all went off to Sunday school as the wicker bowl was being passed round. I watched them leave, feeling sad that I couldn't go too this time, but there was also a tiny stirring deep within me—like the first breeze of a hurricane. Like when the Skeleton Man called me a woman: a mixture of thrill and fear.

"We now take our reading from Psalm 100, which is going to be read to us by Anna Whitear."

"Well that's news!" said Mum, loudly. The she looked startled. "Oops," she whispered, very softly.

I squeezed past her to the end of the pew. As I stepped onto the stage the room went quiet. A few people began whispering. The Bible was propped up on something that looked like a music stand. The minister reached over my shoulder and adjusted the microphone. Then he stepped back. I leaned forward. Breaking the silence felt like making the first footprint on a patch of new snow.

"H-hello. I'm Anna." It sounded odd hearing my voice

booming back to me from the opposite side of the room.

"Hello, Anna!" called out a few people.

There was a bit of laughter.

"Um, I've never done this before." I tried not to let my jaw chatter. "I'm happy to be reading at a service about happiness."

More slight laughter.

"When I lived in London my dad and I had a game about being happy. We called it the Happy Game. In August there was a house fire. I didn't get hurt—I jumped out the window and escaped. But my father died the next day from smoke and burns."

There were some intakes of breath, and more whispers. For some reason I was able to state the facts easily when saying them onstage, to an audience. Perhaps it was because I was just ploughing through, saying it not exactly as me but as a performer-me. Or perhaps it made it easier to detach, knowing what I now knew about Dad.

"I nearly stopped playing the game for a while after that, but then I thought, well, happiness really doesn't count for much if it only depends on good things happening to us, does it? So, I decided to carry on playing it." I hesitated and clenched my fists. "It wasn't easy when I first started playing it. In fact, it was never exactly easy… and these last couple of months have been the hardest it's ever been. But now I've settled in and made friends, I'm happier than ever to be living here, in Mum's house, with her."

Mum pressed a hand to her mouth. The Skeleton Man bent his head.

"Anyway, this is the psalm:
'Make a joyful noise to the Lord, all the earth!
Serve the Lord with gladness!
Come into his presence with singing!'"

"'Know that the Lord, He is God!
It is he who made us, and we are his;
we are his people, and the sheep of his pasture.'"

"'Enter his gates with thanksgiving,
and his courts with praise!
Give thanks to him; bless his name!
For the Lord is good;
his steadfast love endures forever,
and his faithfulness to all generations.'"

I finished with a "Thank you." A few people clapped, and there was some chatter which sounded like bees in a hive. I walked back up the aisle and slotted myself into the pew beside Mum, as the minister remarked that I had my career cut out. Mum put her arm around me and kept it there for the rest of the service, until the last hymn. I felt so happy I didn't hear much of anything else and ended up parroting social scripts rehearsed with my outreach worker when people came up to compliment me afterwards.

Mum was very quiet the next morning. As we ate, her head was turned sideways towards the kitchen sink. She was tense, but it was a different kind of tension from the kind I had seen before. Nevertheless, I decided to keep quiet and let her have her personal space.

When I came out from school she was waiting in the car park. Her eyes sparkled. A folded blue piece of A4 paper poked out from her coat pocket.

"How was your day?" I asked.

"Great." Her voice sounded strained, but again, it wasn't the same kind of strain I had encountered before. She said nothing on the way home, but her mouth worked, as though there was some kind of animal inside her that was struggling to get out. As she opened the garden gate, I noticed she was quivering. Finally, she spoke:

"I went to the solicitor's today. Got some interesting news."

I tried to commit to memory every little detail about her appearance, her habits, the district and her home in two seconds flat, so that if I was taken away I would be able to keep my promise and find her again. "What did he say?"

"Apparently my dad got in touch with them. The

social services have cleared it too, so it's official. The custody challenge is null and void. Do you know what that means?"

"No. What?"

"You're staying here. With me. Forever and ever. WELCOME HOME!"

And suddenly it was as if the real Mum—the Mum I had been so sure existed underneath the defences, and which people had seemingly debated the existence of for years—erupted out of her, like a fully-fledged eagle exploding out of an egg. Her face split into the biggest smile I have ever seen, as she flung her arms wide. For half a second the shock and hugeness of it rendered me utterly immobile. Then I recovered and ran into them. She gathered me up, I buried my face in her shoulder, and even though there was only half an inch between us in height, my feet left the ground.

October came and went, and then November. Mum and I did more and more fun things together. She told me that before I came to live with her, she usually spent her free time sleeping or watching television, and that she ate a lot of packet meals like Pot Noodles and microwave chips. Now that I was here, though, she started to learn new recipes. I didn't tell her this, but Dad was a really good cook. He taught me some recipes like flapjack, pasta bake, and bread. Cooking together was my first ever outreach worker's idea—she thought it would be a good, natural way to teach me teamwork, organisation, time-management, and life skills. Dad didn't write any of the recipes down for me, but, like the Chopin which I hadn't played since leaving the flat, I found that when it came to it, I still remembered them. I wasn't sure how I felt about that. It was nice having something else that I could keep, but after Mum's disclosures I felt quite guilty for wanting to hold on to them, too.

We got into a routine, before bed, of reading passages of books to each other. It sounds babyish but it wasn't, because they were adult books. We read our way through the entire Muriel Spark canon, as well as Tales from Ancient Arabia, and the Cosmic Trilogy by C.S. Lewis. Again, Dad had encouraged my reading, but he and I had never really engaged in it in a joint way. In the same way, I looked up to him as an artist, but have never myself been very good at drawing or painting, or very interested in it as something to pursue. It felt lovely to have someone who encouraged my reading, and who also loved it themselves. Our own little book club.

I got used to school, too. Sometimes Cal, Jesse or Jamie would come round afterwards. Usually we went over to the Skeleton Man's house, since Mum was still at work, and anyway, there was a bigger garden and corridors to run around in. We built another sensory room in Mum's old room, with Christmas tree lights, an oil diffuser bottle and sticks, and fairy jars made with glow-in-the-dark paint. The Skeleton Man put his foot down at fairy lights on the garden shrubs, though.

Cal taught me how to apply nail varnish, lipstick and eyeliner, and how to use face masks. She wanted me to dye my hair purple, too, but I like having brown hair like Dad and red hair like Mum. I was careful not to invite Cal and Jamie round at the same time, because Jamie would definitely scoff at lipstick and eyeliner. The Skeleton Man bought a video gaming setup, too, which meant Jamie rarely played on his Game Boy anymore, so he gave it to me. Most of the time, though, we played rounds of Superkart Track Racing. And when it was just the Skeleton Man and me, we would play and play the piano—Chopin and Handel and Mozart and Bach and Haydn and Liszt. I started working towards my grade seven under his supervision.

There was a parents' evening, too, and Mum got to meet people like Rachel and Miss Marney properly. Afterwards, she gave me a hug and told me how proud she was of me. I had a piano recital back on the last day before the October holidays, during which I played a scherzo. It wasn't as nerve-wracking as a grade, but my hands still got sweaty, making me scared they would slip on the keys. But I only made two mistakes, and I carried on anyway. Afterwards, everyone broke into thunderous applause, but Mum was the only one who stood up, and that meant more to me than all the applause, ever.

Later on in October, Mum told me she wanted to remove the double bed and put a wall up across the middle of her room, so that we could each have our own rooms, albeit half the size. I told her I liked the room and the bed the way they were. She said we would see, but that I was still growing, and that I would need my privacy one day. I didn't believe her at the time. She also signed up for a college course about Asperger's.

We went on walks sometimes—down through the trees and along the river. Once we went to Portobello beach on the train and bus. The tide was far out so we put our things down in the dry sand, ventured out and had a mad game of tag near the waterline. I'm a much faster runner than her so I won in the end, because she couldn't catch me and got tired sooner. Then we built a castle and tried to defend it as the tide came in. One day, when we went up and over Fiddler's Brae, Mum spotted what we thought at first was a clump of sheep's wool. We went to investigate, because I wanted to take it home to try and spin it, like I had seen in a book about the Hebrides. As I approached, it wriggled and whined. Mum leapt back at first, as though it were another bat. Then she relaxed, because it wasn't—it was a tiny puppy, stuck halfway down a rabbit hole and unable to wriggle free. Mum and I dug it out with our hands.

It didn't have a collar. The vet in Livingstone said it was

male, healthy, not microchipped, and about eight weeks old. We put 'lost' posters up, but nobody responded, so Mum thought it was probably dumped there by someone passing down the road in their car. Mum said we could keep him for a week, so I named him Todd, and started training him after school to show Mum that he wouldn't be any trouble or create any mess. He lived at the Skeleton Man's, where I taught him to sit and roll over. Jamie and I wanted to teach him how to jump through a hoop as well. The only problem was that with homework and football and piano and things, I couldn't train him every night. Also, Jamie kept changing the command words, which must be confusing for a dog, who can't understand much English anyway. Even so, he was still there after the week was up. I think Mum must have just got used to him and seen that he wouldn't be any trouble.

On the last day of October something happened that I don't remember at all, but that Mum has since told me all about from her perspective. We're not sure exactly when it happened, but the Skeleton Man says Jamie and I were at his house until about four o'clock, when we asked to go onto the green to play football. Mum says it was almost dark as her drive home from work ended, so it was probably sometime between half past five and six o'clock that evening.

As she was about to turn in to our drive, she saw a black shape spread out along the kerb. She pulled over, jumped out of the car and approached to get a better look, like we did with Todd. In the low light she thought it was a bin liner or a suitcase at first, and then she saw the flash of my butterfly hair clip. I've asked her since what that felt like. She says there are many things she wants me to understand about other people as I get older, but the feelings she had in that moment are ones she hopes I never come to understand, because the only way to understand them would be to actually live through such an experience myself.

When the Skeleton Man found me after I had fallen from the tree he had to move me because he didn't have a mobile phone—but Mum knew the best thing to do was just to not move a person if you find them injured, in case their spinal cord has been damaged. She said it was still difficult to know what to do, though, because she did a mandatory basic first aid course at work, and that said you had to make sure a person's airways were clear by loosening their collar and tilting their chin up—so she didn't know whether she was meant to do that or just not touch or move me at all, and that this was a terrible position to be in because—in her words—she was 'damned if she did and damned if she didn't'. She felt angry at the first aid course writers for not making this clearer and thus putting her in such a position. I can understand that.

What she did by way of compromise was to put the back of her hand to my nose and mouth. When she felt a swell of warmth against it, she knew I was still breathing. She felt for a pulse in my neck, and it was strong. I asked her what my face looked like, and she said she couldn't really see it, because it was pressed into the tarmac on one side, and my hair was over most of the other side so that it looked like a crescent moon. She did see a dried-up trickle of blood that had flowed down from the part of my face that was hidden, though.

At some point, she said, Ben Strachan arrived. She didn't remember calling him, but she must have done. He kept repeating "I'm so sorry this has happened," and his face was white. That surprised Mum—she thought doctors were supposed to be cool with this kind of thing. But he's only human too, and he knows both of us. Mum gave him the key to our house, which was an incredibly brave thing to do given how she'd avoided him for so many years. He got two blankets from inside. He put one over me, and one over her—which took her by surprise because she had forgotten about her own needs. Ben later told me he was worried she would go into shock and there'd be two casualties.

Then it was just a case of waiting for the ambulance to get there and checking to see if I was breathing and my heart was still beating, or if I was coming round—which I wasn't. Mum tried to work out what had happened, to feel less helpless and to try and distract her mind, but also to help the paramedics when they got there. But all she could think of, she told me, was that if I died then she would too. In her mind, I had been her last chance to get things right, and if she lost me it would prove that all she did was cause endless death and damage to all her loved ones. That's not true, of course—I told her that, and so did the Skeleton Man. We both gave her lots of hugs when she told us this bit. She said she knew that it wasn't true really, but that it felt like that to her at the time. She also said she could never shut herself away again—force herself back into her little cave—now she'd felt the sunlight that was me. That made me happy.

She did notice that the pavement was lightly frosted, and that there was a football resting on the grass a few feet away. Jamie Bean wasn't there. Perhaps he'd gone to get help, or perhaps he'd been scared and run away. Not knowing what happened, it's impossible to say. While she was waiting with me and he wasn't there, she wanted to get hold of him and—well, actually she didn't say what she wanted to do—but she hadn't the energy to spare for what she called 'good faith' at that point. And it was only later that she was able to remember that he was just a child. I'm not sure what she meant by that—physically it's very obvious that Jamie is just a child. I think she must have meant that she forgot he was still learning to have the courage to do the right thing.

When the paramedics arrived, they got me onto a backboard, and Mum was able to see my face. She told me my mouth was slightly open, and that my eyes were half-mast. That must have looked terrifying, since she was my mother and I was her child. Mrs Langton used to sleep like that just before she died and her cancer-riddled lungs were using every good surface space to try and exchange enough gas to keep her alive. The blood had come from my right nostril, so it could have been a lot worse—a nosebleed always looks more dramatic than it is. I also had a bruise on my forehead, and a long cut across the bridge of my nose. Other than that, the mud streaks on my tracksuit—and the fact that I was still unconscious—I didn't look badly hurt.

The trip to hospital was only ten minutes long. It would have been longer in a normal car stopping at all the red lights and going at the speed limit, but the ambulance had its siren on. When Mum told me that, I felt quite special—not everyone gets to go in an ambulance with the siren going. I also felt guilty though, since that must have caused a lot of people a lot of trouble and been frightening.

In the ambulance, Mum held my hand. She told me she had a lasting image of it resting palm-down across my chest. It looked like a wilted flower, and my nails needed to be clipped. She turned it over, noticing my long 'life line', which comes from palm-reading, and even though she doesn't believe in that kind of thing at all, it made her feel better. They'd put an IV drip in, and it poked out a mass of tape affixed to the back.

She asked them if I was going to be OK, and they said they were doing all they could. They also called her 'Mrs Whitear'—which made her cringe. It made me cringe too when she told me—after all that my Dad did to her, I could understand why she never wanted to be 'Mrs Whitear' ever again. In fact, she told me she never wanted to be 'Mrs' anybody ever again, even if she re-married.

Unlike most people, who have to sit around for hours until they get a bed, I got through A & E and into the X-ray machine in a matter of minutes. Mum told me the person who talked to her afterwards was a male nurse, who had the facial expression of a funeral director. He said:

"Mrs Whitear, we're working hard to help Anna right now. We're checking for broken bones and whether there's any swelling in her brain. We also want to see if there's damage to her spine." He asked her what had happened, and she said she didn't know. Well, she didn't actually say it as she couldn't speak. She also couldn't cry, which the male nurse just didn't understand at all. He told her it was perfectly normal to cry, which made her feel like a freak. A nurse should know better than that.

When I was little, I thought I knew what different

nonverbal things meant. Tears meant sadness. Smiles meant happiness. Shouting meant anger. Except with Dad, who went very quiet when he was angry. It was only when I got to secondary school that I realised a person could smile bravely. And Mr Langton didn't cry at his wife's funeral. At any rate, Mum bent her head to make it less obvious to the nurse that she wasn't crying. That seemed to satisfy him, she told me. Luckily, Todd was at the Skeleton Man's house. Ben said he'd tell the Skeleton Man about me for Mum. The groceries were still in the car, which was still in the road outside our drive, but none of that mattered any more. Besides, the road hadn't been roped off for investigation.

Once they'd set me up in the ICU Mum was allowed to see me. She told me later that I was surrounded by machines. Old frenemies, she said. They couldn't save Archie, but they tried their best. They did save me, but they separated us from each other. And now they were keeping me alive, but they couldn't save my Dad who—in that instant she realised—may have hurt her immeasurably, yet had somehow still managed to turn out into the world, someone she called 'one of the kindest, gentlest, toughest and most forgiving souls I have ever encountered'. That's when I personally realised it was possible not only to smile bravely, and to be quietly angry, but to also cry with happiness.

While she was there, pushing my hair away from

my face and singing so that only I could hear (except I couldn't hear at this point because I'd been sedated and was asleep), Ben put his hand on her shoulder. She told me that made her leap away and wheel round, simultaneously. I think Mum will always be someone who doesn't do tactile affection easily when she's traumatised or stressed. He got her a chair, even though she didn't ask him to, and also a cup of tea with a lot of sugar in, again to make sure she didn't get ill from shock. But he didn't touch her again.

Mum heard the results of my X-ray from the doctor who cared for me in the coming weeks—Doctor Jenner. She was a middle-aged woman with a stern, bony face but a soft voice, who called Mum into a quiet room. Mum told me she was relieved to see there were no tissues or tea or anything—apparently tissues and tea mean there's going to be a terminal diagnosis.

Instead, Doctor Jenner said: "The good news is that Anna doesn't appear to have any broken bones. There's some mild swelling under the bruise on her head, which we've got under control, but her brain itself looks fine." That was good—it meant I wasn't brain damaged and should wake up soon and still be me as Mum knew me. Assuming I did come round as they expected me to, of course. Doctor Jenner continued: "What we know at the moment is that one of the vertebra in her lower back has been knocked out of place, and it's putting pressure on her spinal cord, constricting its blood supply from about hip level down. Now, it's impossible to say what the long-term effects of that could be, because I gather you don't know how long she was lying out."

Mum told me that when Doctor Jenner said that, it made her feel as if all the blame for any long-term damage would fall to her, for not ensuring I was safe, and then for not discovering me sooner. She asked what the treatment plan was. Doctor Jenner said surgery wasn't the best option because of the danger of further damaging the nerves, especially as my vertebra wasn't actually broken. That's how they'd arrived at the recommendation of traction treatment. I would be put on bed rest, with my spine fixed in the correct position, taking the pressure off my nerves. From there they would see how much function I could recover, before working out how to go forward.

Ben wanted to know how long all this would take, but they couldn't tell him. Only that it would be weeks to months, rather than days. Once the injury had healed, I would go on to physiotherapy and strength training, to heal as much of the nerve damage that had already occurred as possible. Mum says that when she asked if I would walk again, play football again, climb trees again, they avoided answering.

After she'd signed the consent forms, and whilst

they were putting me in traction—for which I was kept
sedated so it wouldn't be painful or scary—Mum went
outside. Livingston Hospital has a tiny little chapel and
a cemetery around the back. I've been there several
times myself now. There's a sweet little gravestone near
the back—not more than two feet high, and made of
smooth, light grey stone.

IN LOVING MEMORY OF
KAYLEIGH KATHARINE STRACHAN
19TH MARCH 1998
AND HER BROTHER, ARCHIE JONATHAN
WHITEAR
22ND—27TH JANUARY 2000
THEY WILL SOAR HIGH ON WINGS LIKE
EAGLES

That last line is a Bible quote. It's a modern translation,
deliberately with no quotation marks or citations. Mum
told me that was so that Dad never realised it was from
the Bible. She told me he hated it when people made any
mention of anything to do with religion, which explained
why he had gone all silent and muttered when I asked to
go to church, and why the church bells had annoyed him
so much each Sunday. According to Mum, his parents
kept him indoors all day every Sunday during his
childhood, except for a brief two hours in the morning

when he was forced to attend Sunday school. There, the teacher had smacked him for not learning and saying his prayers. One time he was forced to take communion—I know what that is now. Another time he was led before a large model cross, and someone hit the backs of his legs so that he collapsed onto his knees in front of it. Neither Mum nor I can see how that helps anyone get closer to God. It's like thinking somebody will learn to swim, and therefore be saved from drowning, by throwing them into the sea. Anyway, if he'd known where the quote came from, he'd never have agreed to its inclusion.

I didn't know what to think about this when she told me. Did Dad's background really explain why he hated church and religion? Mum had not had an easy time with church and religion either. And yet… she still believed. Why?

The last time Mum visited the grave was in May. She'd left a bouquet there, but it had all gone except for a few straggly, brown, drooping threads. She told me what her locket contains: two tiny photographs—one of baby Archie, and one of baby me.

Ben came outside to let Mum know that I was successfully in traction. I nearly asked Mum how he'd known where to find her. Then I remembered that this was a story Ben had, in part, shared. He knew where the gravestone was because Kayleigh was his baby, too. Perhaps he'd even visited it on his own. Mum told me he was holding flowers—winter violets, probably bought from the hospital's shop. He put them where the old flowers had been. New where old had been—just like the two of them, because that's when he put his arms around her, and she didn't pull away.

I don't remember any of that, of course—being unconscious for almost all of it. I do have a couple of very hazy memories of otherworldly sounds, and of light behind my eyes at certain points, but no sense of time or space. Probably that's what it feels like to be a baby in the womb. Here and there a flicker of light, a jolt, a muffled sound that you can't tell if is from your body, your mother's body, or something in the outside world.

The first thing that really registered was when I woke up and thought that the sleeping bag I used to sleep in at home had grown very tight and was giving me burning pins and needles all over my hips, thighs, legs and feet. I was wearing a thin, loose shirt and lying on crisp sheets. There was a sharp pain in my back and a different, foggier pain in my head. Bright lights shone overhead, hurting my eyes. I screwed them up and saw Mum's silhouette. I tried to lift my hand, but she took it in hers and guided it back down. I could feel my tummy under my palm, but I couldn't feel the weight of my hand on top of my tummy. My eyelids felt heavy, and the sound of low whispering was soothing. The lights faded. I tried to drift back to that warm, dark, muffled place where my mind seemed to have been hibernating.

"Anna, can you hear me?"

I opened my eyes again. The lights had been dimmed, and I could see Mum more clearly now. Ben Strachan was holding her hand. Someone in a white coat was standing on the other side of the bed from them.

"I can hear you." My voice was high, crackly and barely more than a whisper. The words were slurred.

"Anna? I'm Doctor Jenner. Do you feel any pain?"

I shook my head, which made my back sear again.

"Don't try to move. You're at the hospital. You've had a wee accident and you've hurt your back. We've put you in traction to keep you still. Do you remember what happened?"

I played back my memories of the day like a video. At school I had researched L.S. Lowry, learned how to describe an isosceles triangle in algebraic terms, drawn the learning support room using a graphics design program, titrated some iodine into some orange juice to measure its vitamin C content, measured the wind speed, and made a vanilla layer cake. Afterwards I was dropped at the Skeleton Man's house by the contract taxi and took a football onto the green on my own to practise some new tactics. After that it was as if I came up against a set of white screens, and try as I might, I couldn't get over, under or around them.

"No." I started to cry, which disconcerted me—I

didn't even feel sad.

"Don't cry, darling." Doctor Jenner patted me on the shoulder. Mum dabbed my eyes with a tissue. "I'd just like to try a few tests, if you'd be all right with that."

"OK."

"Now, this is Lily." Another woman came into view. She wore pale-pink scrubs and had black hair, which was clipped up, the way I like to wear mine.

"Hi!" She waved. I waved back, and saw a drip bandaged on the back of my hand.

"Now, she's just going to brush the sole of one of your feet with a toothbrush. It may be a bit tickly."

I waited and concentrated. I seemed to wait a very long time.

"Right, can you feel me brushing your foot?"

"No."

"OK. I'm going to brush your knees now." I waited a few seconds, hoping to feel something that would make me squeal and squirm away as I had done with Mum. "Can you feel that?" I couldn't. I couldn't feel her brushing my thighs or my lower tummy either. It was as if half my body had disappeared—like a hill fading away into mist. Or more precisely, into a feeling of pressure and pins and needles—the only thing I had ever experienced like it before was when I sat curled up too long, and my legs below my shins went to sleep. The way they felt was like that, but more so, and without sensation returning.

"It's all right, Anna." Doctor Jenner drew away. "Now, Lily's going to check your reflexes. You don't have to do anything, but if you feel any pain or discomfort just tell us and we'll stop. In fact, just tell us if you feel anything at all."

"OK." I waited but felt nothing new. After that they held my calves, pressed the soles of my feet and asked me to point my toes against them, as if I was trying to stand on tiptoes. Then they bent my legs up and asked me to try and push them straight. It was as if they were asking me to wiggle my ears—something I have never been able to do. But at least I can feel things on my ears. I couldn't feel them in my legs or tummy.

"Are my legs broken?"

"No, they're not broken. You knocked a bone out of place, and it trapped your nerves—a bit like when you sit curled up on your leg for a long time and it goes numb."

"So will I feel better in a few minutes then?"

"Well, we've got the bone back into place and freed the nerve, so we'll just have to let it heal and wait and see. It may take a while—it was trapped for a long time. Meanwhile, try and rest. And try not to worry."

After just a few hours I began to get stiff and sore. I would have loved to be able to roll onto my side and curl up, but the straps and blocks didn't allow for it. Besides, my legs would have been left behind.

My nights were filled with frequent wakings from

dreams of being offered up as a human sacrifice. Not being tired physically, I was stuck with impossible-to-fulfil urges to jump up and down, climb things, twirl and run around. They niggled at me like a persistent itch. I had to get used to catheterisations to help me wee, and enemas to help me to poo. A computer controlled where the pressure fell on my back, so that I wouldn't get bed sores. I also had to take several different medicines for pain and muscle relaxation, among other things.

The Skeleton Man visited. He taught me how to play chess. I beat him, two games to one. He bought me a new mobile phone, but I couldn't use it because of the life support equipment. Mrs No and Susan visited too. They brought some beef muck—the making of which was presided over by Molly, apparently—and we practised our burping, with the aim of creating a secret language. Also, Cal came to visit.

One day Professor Morrison, the neurologist, removed the traction device for a few minutes and re-tested my reflexes, sense of touch and ability to move. He wrote something down and left the room without a word. Mum's face looked like it had done when the policeman delivered me back home after I'd made the den at Jamie's. Meanwhile, Ben went around with his eyebrows drawn together and his mouth set in a horizontal line.

Over the following weeks I had two more scans, and in early December the care team held a meeting in my room. The medical staff gathered around my bed, along with Mum and Ben. It felt like a sleepover. I wished I had a midnight feast to share with them, but all I had was some toffee Ben bought me from the shop downstairs. Doctor Jenner cleared her throat.

"Well, Anna, we've discussed your progress, and you've done very well. The bones in your spine are properly aligned, and the inflammation has gone." She smiled at me. "I'm thinking we need to start rehabilitating you now."

"You mean I can work towards getting out of bed?"

"Well, yes. You're a strong girl—I can see that. And I know that you'll come through what I'm about to explain to you." She sat on the side of my bed. "Our goal, as I see it, is to get you to the point of having a happy, independent life at home, whether that's in a wheelchair or on your feet. We put you on flat bed rest for a few weeks to see what nerve function we could recover in your spine. If it were possible for you to recover some sensation and movement in your lower half, we would have expected to see some signs of it by now."

Mum went white. "Are you saying she'll never walk again?"

"Obviously we can't absolutely rule it out, and medicine is advancing all the time, but with what we've got at the moment, it's not looking likely." She swallowed hard. "I'm so very sorry. I wish I had better news."

In many TV shows competitors get a montage of their best moments when they are eliminated. As I struggled to digest what I'd been told with regards to my walking, my brain did something similar with respect to my legs— only it happened in slow motion, and repeatedly—over the course of the next week. I both saw and felt myself, aged five, running across the Cornwall sand towards my granddad, doing long-jump and high-jump, tap-dancing aged eight, kicking a football around, stumbling through knee-high mud on a forest walk during a torrential downpour, scrambling through the branches of Jamie's tree, swimming the length of the local pool with my arms clasped behind my back, using the sustaining pedal on the piano, walking a beam, climbing Snowdon, bounding up the stairs of the flat... I also had a vision of all the things I had hoped to do in Scotland—huge footprints in the snow, learning to skate, dragging a sledge up to the top of Fiddler's Brae, crossing the river with Todd, using boulders as stepping stones. If only I hadn't gone to the green...

"I've referred you to a child counsellor. It's big news to take in, and it's absolutely understandable that you'll need help to adjust." I heard the voice as if I were underwater.

During this time, I almost entirely stopped eating and drinking. The counsellor came and talked to me about how life was still worth living, and gave me a book to read called Rollin' and Rockin, which was written by a man who lost the use of his legs as the result of a skiing accident. It was only after she had gone that it occurred to me that perhaps she thought I was trying to starve myself. In actual fact I would have loved to have been able to eat and drink properly. My stomach felt as if it was turning itself inside out from hunger, and my throat felt dry. Mum brought cheese, ham and tomato toasties into the hospital, and made me hot chocolate, but I just didn't seem to be able to swallow more than a few bites, or a few tiny sips of anything. I felt like the whale in the Just So story, with the raft stuck in his throat, preventing him from eating anything except for very small fish. The dietician put me on special high nutrient chocolate puddings to keep my weight up, and Mum, Ben, the Skeleton Man and the doctors spent a lot of time whispering in the corridor.

I also started a type of therapy called hydrotherapy, to strengthen my upper body. This is where you get into a pool of water—but it's warmer than a swimming pool—and you're there to work, not play. There aren't generally other swimmers there, although sometimes I would see one of the other nurses taking a severely disabled young girl in to swim. I overheard the nurse calling the girl Celia. Celia was a teenager, but she was quite a lot smaller than me. She couldn't control any of her limbs, or her head, and I don't think she could speak. At least, nothing I could understand. She wore a neck float which looked like a travel pillow, but which fastened at the front with Velcro.

Isla—the hydrotherapist—helped me to do certain strengthening exercises. She was from Illinois, and she loved horse riding. When I asked her whether she might teach me how to ride she said, "Sure! I know a riding centre near Uphall—they've got a rehabilitative programme that I help run."

One of the things Isla did was put me in a monofin. This is a type of diving flipper which looks like a mermaid's tail. I learned how to move it a tiny bit by flexing some of my stomach muscles. At the end of each session we took five minutes just to play. Isla had a very good aim—much better than mine—when it came to water fights.

One morning they all gathered together in my room a second time. I braced myself in case they had more difficult news for me.

Doctor Jenner opened the meeting. She just went straight to the point:

"There is a medical trial, beginning in the New Year, which involves using cells from the area of the brain which controls smell, to repair spinal cord injuries like yours. How would you feel about applying for a place on that?"

I opened my mouth to reply, but she cut me off:

"Now, there are no promises of your being given a place on it, or of it being effective—much less enabling you to walk again. But if you are, and if it is, it may at least give you back some movement and sensation in your legs. How much, we can't say. It's early days yet, and preliminary cases are still being followed up. So far it's been different for every patient."

I cleared my throat and chose my words carefully. "So... so I could apply to be in this study... and possibly walk again?"

"Don't count on it. There are a number of risk factors. Even if all goes to plan, regaining any function at all would take a great deal of time, patience and effort on your part. You'd still require wheelchair and mobility training. Even in the best possible scenario you probably wouldn't get all the function back that you had before. But yes, given all those things, there is a chance you could walk again in some capacity. There is also a snag. Participants are required to remain in London for the first phase of the study, for rehabilitative and monitoring purposes."

London. London, with its market places and boroughs, museums and cathedrals, graffiti and tour boats, traffic haze and interminable red lights, Oyster cards and buses, Turnham Green and Richmond Park, Torriano Meeting House, Globe Theatre, British Library, Regent's

Pond, Winter Hill and Kew Gardens. London with Mr Langton, Miss Corrigan and Mrs Taylor, my outreach worker, Alison, my friends from junior school... City of my heart... but not mine. It had been mine because it had been Dad's. This realisation made me feel like an astronaut who is just out of reach of their spacecraft— right in front of it, looking in at the lighted windows, but totally powerless to open the door.

Mum and I looked at each other. "Of course, if it were right for Anna, we would go wherever necessary," she said.

"You might as well put in an application," Doctor Jenner told us both as she handed Mum the forms. "Even if you're offered a place you don't have to take it. There's a waiting list as long as my arm."

On Christmas Eve the ward laid out pillowcases at the end of each bed. I woke in the morning to find mine filled with presents wrapped in snowflake-patterned blue paper. Over the course of the morning I opened them. They contained some chocolate coins, a tiny navy-blue teddy with the Milky Way galaxy printed on its stomach, a Marx Brothers DVD, a country snow-scene, some purple slipper socks, and a ridiculous-looking hat which Professor Morrison tried on. It had lots of stuffed tentacles of different colours sticking up in all directions and made him look like Medusa.

In the afternoon I managed half a potato, a few scraps of turkey, a Brussel sprout and some chocolate pudding, before being wheeled out into the lightly snow-covered garden, where the Skeleton Man let Todd snuffle around my feet, tail wagging almost too fast to see clearly. Todd's tail, I mean. Not the Skeleton Man's.

On Boxing Day I ate some more chocolate pudding, then lay in bed looking out the window. I could see the orange windsock and the helipad where people were brought in and medical crews dispatched. At some point there was a knock on the door.

"Anna?" It was Sophia—the nurse on duty. "You have a visitor."

Simon the minister poked his head round the door. "Hello Anna!" He sat on the chair beside me.

"What's in there?" I pointed at the blue leather satchel he was unslinging from his shoulder.

"Oh, bits and bobs. How's tricks?"

I shrugged.

"Enjoy Christmas dinner?"

I felt myself tense up—so many people had tried to get me to eat, and I wasn't prepared to repeat the truth again; that I really, honestly wanted to, but just couldn't. I shook my head.

"Ach. That's how it goes sometimes, isn't it?"

We played a few games of noughts and crosses, talking very little. I won most of them. "I gather you're considering participating in some kind of cell trial," he said at last.

"Yes." I twisted my fingers. "It's in London."

"Ah." He nodded, looking at me hard. "That must stir up a lot of memories for you."

I set my jaw. "My home is here. I can't see London as my home now. Not when everything my father did was false."

He frowned. "Why do you say that?"

I told him all about the things Dad had done to Mum.

He stroked the beard he didn't have. "Anna, are you forbidding yourself from remembering him as the kind, gentle dad you knew?"

I started to cry. It quickly turned into a howl—a long-overdue howl which counsellors have since told me was a delayed reaction to being bereft, not once, but many times over: of my dad; of my home; of my previous life; and finally, fatally, of my happy, uncomplicated memories of all of these things.

"Oh, Anna…" He offered me a tissue from a packet in his pocket—and his own eyes looked full. "He inspired you to be who you are in so many ways, didn't he? Especially with playing your game. Only now you feel it's all fake—is that right?"

I nodded, feeling unbearably foolish.

"Shall I tell you what I see?"

I waited.

"I see an articulate, open-minded, compassionate, very generous-hearted and attentive young girl who always tries to see the best in people. Am I right?"

"Sometimes." My ears went red.

"Well then. The way I see it, when a person sees the best in someone, and takes those perceptions and uses them to inspire them to grow in those qualities themselves, then even if what they saw turns out to be not quite as faultless as they imagined, they still create something real. Do you see what I'm saying?"

I shook my head, "Not really."

"You saw good qualities in your dad, and you took them and ran with them in full sincerity and made them your own. And they really, truly are your own. And that's because of him. A worthy legacy, don't you think?"

I thought about this. Dad had raised me. Almost single-handedly, until I was ten and he met Mrs Taylor, and even then, he'd still done all the hard stuff. I thought back to the smashed phone—how heavily I had leaned on those messages when I first arrived in the town— and how often I had revisited my memories to help me navigate this new neighbourhood. All courtesy of Dad, for better or for worse. I met Simon's eyes, smiling, and saw that he was smiling back.

"With regards to your Happy Game," he went on, "You're still playing that, aren't you?"

"Um…"

"You'd better be. Because I spent all last night going through this bad boy…" He took a copy of the Bible out his satchel. "There are, as far as I can tell, eight hundred verses and passages calling people to be happy. That averages out at twelve times per book."

"Really?"

"Yep. Sixty-six books, written over a period of fourteen to eighteen hundred years, by at least forty authors, invoking eighteen countries that exist today, spread across three continents. On top of that there are multiple translations in two thousand four hundred languages, and it remains the best-selling book of all time. Even without arguing for or against its spiritual truth, on that basis alone it seems your game has a pretty good following."

This made me laugh.

"I'm not always the most optimistic of people," Simon admitted.

I started to tell him that he was, but he waved my words aside:

"No, really. I find myself lamenting over things a lot in my sermons, by way of conveying points. So, I'm taking that in hand. I'm still making the same points, because they're important and not everything is easy to tackle, but I'm working on their framing. I've started reading a happy passage every week to keep things a bit more upbeat. I have you to thank for that."

I gave him an impulsive hug. He went bright red— red enough to make me laugh.

"Just one more thing," he added, "I came here today as unofficial mail man…"

He undid the buckle of his satchel, and instead of handing me envelopes one by one, he upended the whole thing onto the bed. I stared, unable to process what I was seeing. It was as if a snowdrift had swept in and covered me. I surveyed the pile of envelopes, then looked up at Simon, my throat and eyes burning. In that moment, the messages I wanted to send back to my friends didn't have words.

"I'll leave you to it," he said. "Don't feel you have to write loads of replies—they didn't do this to create a ton of work for you." He nodded and slipped out the door.

Once I was alone, I picked up an envelope. Slowly and neatly, I opened it—carefully crafting the memory. The card inside depicted about twenty cats swarming over the top of a walled garden. One of them—a black and white one—was saying to the others: "OK, troops, let's get to work on Crazy Plant-Man's garden!" The inside was crammed with writing:

Dear Anna,
Hope you like the card—it seemed like your kind of
humour. We'll try and get over to see you before too long.
We moved into the new house last week. Jesus came
too. He's loving his new home. He's already climbed all
the trees and is getting to grips with field mice. Not the

prettiest things to discover half dead under your pillow,
but so it goes... Plus, he's on his third collar. At least
we know they break under pressure, so he won't get
strangled.
Kenny made some changes to the design of the East gable.
We're adding a downstairs bedroom, and bathroom with
a lowered sink, lowering the light switches, and levelling
and widening the doorways. We're also putting a ramp
out front, and a chair-height doorbell. All his idea—we're
in the process of updating the planning permissions now.
Perhaps when you come home you won't need those
things, but they're bound to benefit somebody. We expect
you to come and stay often—and your mum, of course.
You're also invited to the wedding, either in person or by
video-link.
Give our regards to your grandfather.
Anyway, gotta sign off now. Much love and well wishes.
Keep playing your game!
Molly & Kenny xxx

Kenny. He had welcomed me into his home, given me
tea and cake, given me plants for the Skeleton Man—
even though Molly disliked the Skeleton Man at the
time—and trusted me with his feelings and questions
about Molly. And he wasn't even taking her away—
they were adapting their house so they could welcome
me in whatever happened! A stray thought cut across

my mental stream of guilt, like a passing breeze. The clear-cut conviction of it took me by surprise—almost like another person's thoughts plopping into my brain. Kenny didn't hold anything against me. And in terms of what little he knew about how I felt, he didn't take it personally. Furthermore, he wouldn't want me to beat myself up over anything to do with him. I blinked, then smiled.

I opened the next envelope:

Dear Anna,
It's not the same around here without you, but Susan and I are getting on much better these days. I've been going out for daily walks, and my health has improved. I've also been going to cognitive behavioural therapy. If I ultimately have the surgery—and I feel it's in sight at last—I like to think we might end up on the same ward.
With best wishes,
"Mrs No" (aka. Heather Snow!) x

"Mrs No." "Mrs Snow." Molly must have talked to her. I whispered the two names several times and laughed aloud.

The next four envelopes contained hand-drawn pictures from Skylar, Emily, Kirsty and Mary. Joanne had written a longer letter:

Dear Anna,

Joanne here. Hope you're doing well. We all miss you! Following your reading the church seems to have become a much brighter, warmer place. Some people aren't entirely enamoured with that, but such is the way of things, I suppose.

I thought you might be interested to know that Sam and I are renewing our wedding vows. We sat down and had a long talk. We know we have a lot of patching up to do, but we realised there's no 'right' time to do such a thing—if we really want this, we'd better just go for it. Anyway, I thought that news would make good ammunition for your game.

Big love from the Adamson clan!

Joanne et al. xox

Next there were five letters from other members of the church, and ten short notes from casual acquaintances at school. Miss Marney had sent me a card, which simply read: *"Come back soon! There's a wheelchair basketball team in Livingston if you're interested. x"* There was one from Rachel too, and a letter from Cal, written on what looked like a page torn from an exercise book:

Dear Anna, I hope your doing well and that youll be back soon. The sensory tents just big enough for a wheelchair! Do you have instant messanger or videolink? I'm listing

the things you and me can do when your back. Jess says
hi. Anyway got to go, I'm making a dining room chair,
talk to you soon!
Love Cal xox

One of the remaining envelopes was cream-coloured,
and heavier in texture than the others. My name was
written on the front in a small, slanting hand which
added loops to lower-case 'L's and 'Y's. The ink lay on
the paper more thickly and uniformly than it does with
a biro, making less of an indentation on the paper. The
lines were narrower on the vertical strokes of letters, and
wider on the horizontal ones.

Dear Anna,
You wouldn't think I had much left to tell you, given how
often I visit. Todd has learned how to dig on command,
so I've set him to work digging a vegetable patch. By this
time next year we'll have home grown turnips, peas,
broad beans and potatoes in the freezer. Jamie has been
helping, of course.
My cast got adjusted again last week.
There is something I've been wanting to tell you for a
while, but have held off on to be sure, and until a suitable
moment arrived. An incident occurred in December
involving Jamie, some other schoolchildren, a knife
hidden in a sock, and an attempted attack on me in the

dead of night—Chopin-time, to you and me. As it turned
out, Jamie had gone along with the intention of defending
me. Luckily, the police turned up before any serious
damage was done to people, pets or property.
Following the incident, Carol felt she could no longer
care for Jamie, and gave him up to the children's home.
However, I have had a long think about this, and if the
relevant authorities are willing, I shall be taking him in to
live with me as my foster-son, as soon as I have finished
undergoing the necessary training and disclosure checks.
It shouldn't be too long.
Of course, this does not in any way mean that I am
attempting to replace you. Nothing and nobody could
ever do that. I just remembered you telling me how
worried you were about him, and I realised that both
he and I need a friend. Consider my telling you a late
Christmas present.
With love always,
Grandpa, aka 'The Skeleton Man'

So, Jamie would soon be safe from the Children's Home.
Well, safe for a while at least. Perhaps the Skeleton Man
would adopt him later. Then neither of them would
ever be lonely again. And the grandchildren's room was
so much nicer than his room at Carol's. I hoped there
wasn't a parent like Mum somewhere, missing him and
fighting to get him back. Not just because that might

mean him going away, but because I wouldn't wish that on any parent, knowing Mum and all she'd gone through. A funny thought came to me: if the Skeleton Man was now Jamie's foster father, that made him Mum's foster-brother, and therefore my foster-uncle! By coincidence the next envelope contained a note from Jamie himself:

Dear Anna,
Grandpa John has been working with me on spelling and grammar. Can you tell? I hope you're happy and that the food is ok. Grandpa John says the food was terrible when he was in hospital.
See you soon,
Jamie.
P.S. Here is a paw print from Todd. I dropped the letter and he trod on it.

I experienced a jolt when I opened the last envelope and saw a folded piece of blue A4 paper. Perhaps this wasn't for me at all but for Mum and got muddled in with the rest by mistake.

Perhaps there had been a mistake with the custody challenge being dropped, or the social services had revoked their decision… Well if that was the case then Mum and I would deal with it together. I opened it.

Dear Anna,
Knock 'em all flat!
With best wishes from everyone at McCauliff & Co.

In a different colour, at the bottom of the card:

(Especially Anna. P.S. Gary's behaving much better these
days.)

A week after my accident Mum quit her job. She said
she was glad to get out. Layla, her boss, had it in for her
for a long time because I was reducing the number of
evenings she could work late, and the amount of work
she got done at home. The idea that I had unknowingly
been contributing to Mum's stress in yet another way
made my ears go red and my hands clench and unclench,
but she said that I was far more important than 'a load
of bickering harpies'. She also said the Skeleton Man had
offered to help us out until she could get something new.

To get the Happy Game going again I decided to
be happy that Mum had escaped a horrible workplace
that she might not have escaped had it not been for my
coming. Then I realised I'd never told her about the
Game, because she'd told me never to mention Dad or
his flat or our lives together. She knew of it from when
I mentioned it in church, but nothing about how it was
played. Apparently, though, Molly had told her already.

Mum called the Game 'beautiful'. I realised then that we would have to think of a new way to break in the morning if I didn't get my walking back. If she pushed me in a wheelchair instead of my running around, it would be a joint effort. That thought felt good. It felt odd talking about the Happy Game to her after such a long time of being so careful not to share anything about Dad.

All these things floated around in my brain, especially at night around three o'clock in the morning, when I would often wake up. Shadows and light played across the curtained window in the wall between the corridor and my room, reminding me of the flat in London. Five hours until breakfast. After Simon visited, my appetite returned quite quickly. Hospitals have a reputation for serving bad food, but I don't know why because Livingston served lovely meals. They gave you a menu card, and you ticked items from a variety of subcategories. My favourite for lunch was soup and a roll, a banana, and some apple juice. I also liked having sliced hard boiled eggs, bacon, toast and avocado for breakfast. Shepherd's pie was my favourite dinner, but it was a gamble because the baked potatoes—which I think were probably the frozen microwaveable kind— sometimes weren't cooked all the way through, and their skin went slimy, which made me gag.

One time, Mum and I had a tea party. It was the first time I'd actually drunk tea—before then I'd only had hot chocolate, water, milk, milkshakes, smoothies, or fizzy or flat juice. I had mocha coffee once at a cafe with Dad, but I didn't sleep for twenty-four hours afterwards, so we didn't try that again. This time Mum got two plastic cups of tea, and two single biscuits—each in their own packet—from a vending machine in the waiting room of the outpatients' department. Mum and the Skeleton Man used to have tea parties when she was very little, she told me. Had we been having a proper tea party we would have been drinking out of china tea cups, with our pinkies raised. The plastic cups didn't have handles, though, so we couldn't do that as easily this time. I made up my mind to design a single use, but pretty, tea cup with a handle. Perhaps it could be part of a range, including table cloth, saucers, plates, teapot, milk jug, sugar bowl spoons and knives. All materials that could be recycled so that places like the green wouldn't get littered.

Mum was asleep on the little bed beside me. Some people get frustrated lying awake at night. That was one thing Mrs No got frustrated about sometimes. I have always loved it, though. Dad also taught me a variation of the Happy Game that he liked to play when he was lying awake at night. You think of three things to be happy about from the day you've just had. Then if you remember them, you think of three things to be happy about from the day before, and then the day before that, and so on. It gets harder and harder the further back you go, because of having to remember all the details from each day, but it makes playing the day by day version easier as the habit grows. It's probably also why I find it easy to remember stretches of time, and objects and places, in fine detail—and certain conversations nearly word for word.

I don't know when I fell asleep, but when I woke up, the sun was out. I could see through my window that it had a halo of ice crystals around its circumference. Mum was pulling on her coat. She had already tied her hair back and put her boots on.

"What are you doing?" I asked her.

"Oh, sorry—didn't mean to wake you," she said. "I'll be back soon. I'm just nipping out for a few hours. Is that OK?"

I didn't want her to go—she had been there nearly all the time with me, and a few hours felt terribly long to be without her. Still, she had definitely earned it, so I tried to be brave and not make her feel guilty for leaving. I was a teenager, after all. And I had managed long periods of time without her when I first came to live with her.

"Are you going to see Todd?" I asked.

"Might look in on him, yeah," she answered. "I'll give him cuddles from you."

"Thanks," I said.

"I'll probably be back about lunchtime." She gave me a hug and a kiss, and then hurried out the room. I heard her footsteps receding down the corridor, and then it was quiet.

A trolley wheel squeaked. A baby cried far away. I was still only halfway through Mrs No's gigantic volume of Greek myths and legends. A few days ago, Ben and Mum acted out the story of Orpheus and Eurydice, with Todd as Charon's dog, Pluto, in the hospital garden, while I watched through the window. Now I picked the book up and began to read about Athena the weaver.

Mum got back just as I was finishing my soup. As soon as she entered the room I noticed something different about her. The way she carried herself—she looked solid but graceful—like a dancer. Her face was relaxed, with smile lines around her mouth. Her eyes had a softness to them, but she looked strong as well. When she spoke, her voice was gentle and smooth—not abrupt, as it had been when I first came to her. Even after the custody challenge was dropped her words tended to jerk out, rather than to slide out. She reminded me much more of Dad. Much more of Molly. Much more of Ben. She hung up her coat and sat down.

"Where did you go?" I asked. I meant it to come out lightly, like any other conversation, but I probably sounded especially curious.

"I went to see Simon, the minister," she said. "You just looked so different, and seemed to change so much, after he visited you. I wanted to see if he could help me in the same way."

"Did he?"

"Well, not exactly..." She tilted her head. "I went to his house but he was at a session meeting. I saw his wife, Helen. Did he tell you she had her baby?"

"No!" My face split into a huge smile. "Oh, they must be so happy! I'll have to do them a card! Does the shop here sell coloured pencils or anything? Is it a boy or a girl? What's it called?"

"Yes, yes, yes, girl and Lizzy, respectively!" Mum laughed. Then she looked down, and her eyebrows and mouth worked. Now I understood what that look meant—for all she was trying to smile bravely, babies made her feel very raw in her heart, just like Dad felt in mine. Not exactly in a bad way, just a way that means you choose who to share with, and how to share, very carefully, so that you feel comfortable. But despite looking emotional, she didn't lose her new, soft strength.

"I've got to admit, I was a bit of a wreck when I went there. And when I saw Lizzy it felt like... well, it felt insensitive for her to be there, in my face, as soon as Helen opened the door, but how could it be insensitive? I'd chosen to go there. It was her own house. And it's not like Helen had Lizzie with her just to make me feel bad."

"Did you like Helen?" I asked. "I know her a bit from Sunday school, but not very well."

She twisted her fingers. Perhaps this was her equivalent of clenching and unclenching her fists. "I felt kind of weird going past all the things in the hall."

"What kind of things?"

"Oh, just normal baby things, you know. Pram. Carry-seat. Baby socks on the radiator. And I didn't like it at all when she breastfed in front of me. Actually made me want to kill something."

"Why?"

"Because I wanted to do that so badly for you when I had you, and it just didn't work for me. Jealousy, I suppose. But then, she doesn't know anything about me or the things that have happened."

"Did you have tea?"

She smiled again. "Yes. And chocolate chip cookies. And then I felt a bit better about it all. She's still human! I mean, I'd have had my doubts if she'd had a kale smoothie or something!"

"What did you talk about?"

"I...well I...I just said things to her...more like at her, actually—that I didn't think I could say to anyone else. Not even you and Molly."

"Like what?" As soon as I asked I realised it was a silly question—she'd just said she couldn't tell me. "Sorry," I added, hastily, "You just said you couldn't say."

"That was before though," she smiled for a second again. "I said I didn't think I could do parenting. And that I was fed up being a bad thing for people, and with God's mysterious ways. Everything happens for a reason. Blessings in disguise." She was spitting her words out again now, and I felt worried that this last one meant she didn't want to play the Happy Game anymore. Suddenly she shook her head and her face relaxed again. "Sorry," she said. "I didn't mean to work myself up. But I'm through with all of it—all that cr...all that nonsense. Not with God—" she added, quickly, "—Just with people saying things like that. "

"Did you feel like a bad parent because of my accident?"

She frowned. "Not just that."

"Because of Kayleigh and Archie?"

"I really don't know. No one thing, I suppose. And it's still all so new, even though I've been a Mum, like forever. Half my life, since Kayleigh's still my baby. I thought I was doing well with you with school, and Todd, and your friends and cooking and everything. I had Chrismas all planned out, too. We were going to have lunch at Dad's with him and Jamie, and then meet Molly and Kenny in the afternoon for silly games."

"You were doing well!" I said, emphatically. "You still are!"

"Thank you, Anna" she replied quietly. "That means the world to hear. And I know that really. It's just that... it's like, my head plays tricks with me. And then I want to do and say things and I can't. Or I want to not do and say things and I can't stop myself. That's why I'm horrible sometimes. I don't want to be like that. I don't know why it happens. I want it to stop..."

"What did Helen say?"

"Well, I thought she was going to say things about sin and the sinful self. I'd have got up and walked right out if she'd done that—had enough of that kind of talk in the past already. She didn't. She just said she didn't know me very well or what it was like in my head. But that she gets that sometimes, too."

"Did she say anything else?"

"She asked me a question. She said she wouldn't ask it of a nonbeliever." I clenched and unclenched my fists. I was pretty sure I believed in God now, and in Jesus too, but I wondered if I believed enough yet. Maybe it only counted if you believed past a certain point. "She said she was the kind of person who had a place for everything and everything in its place. Then she said she expected having children tested that to the limits!" Mum chuckled, and then was quiet again. "But she said it took her a long time to work out where her own guilt about things belonged."

"Where did it belong?"

"Well, that's the thing. I immediately said on the cross, because the Bible makes that very clear. But that's always felt like the easy answer, to me."

"It can't have been very easy for Jesus..." I murmured.

"That's what she said. Well, actually she just asked me for whom it was easy, and then I understood what she meant. And I felt so small and so stupid. And right at that moment, Anna, this gust of wind blew a branch on a tree outside her house and sent it knocking at the window. Then she said she could dig around for something about God clearing obstacles rather than laying them in our places, and about him being a God of grace and not of debt—but, she said, she gives herself that lecture all the time, and a fat lot of good it does her! Plus you only have to look at a newspaper to wonder if that isn't too simplistic an outlook."

"That's true," I said, and I knew now, in a way I hadn't known before, that it was. The Happy Game couldn't simplify life. It couldn't be used to dodge problems. It couldn't solve problems all on its own. But I also knew that complexity and difficult, awful things didn't make good things any less real or less significant, or less worthy of celebration. That was what it was about.

Mum broke in on my thoughts. "She said she was sorry for all I had been through and was going through. And that she was glad we had a chance to talk properly. She had this intense, luminous look of compassion about her—I can't really describe it. Not like the sympathy grimace of someone who cares-but-doesn't-really, or who thinks they're so wise." I didn't know what she meant by that, but then, I still have a long way to go connecting up things like the size of the eyes, a twitch of the mouth or eyebrows, a blink—with highly specific emotions and nuances. I don't think you ever stop learning that kind of thing. I think there's learning involved for everyone— only some people just don't have to think consciously about it. "Then she said she didn't really feel equipped to leave me with any party-bag of helpful placations to take home."

"A party-bag—I like that phrase," I interrupted.

"Me too," she said. "But she did say that when she gets a guilt-attack, or a lack of confidence, the way she thinks of it is that both shame and Jesus died on the cross. Except Jesus was resurrected and shame wasn't, so she always tries to leave it that way. And that made me wonder what things she's been through herself."

"Did you ask her?"

"No, it isn't my business."

"Did she tell you?"

"No."

"You can't tell from the outside, can you?"

"No, you can't," she agreed.

That night I dreamed I was a ship, sailing across a great, Grecian sea. Other ships sounded their horns as they passed me. Some hoisted their flags. In this way we met and parted, travelling across the shipping lanes, never knowing what was in each other's holds.

Something good, perhaps, like wine, grain, medicine or honey. Something bad like slaves, unwilling brides, ammunition or prisoners of war. Or maybe something else...something nobody had ever seen before, that was about to sweep across the globe and change it forever.

When I awoke in the still, quiet pre-dawn, a weight seemed finally to have dropped away through the trapdoor of my soul.

Open Letter from Anna Whitear, Featured in Alive!

First of all, thanks to Joanne and Helen and the other editors for publishing this, even though it isn't very religious. I was really touched by all the letters you sent, so it seemed right that I should write something to you in return. I loved the surprise party—thank you for not having any party poppers or rubber balloons or anything like that, for being gentle, and for coming into view one person at a time. How fortunate that there wasn't enough room for everyone in the visitor's lounge! Holding it outside meant I got to see Todd and hear the birds, and also to see my brother's and sister's gravestone. Seeing it made them truly real—I have a brother and a sister! I believe I'll meet them somehow, at some point. It was also fortunate that there wasn't any rain or sleet.

Skylar—thank you so much for laying the wreath for Dad—it meant more than I can ever express. And

ANNA

Simon, thank you for marrying Mum and Ben—they caught you off-guard asking you to do that, didn't they!

It's been a month now since we settled into our Sunshine Flat. There was a winter storm as we were coming down in the van, but I didn't mind that, because I knew where we were going, and why we were going— and I was excited, even though I knew it was going to be hard. Mum and Ben were with me, and I knew you were all with me in spirit, too.

The flat is FANTASTIC! We're staying with two other girls. One of the girls is called Katy. She's twelve. She hurt her spine playing on a swing which broke. She's still recovering from surgery and has the most beautiful collection of hand-made nightgowns which have been passed down through her family. The other girl is Clara. She's been paralysed on one side for most of her life. She's in a lot of pain which nobody can really explain, but she's taking a few steps. We have a chore rota which the wardens have set up—it's supposed to make it feel more like home. This week I'm washing up, Clara or her mum are taking out the bins, and Katy or her dad are vacuuming. The next week it all changes round so we don't get bored. They have a really fun sit-on vacuum cleaner. All the sinks, shelves, light switches and work surfaces are lowered so we can reach everything easily from our wheelchairs, and the door frames are much wider than most.

In the living room there's one of those wide-screen TVs, as well as a really good electric piano which I can play any time I like. It's better than the keyboard in the church, though not as good as a real piano. I'm learning a few mazurkas. If people are sleeping or wanting peace and quiet, I just plug in the headphones. Ben found me a sustaining pedal which I can operate using my tongue, so I've been getting used to that. It's not as big a change as you'd think. I'm thankful that the vertebra I knocked out of place was low enough down that I still have full use of my hands and fingers.

I miss home. I miss going to church, going to see Mrs No with Molly, gardening with Jamie and the Skeleton Man, and just venturing down the street and seeing people I know. Mum misses it too. She's getting counselling to help her re-learn how to make friends and cope with her own problems. She has step by step guides for talking to people in different situations, in order to make and keep connections. It's not unlike the social stories I used to have when I was little. It isn't that she doesn't know how to do these things—it's just that it's been such a long time she's got a little bit rusty. She's also got Post-Traumatic Stress Disorder, which is when certain everyday things stop you being able to function because your subconscious mind associates them with bad experiences from the past. The type of help she's getting is called 'dialectical behaviour therapy', which is a new one from America. It involves talking back and forth, learning to name your feelings, telling yourself it's OK to feel them, and then using problem solving strategies to work out what to do with them, instead of letting them rule you.

Sometimes I get scared you might all forget about us while we're away, and that everything might have changed by the time we get back—but I know those are silly fears. Even if things did change it would still be home, and you would still all be you.

Anyway, I'm running out of space so I'd better stop. There's so much I'd like to say! I still haven't told you about the clown-doctors who came round last Friday, or the Bubble Lady who created a giant bubble around Mum, or the couple with the therapy dog, or the two creative writing students who got Katy to write her first story. She has the wildest imagination of anyone I've ever met—it gets her into trouble when she does things without thinking. Meanwhile, Clara is producing a pamphlet of poetry—mostly about goats.

As for me, they're saying I should consider turning my bits of notebook-writing into a proper memoir. I don't know about that—I don't know who would read it—but I'll certainly give it some thought.

My life is full, I feel all your prayers, and I'm happy. I am happy. I am so happy.

ABOUT THE AUTHOR

Laura Guthrie grew up in the rural Scottish Highlands ("I come from where the planes don't fly") and currently lives in Inverness.

She has an honours degree in biological sciences from the University of Edinburgh, and a PhD in creative writing from the University of Glasgow.

She is a member of the Dingwall-based Ross-Shire Writers, and has produced two of her own plays with her theatre company, Sunrise Theatre. Her poetry and short fiction have been anthologised by several Scottish presses. She is the winner of the 2016 Exeter Story Prize. *Anna* is her first novel.

Follow Laura on Twitter:
@catherinespark

ACKNOWLEDGEMENTS

This novel owes many things to many people, without whom I wouldn't be able to share it with you. I would like to thank those at Cranachan who took on its publication—who line-edited, encouraged and crafted the design you see here: Anne Glennie, Kelly MacDonald, Natalie Jayne Clarke and Adam Scott. Thank you to the Ross-Shire writers, particularly my friend Cheryl, who first introduced me to Anne and to Cranachan.

Thanks also to those folks with whom I crossed paths at Glasgow University, who believed in me, and whose feedback, tutoring and questions helped me create a plot that hangs together: Kei Miller, Vahni Capildeo, Carolyn Jess-Cooke and Elizabeth Reeder in particular; as well as the many MLitt, MFA and PhD students with whom I was privileged to study.

My family have offered moral support, ideas and queries, proof readings and an audience for early readings-out-loud. They put me back together when I fell apart, reasoned with me when I lost my head, and endured many tears and passionate, pacing, all-consuming monologues. Thank you for being you. Finally, thank you to the many friends—writers and non-writers alike—who have offered public and private, written and spoken words of encouragement, praise and anticipation along this journey. May this, the final result, bring all of you great joy and comfort.

AUTHOR'S NOTE

I was diagnosed with Asperger's syndrome when I was fourteen. Since then I've always been interested in the creation of specified Aspie and autistic characters in fiction, especially first person narrators. One thing I felt about a lot of the works I read, was that despite engendering the reader's sympathies, the characters with Asperger's were never exactly 'lovely' people, nor did they have expansive imaginations or rich uses of language. Another thing that bothered me was the subliminal implication, through omission or suggestion via fictional representation, that someone with Asperger's was, or should be written as, somehow incapable of being lovely, and not desiring of social relations by dint of diagnosis. I know I myself care deeply about many people.

Then there was the notion that a character with Asperger's has to somehow either develop away from their traits, or other characters have to modify their own ways of being, with this modification only being on an as-needs basis to rub along with the character with Asperger's. I wanted to see a work of fiction in which a person with Asperger's does not have to leave their basic self behind as part of the process of overcoming their struggles, and in which they, as they are, actually change their story world for the better. This is very different from simply being accommodated, and other fictional characters without labels to their names are granted such privileges within their plots.

In writing Anna, I haven't tried to hold an impartial mirror up to the world. What you've just read is a story inspired by things as seen and interpreted through my own personal lens, and your imaginings along the way will be coloured by that lens, as well as your own. Therefore I trust you to read with open eyes and open minds, and if you feel you have been led to a general conclusion about something real as a result, look out into the real world too, and question yourself as to whether the fiction presents a reasonable representation. If readers can do this, fiction need not be dangerous. If they can't, then fiction may fall prey to strangleholds in the name of completely watertight representations.

In 2013 Asperger's syndrome became Autistic Spectrum Disorder Level 1. Within the story's time frame, Anna was diagnosed before the change came about, and thus uses the term 'Asperger's'. Some autistics feel the term unfairly suggests that certain autistic people have greater mental function than others, and thus have more of a right to a voice of their own about their care and treatment. I don't mean to condone such prejudice in my use of the term. I know some people will not feel comfortable with this, but rest assured that there is nothing more behind its use as far as my thinking is concerned. Just remember that not everyone agrees with it as a label.

Another thing: the original *Pollyanna* treats Anna's possibly-permanent paraplegia as a giant tragedy. Having read several discourses from wheelchair users who felt the negative impacts of such representations on their own lives, I decided not to replicate this regard within my interpretation of the story. Disabilities only become tragedies when non-disabled people turn them into things that block opportunities, or treat people with them as somehow pitiable, incomplete, marred or at worst, dispensable. I didn't want Anna's happiness to hinge on the prospect of being able to walk again, or for her disability to seem like the be-all and end-all. That being said, I believe in people having the chance of augmented function where they desire it, if that chance can be given. That is simply a case of respecting a person's personal choice, and this idea informed my crafting of the end of *Anna*. I also think there is a big difference between being disabled and *becoming* disabled. The latter naturally requires a period of adjustment which, for a while, may feel like grief. That's not necessarily a reflection of the person's regard for that particular disability; it's simply the process of adjusting.

And now I must congratulate you on your creation. You have imagined so many characters, voices and landscapes during the reading of this novel. Since nobody else has your brain, nobody else in the world has read, or created, quite the same story that you have. I hope you've enjoyed it, and that we can soon collaborate on another book.